FPL
M

W9-BTF-289

INB
026.00

DISCARD

JUN 0 5 2015

FRAMINGHAM PUBLIC LIBRARY

### Books by Rita Mae Brown & Sneaky Pie Brown

WISH YOU WERE HERE • REST IN PIECES • MURDER AT MONTICELLO
PAY DIRT • MURDER, SHE MEOWED • MURDER ON THE PROWL
CAT ON THE SCENT • SNEAKY PIE'S COOKBOOK FOR MYSTERY LOVERS
PAWING THROUGH THE PAST • CLAWS AND EFFECT
CATCH AS CAT CAN •THE TAIL OF THE TIP-OFF • WHISKER OF EVIL
CAT'S EYEWITNESS • SOUR PUSS • PUSS 'N CAHOOTS
THE PURRFECT MURDER • SANTA CLAWED • CAT OF THE CENTURY
HISS OF DEATH • THE BIG CAT NAP • SNEAKY PIE FOR PRESIDENT
THE LITTER OF THE LAW • NINE LIVES TO DIE • TAIL GAIT

### Books by Rita Mae Brown featuring "Sister" Jane Arnold

OUTFOXED • HOTSPUR • FULL CRY • THE HUNT BALL
THE HOUNDS AND THE FURY • THE TELL-TALE HORSE
HOUNDED TO DEATH • FOX TRACKS • LET SLEEPING DOGS LIE

### The Mags Rogers Books

MURDER UNLEASHED • A NOSE FOR JUSTICE

### Books by Rita Mae Brown

ANIMAL MAGNETISM: MY LIFE WITH CREATURES GREAT AND SMALL
THE HAND THAT CRADLES THE ROCK • SONGS TO A HANDSOME WOMAN
A PLAIN BROWN RAPPER • RUBYFRUIT JUNGLE • IN HER DAY
SIX OF ONE • SOUTHERN DISCOMFORT
SUDDEN DEATH • HIGH HEARTS
STARTING FROM SCRATCH: A DIFFERENT KIND OF WRITERS' MANUAL
BINGO •VENUS ENVY
DOLLEY: A NOVEL OF DOLLEY MADISON IN LOVE AND WAR
RIDING SHOTGUN • RITA WILL: MEMOIR OF A LITERARY RABBLE-ROUSER
LOOSE LIPS •ALMA MATER • SAND CASTLE

# Tail Gait

# Tail Gait

## A MRS. MURPHY MYSTERY

# RITA MAE BROWN
# & SNEAKY PIE BROWN

Illustrated by Michael Gellatly

BANTAM BOOKS

NEW YORK

Tail Gait is a work of fiction. Names, characters, places, and incidents either are the product of the author's imagination or are used fictitiously. Any resemblance to actual persons, living or dead, or locales is entirely coincidental.

Copyright © 2015 by American Artists, Inc.

All rights reserved.

Published in the United States by Bantam Books, an imprint of Random House, a division of Penguin Random House LLC, New York.

BANTAM BOOKS and the HOUSE colophon are registered trademarks of Penguin Random House LLC.

Illustrations copyright © 2015 by Michael Gellatly

Library of Congress Cataloging-in-Publication Data
Brown, Rita Mae, author.
Tail Gait : a Mrs. Murphy Mystery / Rita Mae Brown & Sneaky Pie Brown ; illustrated by Michael Gellatly.
pages cm
ISBN 978-0-553-39236-4
eBook ISBN 978-0-553-39237-1
1. Murphy, Mrs. (Fictitious character)—Fiction. 2. Haristeen, Harry (Fictitious character)—Fiction. 3. Women detectives—Virginia—Fiction. 4. Women cat owners—Fiction. 5. Cats—Fiction. 6. Mystery fiction. I. Brown, Sneaky Pie-author. II. Gellatly, Michael, illustrator. III. Title.
PS3552.R698T33 2015
813'.54—dc23
2014049098

Printed in the United States of America on acid-free paper

www.bantamdell.com

2 4 6 8 9 7 5 3 1

First Edition

With gratitude to
Carol Tanzola

# Cast of Characters

**Mary Minor Haristeen**—"Harry," just forty-one, is a Smith graduate who wound up being Crozet, Virginia's postmistress for sixteen years. Now she's trying to make money farming. Having survived breast cancer, Harry prefers not to think about it. She more or less lives on the surface of life until curiosity pulls her deeper . . . as it inevitably does.

**Pharamond Haristeen, D.V.M.**—"Fair" specializes in equine reproduction. After graduating from Auburn he married his childhood sweetheart, Harry. A year older than his wife, he reads people's emotions much better than she does.

**Susan Tucker**—Outgoing, adept at any and all social exchange, she's Harry's best friend since cradle days. She loves Harry but worries about how Harry just blunders into things.

**The Very Reverend Herbert Jones**—A Vietnam veteran, Army, he is pastor at St. Luke's Lutheran Church, which is well over two hundred years old. A man of deep conviction and feeling, he's known Harry since her childhood.

**Deputy Cynthia Cooper**—Tall, lean, and Harry's next-door neighbor, renting the adjoining farm. Cooper loves law enforcement. From time to time, Harry meddles in Cooper's business, but in her defense the Smith graduate has an uncanny knack of uncovering crucial information.

**Sheriff Rick Shaw**—The sheriff of Albemarle County, he is over-burdened, underfunded, and overworked. Despite that, he likes his job and has learned to trust Cooper. (Originally, he wasn't thrilled with having a woman in the department.)

**Dr. Nelson Yarbrough**—Quarterback of the 1959 University of Virginia football team, his pro ball career was ended by an injury. He and his wife, Sandra, practice dentistry and good works in Charlottesville.

**Marshall Reese**—This defensive lineman on the 1959 UVA team has become a successful developer by building carefully detailed houses, conscientiously following history as much as possible.

**Paul Huber**—On the 1959 team, Huber was UVA's right halfback. Now he runs a landscaping company founded by his father and works closely with Marshall. He specializes in eighteenth-century plantings and gardens.

**Willis Fugate**, fullback, 1959; **Rudolph Putnam**, fullback, 1960; **Lionel Gardner**, offensive lineman, 1961; **Tim Jardine**, linebacker, 1970—These charming old boys are all former UVA football players.

**Frank Cresey**—He was a UVA halfback, and in 1975 was All-American, which keeps his old friends loyal to him. Supremely gifted athletically, Frank was at one time popular with the ladies and a good student. That was before he destroyed himself with drink.

**Professor Greg "Ginger" McConnell, History Emeritus, University of Virginia**—His writings on the lives of the common man and women in Revolutionary and post-Revolutionary America made him a world authority on same. Overflowing with enthusiasm for his subject, Ginger remains delightfully young and is universally loved—or perhaps not.

**Trudy McConnell**—Wife to Ginger and mother to Olivia and Renata "Rennie," the two daughters are now middle-aged. Like the wives of many prominent men, Trudy is Ginger's anchor.

**Olivia Gaston**—After a disastrous romance with Frank Cresey when she was in her late teens, she's made a good life for herself with a wonderful husband in New Orleans.

**Snoop**—Possibly middle-aged, it's hard to tell, he's an alcoholic who "lives" on the Downtown Mall. The well-mannered African American doesn't talk about his past. Most of the Mall Rats, as they are known, don't.

# Cast of Characters

## 1777–1782

**Captain John Schuyler**—Captain Schuyler is twenty years old, powerfully built, and a good man. After fighting in the Battle of Saratoga, the American soldier takes a British lieutenant prisoner; from that moment on, their fates are forever linked.

**Lieutenant Charles West**—At nineteen, in the British Army, he's the second son of an impoverished aristocrat. Artistic and quick-thinking, he's captured by Captain Schuyler, along with several of his men.

**Ewing Garth**—Highly intelligent, a successful businessman with holdings in Virginia and North Carolina, he is an American patriot.

**Catherine Garth**—Bold, strong of body and mind, she admires her father. She is also beyond beautiful, and at eighteen coming into full bloom.

**Rachel Garth**—Two years younger than Catherine, she, too, is a beautiful girl. She's not as bold as Catherine but she's observant and no fool.

**Jeddie Rice**—A young slave with a gift for training and riding horses. He and Catherine have a natural affinity.

**Roger**—The butler, and therefore a powerful slave.

**Weymouth**—Roger's son, who will one day inherit this most coveted position.

**Corporal Karl Ix**—A captured Hessian soldier who endures an eight hundred mile march alongside Lieutenant West. Over time, the two become friends. Ix is an engineer in his late twenties.

**Thomas Parsons**, **Edward Thimble, Samuel MacLeish**—Captured along with their commanding officer, Lieutenant West. Their resourcefulness and toughness keep them alive in The Barracks, the prisoner-of-war camp just outside Charlottesville, Virginia.

**Captain Graves**—Of the Royal Irish Artillery, he's also captured at Saratoga. In time, he's the first to understand what this new land has to offer.

# The Really Important Characters

**Mrs. Murphy**—She's a tiger cat who is usually cool, calm, and collected. She loves her humans, Tucker the dog, and even Pewter, the other cat, who can be a pill.

**Pewter**—She's self-centered and rotund—even intelligent when she wants to be. Selfish as this cat is, she often comes through at the last minute to help and then wants all the credit.

**Tee Tucker**—This corgi could take your college boards. Deeply devoted to Harry, Fair, and Mrs. Murphy, she is less devoted to Pewter.

**Simon**—He's an opossum who lives in the hayloft of the Haristeens' barn.

**Matilda**—This large blacksnake has a large sense of humor. She also lives in the hayloft.

**Flatface**—A great horned owl who lives in the barn cupola, she forever irritates Pewter, even as the snooty cat realizes the bird could easily pick her up and carry her off.

**Shortro**—This young Saddlebred in Harry's barn is being trained as a foxhunter. He's very smart and good-natured.

**Tomahawk**—Harry's older Thoroughbred. He and Shortro have been friends a long time.

**Piglet**—This Welsh corgi goes through war and imprisonment with Lieutenant Charles West. As far as he is concerned, an American canine is as good as a canine who is a subject of George III. Still, he keeps this to himself.

## The Lutheran Cats

**Elocution**—She's the oldest of the St. Luke's cats and cares a lot about the "Rev," as his friends sometimes call the Very Reverend Herbert Jones.

**Cazenovia**—This cat watches everybody and everything.

**Lucy Fur**—The youngest of the kitties: While ever playful, she obeys her elders.

# Tail Gait

# 1

*October 7, 1777*
*Bemis Heights, near Saratoga, New York*

Lieutenant Charles West slipped through the heavy woods with a handful of his men, all selected marksmen, part of Captain Alexander Fraser's 34th Regiment. Below, other soldiers of Fraser's 34th Regiment could be heard firing at the Continental forces. Any hope of the brave British lieutenant's piercing the American rebels' line was fading. The barrage was intense. Wearing green coats helped to conceal West's Rangers, but the enemy knew the territory and had learned a great deal about fighting in such terrain from the Mohawks. The Continentals also carried rifles made in Kentucky or Pennsylvania, far more accurate than the British-issued musket, Brown Bess.

Senses razor-sharp, the nineteen-year-old lieutenant hoped to push forward, verify the flank of the rebel army, and report back to Captain Fraser. With only twenty men and his dog, Piglet, he searched for the back of that enemy flank. If only he could find it, then surely some of them would survive and return to their commander with that vital information.

Lieutenant Charles West, intrepid, and his men stealthily moved forward. At the young man's heels trod his alert herding dog, a tough little fellow favored by the Welsh. While not Welsh, West

3

hailed from the borderland with Scotland, had played as a child on Hadrian's Wall. He'd learned to prize the ability of corgis.

Piglet was named for the king. With senses far superior to his master's, he was accustomed to rifle fire and the boom of cannons. Stopping for a moment, he lifted his head and inhaled. A low growl and raised hackles alerted the dog's beloved master. Charles halted. Looking down at Piglet bristling, he held up his hand for a halt. The twenty men under West's command did as ordered but for Angus MacKenzie, twenty yards ahead.

A shot rang out directly in front of Angus, then a second to his left. The sturdy Scot dropped.

"If you want to live, stop," a deep voice called from the woods while Angus struggled for breath. "Throw down your muskets."

West looked around. A shot was fired over his head, then another and another. He put down his musket and hurried to Angus's side. The men in West's far rear carefully withdrew and were soon out of sight. Four other British soldiers remained with the lieutenant.

"MacKenzie, hang on, man." Charles knelt to lift the older man's grizzled head so gently the wounded man smiled.

Piglet came over to lick Angus's face.

"Piglet, no," Charles softly said as nearby a rebel rifleman rose from the brush and moved toward him and his men.

"I'll carry you to wherever they take us," West assured poor Angus.

Angus tried to smile through clenched teeth as he finally was able to mutter, "No time."

Lieutenant West laid Angus gently down as Piglet whined a bit. Angus was gone. The officer in charge of the rebels, a young man close to Charles West in age, took note of the care his counterpart evidenced toward a simple soldier.

"Lieutenant," the dark fellow said. "You and your men are my prisoners."

"Charles West." He inclined his head slightly.

The handsome young fellow prayed no one would be foolish. The four men close to Lieutenant West laid down their arms. The marksmen had done all that was asked of them.

With a flick of his hand, Captain John Schuyler sent some of his men to search for the other fleeing Brits. Six stayed behind with the captain.

Captain Schuyler strode up to Charles. Glancing down at the handsome flintlock pistol shoved into the lieutenant's breeches, Schuyler plucked it out.

"A beauty." Tall like Charles, Schuyler looked him right in the eye.

"A parting gift from my father."

Stuffing the captured sidearm behind his belt, Captain Schuyler smiled broadly. "The fortunes of war."

Oddly enough, the two strapping fellows were mirror images of each other, even as Schuyler's black hair and brown eyes were in contrast to West's blue eyes and blonde hair.

Knowing he could not possibly keep a sidearm as a prisoner, West was stung by the loss of his one prized paternal gift. However, West had more important worries.

"I shall assume," Charles said, "that there is no time to bury MacKenzie?"

"I'm afraid not," Captain Schuyler replied. He heard intensified gunfire below, as well as a bugle call abruptly silenced. "But you may retrieve from the body any such keepsake to send to his family."

"Thank you, Sir. Most kind." Charles again knelt down. Removing a letter from the inside of the dead man's green coat, he also took a worn wedding band off Angus's left hand. Feeling through his pockets, West pulled out a few coins, which he handed to Captain Schuyler.

The darker officer gave them back. "No, no, send what you can to his wife," he said, for he noticed the wedding ring. "From the prison camp, you'll be able to send letters, receive same and funds." Observing West's quizzical expression, Schuyler said, "We aren't savages, man."

West stood up, Piglet intently studying his master's face. "What you are, Captain, are damned good soldiers."

Grins appeared on the rebel faces. These cocky Brits thought they'd roll right over them, or, even worse, they thought most colonists would stick with the Crown. Hearing the battle raging below, the Americans liked the acknowledgment.

Captain Schuyler and his men surrounded his small harvest of captives. "Jacob, each one of you men take a musket." Jacob and the others did as ordered.

The long march to an uncertain future began.

As an officer, Captain Schuyler walked with his British counterpart. He was intent on showing these people the rebellious colonists were civilized and understood the rules of war. Looking down at the corgi, he asked. "What is his rank?"

Despite himself, West smiled. "Private Piglet, Captain, eager to do my bidding."

Voice low, slightly conspiratorial, Captain Schuyler replied, "Ah, now there's a good soldier."

Piglet, pleased, trotted along. Cannon fire could be heard at a distance, mostly from the rebels' side. The British struggled to haul their big guns over the uneven ground. The little fellow was not afraid. He had liked Angus, would remember him in his fashion, for the older man would occasionally share a biscuit with him, speak to him in his accent, a soothing sound.

Piglet knew war as well as any canine, and he would protect Charles to the death. Through searing heat, driving rain, biting sleet, and heavy snows, Piglet didn't care, as long as he was with his young man, a battle-hardened young man with a heart of gold.

Even this terrible war couldn't kill that, and Piglet knew it. But then dogs know the things about humans that humans work to conceal from other humans.

On that day, October 7, 1777, Fate tossed together three lives. Lieutenant Charles West, Captain John Schuyler, and Piglet, three lives that would be entwined until their own deaths years later. What the American Captain Schuyler knew that neither Lieutenant West nor Piglet could imagine was that an old order was dying and a new country was being born.

# 2

*L*ong, low, pale golden rays washed the western side of the stone wall around St. Luke's graveyard. Many of the souls therein had been sleeping since shortly after the Revolutionary War. The church itself—of hand-laid stone, much of it pulled from the fields— matched the deceased in age. The architect of this peaceful sym- metry had fallen in love with central Virginia and a young Virginia beauty while in a Revolutionary War camp a few miles away. Three arched walkways connected the church at one end and the rectory office at the other. St. Luke's inner quad was bounded on the north by the main arcade. At each corner the two shorter arcades created a quiet rectangle; a longer arcade duplicated the front arcade. The proportions of this old rectangular plan were graceful, simple, timeless. The shorter arcades were anchored by one-story stone buildings with the handblown glass wavy in their paned windows. Originally used as classrooms, one lower school and one upper, the space was now used by different church groups. The men's building reposed on the north. The women's sat on the south, each a dupli- cate of the other, as with the arcades. The men's building was so clean one could eat off the random-width heart-pine floor, a clean- liness that had each wife wondering why this was not the case in her home.

Bordering this inner quad was a large outer quad, big enough for football games and gatherings in good weather. The far border was the graveyard, enclosed by a gray stone wall, the same stone as the church's structures.

From the large quad, the pastor's house was to the left of the graveyard. The dwelling had grown over the centuries, with additions as well as a two-car garage. Originally a stable with living quarters overhead, the parsonage had been constructed of clapboard painted white. Its shutters were midnight blue, each with a cross cut into the top.

As St. Luke's was a Lutheran church, it was high church, but the décor, while testifying to a brief flirtation with gilt, was more subdued than that of the Catholic church down the road. However, it was not nearly as barren as the local Church of the Holy Light.

Inside this delightful, warm home, a dinner party brought together friends. The Very Reverend Herbert Jones, at long last emerging from the shadow of his wife's death, had decided to entertain this evening. Although his wife, a great beauty in her day, had passed away seven years ago, it had taken the good man that long to rebound.

Inside, Harry and Fair Haristeen, D.V.M.; Susan and Ned Tucker; Nelson and Sandra Yarbrough, both dentists; Professor Greg "Ginger" McConnell and his wife, Trudy; Marshall and Joyce Reese; and Paul and Anita Huber all sat in the simple, pale yellow living room with Reverend Jones and his dear friend, Miranda Hogendobber. After Harry's mother died, Miranda was a surrogate mother to her and a good friend to all. Miranda also possessed a singing voice touched by an angel, a voice in the service of the Church of the Holy Light, an evangelical house of worship.

The caterer could be heard at work in the old country kitchen.

"I don't know why you didn't let me cook tonight's repast," said Miranda, looking quite nice in a peach dress.

"Because then you'd fret." Herb smiled as Lucy Fur, a Lutheran cat, leapt to the back of his big easy chair.

"I've forgotten how lovely this house is," Trudy remarked. "Like walking back in time."

"Well, at least there's no television in the living room," remarked Susan, in her early forties. "Drives me crazy."

Harry, Susan's friend since cradle days, reached over to pinch her. "Oh, Susan, everything drives you crazy."

"There, she said it, I didn't." Ned laughed. Ned was the district's representative to the state legislature, which he usually referred to as the House of Burgesses, as it was known before the Revolution. He also, not for public consumption, referred to it as "the Asylum."

"She's a perfectionist in everything, but most especially deportment," Fair complimented Susan, using the word his mother had always used to chide him. In his head, he could still hear the voice: "Pharamond, a gentleman always walks to the outside of a lady. In this fashion, should a conveyance drive through a mud puddle, he will be besmirched, not she."

And so, since age five, Fair had always walked on the outside as well as performing all the duties a Virginia gentleman was supposed to perform. These duties were ironclad, regardless of race, religion, age, or class. His father's way of enforcing the same standard was to mutter, "Don't be a dolt, son."

All of the assembled that evening at Reverend Jones's home had been raised with strict rules of behavior. While other parts of the country might see such rules as imposing on their self-expression, every Southerner knows that the way to truly insult someone is with impeccable manners. One slight shift of tone, one turn of the hand, jingling coins in a pocket, could be like an arrow shot from the bow. While none of the people there dwelt on it, each one knew manners provided vital information on social and emotional levels. To not know them was like reading with one eye closed.

The Lutheran cats, however, were under no such dictates. At that moment, Cazenovia was in the kitchen, clawing the leg of the caterer in hopes he would drop a morsel. "Damn cat," the caterer was heard to exclaim.

The Reverend Jones rose, entered the kitchen to confront the unrepentant calico. "Where are your manners?"

Elocution, the third of the Lutheran cats, sauntered into the kitchen but was prudent enough not to meow.

"Sorry to curse," apologized Warren Chiles, a parishioner and the caterer.

The Reverend laughed. "I do it all the time. My hope is that the Good Lord has bigger fish to fry than a pastor who cusses."

"I think he does." Warren nodded. "Dinner's ready."

"Good. I'm starved. Bet everyone else is too."

The Reverend Jones returned to the living room and rounded up his guests. They filed into the dining room, which was painted a flattering deep ivory. A small chandelier from 1804 cast soft light on the table. An embroidered tablecloth covered many a scratch—not from the cats, of course.

As pork roast was served and wine poured, outside the windows the sunset's last golden rays turned deep salmon, then exploded in fire.

Harry called their attention to it. "Look at that sunset."

The others paused to turn around.

Trudy, originally from Michigan, stared at the fireworks. "I never tire of the beauty of this place."

"I remember beautiful sunsets over Tampa Bay when I was a kid, but there's something about watching the mountains turn colors with the sunset, then twilight," Nelson remarked.

"It makes me wonder who else is watching this and where?" Sandra wondered. "Is it this beautiful right now in Asheville, North Carolina, or up in the Hudson River Valley?"

"Or who watched this valley's gorgeous sunsets back in 1820?" Marshall mused. Like Nelson and Paul, Marshall had studied history under Professor McConnell when they'd played football for the University of Virginia back in 1959.

The dinner conversation covered sunsets and sunrises, moonrises, and whether it was better to live on the water or by the mountains. These were gentle conversations among people who had known one another for decades. After dinner, they repaired to the living room. The Reverend Jones started a fire in the fireplace. The three cats—now full—quickly plopped in front of it.

The last frost was usually about mid-April, but last year, there had been frosts into early May. You never knew. Frosts or not, the daffodils were up already, redbuds swelled but had not yet opened. It was early spring in the Appalachians, a magical time.

"When is your next class reunion?" Ginger asked Nelson.

"I don't know, but I know the team will get together in Richmond at the end of the month. We used to get together at Wintergreen," the dentist said, referring to a skiing community west of Charlottesville, "but it's gotten to the point where some of us can't climb those steep stairs."

"Goes so fast," murmured Harry, who, though much younger than the University of Virginia men, couldn't believe how time flew.

Miranda, in her seventies, smiled. "Everyone says that. Ever notice?"

"People have been complaining about time since Pericles's Athens." Ginger laughed. "Before, even. I chalk it up to the human condition."

"Which reminds me, the human condition. How is your research going on your book?" asked Nelson.

Trudy interjected with good humor, "If the book doesn't kill him, I might."

Ginger put his arm around his wife's shoulders. "Honey, I've been a trial for decades, what's one more?"

"Decade or trial?" she shot back.

They laughed, then he answered. "The writing is slow because I fall in love with my research. Always have. I think I have visited every church built before, during, and immediately after the Revolutionary War, including this one. I've read the rolls of parishioners, visited the graves, noted those who were soldiers or sailors during the War, those who were prisoners of war at The Barracks just down the road from here. They all feel like people I know. I've read their property purchases, lawsuits, if any. In short, the detritus of everyday life. Well, Trudy has heard this so many times, but sometimes I feel they are reaching back."

"That's why you were and are such a good teacher. You brought them to life." Nelson paid Ginger the ultimate compliment.

"Indeed," said the Reverend Jones. "I've never had the good fortune to attend Ginger's classes, but I've read his books. I'm a bit of a history buff too, which you know, but I blunder about. I've always been interested in how the various faiths took root in this new land and, given the distances people had to travel for spiritual comfort, I often wonder about, say, a Catholic priest comforting a dying Quaker because he was the closest to the suffering man." The Reverend Jones was an original thinker.

"I never thought of that," Harry said.

"Me neither." Susan leaned forward. "So many people, so many different ways of worshipping, thinking."

"Smartest thing we ever did, separation of church and state, and we can thank Madison for drawing up those Articles for Virginia when we were a colony." Ginger's tone brooked no interference, but then the rest agreed on this issue.

"Who was your best student?" Miranda asked him.

Nelson quickly laughed. "Not me."

"You made good grades. History wasn't your passion, not like Marshall and Paul here."

"Because of you, I studied on my own. Eighteenth- and early nineteenth-century gardens," said Paul, the 1959 team's right halfback. "Freedom gardens, as some were termed. But then, I always knew I'd take over Dad's landscaping company. It made sense."

"Helps me." Marshall smiled.

Joyce beamed, always ready to praise her driven husband, a defensive lineman from those same days. "You must see what Marshall and Paul are doing at Continental Estates."

"Now, honey, they don't want to hear about that," Marshall drawled.

The Reverend Jones encouraged Marshall and Paul. "Of course we do."

"As you know, for the last fifty years I've created developments that preserve land, sometimes even reconstructing the original dwellings. I really got the idea in Ginger's classes. He showed me how to track ownership so I could be accurate, so I could build houses of the time but with all our conveniences."

"And if possible, I landscape them as they would have been done in, say, 1790," Paul chimed in.

"Don't you receive state and federal tax credits?" Fair asked.

"I do, Paul doesn't. But as the developer, I do. The paperwork is overwhelming, and of course both Paul and I must go before the Albemarle County Planning Commission."

Paul jumped in. "Not just with historical planning, but also with environmental studies and now even wildlife habitats. Sometimes the paperwork, the prequalifications, take over a year."

"Public hearings too." Marshall nodded.

"Well, the tax credits are worth it," Ned said, and he would know.

Marshall agreed. "Since 2000, Reese Builders have received sixteen million dollars in state and federal tax credits." He held up his hands. "And I promise you, half of that goes toward the studies, the artist's renderings, the soil tests."

Joyce added, "And if there were just one misstep, you can bet Marshall would be vilified in the newspaper, smacked with lawsuits. It's absurd."

Harry said, "It's certainly overkill, but then most developers are probably not as careful as Marshall."

Marshall replied, "Most are. There's a rotten apple in any barrel, but you'd be surprised at how most people in this business want a good name." He smiled at Ginger. "We got off the track. You were telling us about your book."

With a small brandy snifter in his hand, Ginger chuckled. "The people who fled to Nova Scotia or back to England during Revolutionary times have been swept under the rug but they also helped create this country. Many lived over on Twenty South, the main road to Scottsville. And, of course, a few lived right here in what is now Crozet." He sipped, then continued. "Over decades, I've tracked these men and their wives through Oxford and Cambridge. A young assistant will call me tomorrow with the latest findings. As there is a five-hour time difference, it won't be long after that until tee time!"

"Speaking of golf, I can't wait to get back out." Susan sat upright, enthusiasm on her face.

"If I played as good as you do, I'd be thrilled too." Paul laughed. "For me, it's a fair amount of wishfulness, but I will prevail."

"That's what we all say." Nelson teased him and they all laughed.

The pleasing aroma of the burning wood added to the closeness of the evening.

"I'm eighty-two now and I wish I had eighty-two more years." Ginger smiled. "I'm just getting to the point where I see how it all fits together, the puzzle of the centuries. I will not live to see the next generation of historical breakthroughs. I hope UVA is at the forefront of these." The others, startled, looked at him with alarm, except for Trudy, who knew how her husband truly felt.

Nelson spoke lightly. "Ginger, you will forever be the history professor at UVA, and the department will continue your research without regard to political fashion. And you will always be a tolerable golfer."

They laughed again.

The Reverend Jones shared Ginger's emotions. He was in his seventies, and a lifetime of living and learning had only just begun to truly fall into place. He was only now understanding what Vietnam had meant to him when he was a young combat soldier in the Army. Despite the treatment at home, which both he and the nation finally overcame, he was grateful because he had learned to lead. Those lessons of being responsible for other men never left him, and he believed that sense of duty had made him a decent pastor.

Those who attended St. Luke's would have amended that to "a great pastor, a man of feeling, conviction, and love."

As the evening finally broke up, Susan reminded Nelson of tomorrow's tee times.

"I'm at one o'clock. My goal is to score my age on my birthday." Ginger smiled.

"If anyone can play his age, it's you," Susan complimented Ginger. "That's what Nelson meant by 'tolerable.' "

Driving home, Harry turned to her husband, all six feet five inches of him. "Honey, what's the big deal with shooting your age?"

He shrugged. "I'm not sure, but it is a big deal. Aren't you caddying for Susan? I'd think you'd know these things."

"Ha! The real reason I caddy for Susan is usually whoever is play-ing with her that day asks me to do it. She obsesses over what club to use, wastes time and more time. I just whip out a club and hand it to her."

"But you don't play. How do you know?"

"Years ago, when we were all in high school, I asked the school coach to tell me. Then I read some and watched some."

"God, Terry Baumgartner! Hadn't thought of him in years." Fair slowed for a patch of ground fog.

"Golf is a beautiful game. I just never had the patience for it. I need speed, whether my own or my horse's. I'd lose my mind standing over a little white ball and whacking it."

"Honey, millions of Americans are losing their minds. It's a heartbreaking game."

"Isn't that the truth! Susan can remember greens, weather, you name it, from thirty years ago when she was twelve! I can hardly remember last week."

"You remember a lot." He smiled. "But this shooting-your-age thing. Hardly anyone ever does it."

# 3

April 11, 2015

BoomBoom Craycroft and Susan Tucker rode in one green golf cart while Nelson Yarbrough and David Wheeler rode in another. Harry, as promised, rode in a third cart, along with her two cats, Mrs. Murphy and Pewter; Susan's golf bag; and a small thermos of hot tea sitting in the cupholder.

Brilliant sunshine flooded the fairways, yellow buds swelled on willows soon to open to a light green unique to the season. Spring, long and cool, promised more floral glory shortly. A ten-mile-an-hour wind from the west ensured that the day would feel cool even if the mercury climbed into the low sixties. As it was, the temperature at 2:30 hung in the high fifties, sweater weather.

The carts pulled up at the third tee. Despite a lingering light frost, people were eager to get out and begin a new season. Of course, this year their game would improve. They just knew it.

The foursome, having played together over the years, kept to a well-oiled routine. The ladies drove first off the ladies' tees, then the men followed from the men's tees.

BoomBoom, an 11 handicap, never one to dally, pulled her three wood from her bag, teed up, and hit a beauty straight down the long, long fairway. This course was built in 1927, land was cheap back then, and five-par holes could be built without destroying the

budget. Four- and a few five-par holes were common on these grand old courses. Farmington didn't need a lot of doglegs. If you could hit straight and true, read the roll of the land, you would enjoy playing the old course the old way. Still, sand traps, some tricky fairways, and deceptive sight lines here and there forced a player to think.

But then thinking is the easier part of golf; executing is another story. Susan, a 4 handicap, watched BoomBoom, another childhood friend. BoomBoom could drive. Her short game often let her down, but a woman really had to blast to match the tall blonde off the tee.

Susan was fussing. "Four wood? No, no, there's that hidden little bunker up there."

"Here. Just hit the damn thing." Harry handed her a three wood.

Irritated by Harry's directness, Susan stared at it. "All right."

She grabbed the three wood. The banter with Harry energized her. She could take it all out on the ball.

Mrs. Murphy and Pewter were allowed on the course because they were not destructive. Plus, they could find golf balls better than the humans. The two cats watched Susan tee up.

She was a natural. Gifted with a fluid swing, Susan made golf look easy. As a child she had watched the incomparable Mary Pat Janss, dreaming to rise to the competence of her idol. As Mary Pat had played internationally, that was a far putt, as they say. But the older woman recognized talent and happily worked with Susan, who adjusted to Mary Pat's take-no-prisoners attitude.

Golf had changed, as had everything, it seemed to Susan. Now promising young golfers needed sponsors and special coaches. Kids were slotted for same by ages twelve or thirteen. Could she have made it in the pros? Who knows? She didn't dwell on it. If she dwelled on anything, it was becoming club champion so her name would be inscribed on the list that many times included Mary Pat's.

Susan knocked one just a bit beyond BoomBoom's. Both balls sat squarely in the middle of the fairway.

David, also quite good, smiled at Nelson as he walked up to the tee. "I'll outdrive her. Then we can watch her frazzle."

"You can outdrive her, it's her second shot that kills you." Nelson smiled. "That woman has such control, and of her temper too."

Pewter found the entire process mysterious. *"Why do people hit this little thing, get in a cart and drive to it?"*

*"We've been doing it since we were kittens. Why ask now?"* replied Mrs. Murphy, the ever-sensible tiger cat.

The gray cat frowned. *"I've asked ever since we were kittens. You never answer."*

*"Because I can't. Pewter, why worry about it? We get to leave the farm, we ride around in this silly cart, and they are blissfully happy."*

Pewter eyed her friend. *"Then why do they curse so much?"*

Mrs. Murphy didn't answer. Instead, she watched David.

The ball came off his club head low, then rose and soared, gaining speed like a guided missile. David outdrove the ladies by a good thirty yards. It was a terrific shot, but the ball nudged the edge of the fairway. In slightly taller grass, his second shot to the green would take just enough power and a bit of a curve to land safely, as the sand traps guarding this green were notorious.

Nelson also blasted one. Not only had the tall man played quarterback for the University of Virginia, he'd also played pro ball in the Canadian league. If there was one thing Nelson possessed, it was power. He also hit a good clean shot, which, unlike David's, landed more to the left. His 15 handicap was deceptive because some days Nelson played to a much lower handicap than other days. Fifteen was a good average. The erratic nature of the game kept a player on cloud nine or in the dumps.

Everyone's second shot was pretty decent except for Nelson's. At the last second before contact he turned his clubface slightly, mishit the ball into either high rough or the bordering woods. He couldn't tell, but a search was in order.

Walking through the higher grass, no ball. Accepting his fate, Nelson trotted into the woods. He hated holding up play. Nestled under a fallen limb was his bright white ball.

Wisely he accepted the penalty shot, but before he stepped out of the woods back into the high rough, Nelson heard gunfire close by.

Looking around, he saw nothing, but he heard a yelp. Hurrying back to the cart, he said to David, "Did you hear that?"

"Did. Sounded like a pistol." David looked in the direction of the earlier sound. "I've often wanted to shoot myself after a bad shot. Hope no one did."

On the green, the five friends remarked on the strange sound, then settled down to putt. All made par but Nelson, thanks to his mishit.

Just as the players climbed into their carts, a course patrol drove up in a cart. Teenager Bobby Thomas's face was unusually grim. "Folks, please stay here until I return and tell you what to do next."

As he was speaking, a siren wailed. The foursome saw the lights flashing as an ambulance turned and drove on a cart path between their green and another. They couldn't see more than that, but they could hear the ambulance moving up ahead. Next came a squad car, sirens on, as the sheriff maneuvered the same pathway. Out of nowhere, it seemed that all the carts began to converge on the same path.

"Bobby, what's going on?" Susan asked.

"I can't tell you, but I will be back."

Out of the cart first, Susan walked the few steps to the men's cart. They, too, stood. Harry and BoomBoom then joined the others. The cats stayed on the seat.

"I don't remember any ambulance coming this far onto the course." BoomBoom frowned.

Nelson spoke. "Actually, I don't remember any ambulance, ever."

"What about Kirsten Menefee's heart attack?" Harry said.

David replied, "Driving range."

They listened intently after the sirens stopped. As beautiful as the spring day was, the four felt restless after forty-five minutes. They were instructed—commanded, actually—to stay right where they were. After an hour, Bobby Thomas returned.

"What's going on?" David politely asked.

"Ginger McConnell has"—he paused—"died."

"Of what?" Susan exclaimed.

"I don't know." A troubled look crossed the teen's face. "You are all to return to the club and wait there. A deputy wants to talk with you."

Harry blurted out, "Deputies don't show up for heart attacks."

"Mrs. Haristeen, I'm supposed to make sure you all go back to the club and remain with your carts."

"I'm sorry, Bobby. I didn't mean to put you on the spot." Harry felt guilty for pressing the young man.

Driving back to the cart return, Harry noticed carts streaming in from all directions, their occupants grim-faced and worried.

By the time her group reached the parking lot, a line had formed. An officer from the sheriff's department stood in the road, directing cart traffic. No cars moved anywhere. It was all golf carts.

Up ahead Harry saw deputies questioning players. Sheriff Rick Shaw emerged from the golf shop with the pro, Rob McNamara.

After twenty minutes, Harry's neighbor, Deputy Cynthia Cooper, reached the foursome. Each of the group had enough sense not to blurt out questions right away.

Cynthia acknowledged her neighbors, as well as Nelson and David. She scribbled something in her notebook.

Nelson noticed Marshall Reese and Paul Huber in a cart right behind them. They sat with Willis Fugate and Rudolph Putnam, two other former UVA football players. So many college athletes remained in Charlottesville, most becoming successful financially.

"Did anyone see a person run across the golf course?" Cooper asked.

Each of them said "No."

"Any suspicious movements at all?"

Same reply.

"Did anyone hear a motor? Not a car, but something like an all-terrain vehicle?"

"No."

"Any strange noise at all?"

Again, "No."

She then said, "If I need any of you, I'll call."

No sooner did she say "I'll call" than the television station's mobile cam truck appeared, slowly creeping down the main drive. Cooper stared, then said, "Danny will hold them up, but they'll park by the side of the road and nab people on the way out. Dammit!"

Danny was the young officer directing cart traffic, and he was already making his way over to the white van with the station's logo painted on its side in huge letters.

"Their job is to report the news. Our job is to prevent or solve crime. Rarely does misinformation or too much publicity help." She grimaced.

"Can I help?" Harry offered. "All of us would, you know."

Cooper held up her hands. "Harry, that's a frightening offer."

"*Got that right.*" Pewter, like the humans, recognized the danger of Harry's curiosity.

Cooper looked down the long, long line, other officers now showing up. "I'd better hop to it here." She then looked at each of the foursome. "Ginger McConnell has been shot and killed. If any of you can think of a reason why he would be targeted, let me know. You all knew him and maybe something will occur to you. Oh, you can turn in your carts now, and thanks." She moved to the carts behind them.

Face ashen, Nelson spoke to David. "Will you turn this in?"

"Of course."

Then the tall man made his way to his old teammates.

Next to BoomBoom, Susan remarked, "We just had dinner with Ginger and Trudy. This is hard to believe."

Harry was right behind the two carts, and turned hers in. She bid David good day, as well as BoomBoom. With the cats trailing behind her, she got into Susan's Audi station wagon.

The cats sat quietly in the back as Susan waited for a signal from Danny to pull out of the lot.

"I'm not stopping," Susan growled as the reporter attempted to flag her down.

"Good move," said Harry. "We don't know anything anyway."

Susan was teary. "Harry, a man of Ginger McConnell's stature, a renowned scholar, doesn't just get killed on the golf course. This is terrible."

Harry opened the glove compartment, yanking out a Kleenex. "Here. Would you like me to drive?"

Susan waved off the offer but took the Kleenex. "How can you stay so calm?"

"On the outside," came the tense reply.

"Maybe there's some mistake."

"Susan, how can there be a mistake if Coop tells us he was killed?"

Susan again waved her hand, then pulled over to the side of the road. "Maybe you better drive after all."

Sliding behind the wheel, Harry glanced into the rearview mirror. The two cats, eyes wide open, observed everything she and Susan did.

Harry thought to change the subject. "Hell of a shot you made back there off the tee."

Susan cried all the harder, so Harry drove her the rest of the way home in silence. She tried to remember everything from the last three holes. They'd been told that Ginger was on the eleventh hole, close to where they were when they heard gunfire. The eleventh hole is catty-cornered from where? A variety of ideas flitted through her mind, which she carefully did not share with Susan, whom she walked to her door.

"Want me to stay with you?" Harry asked.

Sniffling, Susan said, "No, no. Ned will be home soon. I expect he was called. If Sheriff Shaw ever needs any state support, he knows Ned is right here and will see he gets what he needs."

"All right, then." Harry handed Susan the keys to the Audi and returned to her truck, which she had left at Susan's house.

Lifting the cats in, although they could climb in themselves, she stepped on the foot rail to swing herself up. Harry didn't cry until she got home.

# 4

*B*umping along, the old John Deere tractor called Johnny Pop emitted the noise from its exhaust pipe that gave it its name. Harry could always think better when she was outside doing a chore. The crevices on the east side of the Blue Ridge Mountains had not yet escaped winter, but the sides flashed the first blush of red in the swelling leaf buds. She often wondered about that color when the sun hit the buds just before they opened. Why the red color and not green? She made a note to look that up when she returned to the farmhouse.

Red, the color of blood, dark if flowing from a vein, gorgeous red if spurting from an artery. One can't grow up in the country and not have seen cuts, wounds, or even worse. She wondered if Ginger had been covered in blood.

Turning the tractor around, she headed back toward the barn, a quarter of a mile away. She saw Cooper stepping out of a squad car, by the barn.

Tucker, the corgi, sat at the tall officer's feet. The intrepid dog trusted the deputy because Cooper always smelled safe.

The cats were sprawled in the tack room office. They paid no attention to the crunch of tires, the closing of a door, or the *pop-pop* of the tractor pulling up outside. Harry cut the motor. The John Deere let one last loud report, almost like gunfire.

Harry climbed down as Tucker walked over to her.

"Hey, what are you doing out here at this time of day?"

Cooper leaned against the door. "Aunt Tally called. She said her sidesaddle was missing, and she proceeded to inform me of the value."

"So Rick sent you out here?" asked Harry, mentioning the sheriff.

"Aunt Tally's important," Cooper simply answered. "They've got a team on Saturday's murder. I could be spared, the reason being that I can get along with Aunt Tally. Few can. Also, she knows everybody, their parents, their grandparents, their great-grandparents."

"That's a fact." Harry nodded, as Aunt Tally was now 102. Surely, she'd be the first human to reach two hundred years.

"Turns out that her great-niece took the saddle to her house to clean it up. One problem solved." Cooper brushed her hands together. "And Aunt Tally had no idea why Professor Ginger McConnell would be shot."

"Come on and have a cup of tea with me," Harry invited Cooper. "I could use a pickup."

"You know, I could use one too."

So different in backgrounds, the two women walked up the old brick path across the lawn to the screened-in porch door. Tucker hurried in to accompany them. The cats would miss extra treats, plus the chat between the humans. Already Tucker relished dispensing information only she had. That would irritate Pewter to no end.

In the kitchen, Harry asked, "Constant Comment? A green tea? I even have white teas, and if you want a real bomb wake-up I have my Yorkshire Gold."

"Yorkshire. I don't know why I'm sleepy today."

"Low pressure. Be raining mid-afternoon, one of those soaking, steady April rains." Harry pulled out two small silver tea balls, into which she put the correct amount of leaves. If you're going to make a cup of tea, do it properly. She then opened a cabinet door with a squeak, lifted out an old Brown Betty teapot, beloved of her mother.

A few minutes later, cup finally in hand, Cooper sipped the restorative beverage. "You've known the professor since childhood?"

Sitting opposite her, Harry remarked, "And I thought this was a social call."

"It is. You, Fair, Miranda, Aunt Tally, all of you born and bred around these parts, you know everyone and sometimes have insights I don't."

"I'll take that as a compliment."

"It is until you think you can be an amateur detective."

"Me? I wouldn't think of it!"

They both let that fat fib sit on the table. Below the table, even Tucker stifled a small bark.

"You didn't study with him," said Susan. "You were at Smith. Can you think of anyone who would want to kill Ginger McConnell?"

Harry leaned forward. "No, but Ginger bore the brunt of displeasure, that's the only way I know how to describe it, when the push for clarity about Thomas Jefferson's relationship with the slave Sally Hemings began to make news. The debate grew fiercer. I remember the uproar beginning in the eighties. Might be off a year or two, but the controversy kept going until DNA settled it, more or less."

"And?"

"Well, Ginger publicly said and was quoted in papers—even national papers—saying what any true historian would say, 'No line of inquiry should be shut down for ulterior considerations.' It was that word *ulterior* that was the match in the tinderbox."

"You mean for those who denied the possibility of a relationship between the two?" Cooper's eyebrows raised.

"No, both sides. The racists, naturally, blew a fuse. Maybe *racists* is the wrong word. They didn't think of themselves that way, they thought of themselves as defending the honor of a great man, while others didn't want to think about it. The descendants of Jefferson's liaison with Hemings thought they were being accused of seeking monetary gain. It was such a mess, but Ginger kept his hand on the tiller. He wouldn't cave to pressure from either side. He kept insisting we must collect and study all the evidence. Personally, he believed Hemings was Jefferson's mistress, but he never publicly said this. He truly believed no line of inquiry should be shut down." Harry added, "Today is Jefferson's birthday, by the way. April thirteenth, 1743."

Cooper held up her cup to clink Harry's, a toast of tea.

"Did he ever explain to you what he meant by *ulterior*?"

"He did. To Ginger, anything other than seeking the truth meant an ulterior motive. He was quite strict that way. Maybe a little too strict." She drained her cup, thought for a moment. "Do you think someone killed the professor over that? Now?"

"No. Well, let me back up a minute. Could a nutcase become inflamed reviewing that old issue? Sure. A nutcase can find a reason to kill you if you wear cargo pants. You never know."

"How was he killed?"

"High-caliber handgun. Two shots. Chest."

"Dear God!" Harry's hand covered her own heart. "Fair and I were going to go see Trudy, but Reverend Jones said to wait. He would tell us when she was ready. In the meantime, I know Trudy's friends and her daughters are doing all that can be done. The house has to be opened, and people have to come by, you know."

Cooper sighed. "I know. Back to his work. We've interviewed colleagues. We have heard all their descriptions of his research.

Most of them too technical, really, but that's why they do what they do. How would you characterize his work?"

"Let me think a minute. He had such a wide-ranging mind. He'd talk about most anything, but his area of expertise was the Revolutionary War and the years immediately following. Not political stuff like the collapse of the Articles of Confederation followed by the Constitutional Convention, but economic growth in the Mid-Atlantic, especially Virginia road building, movement of goods, population growth, which also included a swelling slave population. Remember we hadn't outlawed bringing in people from Africa yet."

"What do you mean?"

"In 1807 congress finally agreed to no more slave importation after 1808. No more slave ships. I add that the North had slaves, too."

"That I knew, but let me back up here. His focus was on the average person?"

Harry smiled. "Now, Coop, you know there are no average people, especially in Virginia, and especially on the day of Jefferson's birth."

"Right."

"It's obvious you think that Professor McConnell's murder has something to do with his work."

Cooper sighed again. "We have to consider every possibility just as Ginger would. This was a historical issue. No obvious deep-seated family troubles. You can only cover them up so much. No heated jealousy among his colleagues, many of whom are also retired. Professor Brinsley Sims kept up a close working relationship with him. Sims has been helpful. Nothing that Professor McConnell worked on had any bearing on a corporation's profits. It wasn't like he was investigating something that could be tied to climate change." She shrugged. "But you don't kill someone on the golf course without a powerful motive."

"Could this have something to do with golf?"

Cooper shook her head. "I know people get mad enough to kill, but still—"

"It's a game that's good for business," Harry shrewdly commented, "especially for older women, women who went to school before Title Nine, can't pull together like Nelson Yarbrough and his football teammates, but if they play golf, they can go out and hit with their corporate bosses and coworkers. They'll learn the rudiments of teamwork. Maybe I should say teamwork as defined by men."

"Hadn't thought of that." Cooper rested her hand on her chin. "Harry, would you make me another cup of tea? I am just dragging my ass. This one cup helped a little."

"Sure. I could use a second one too."

As Harry boiled water, Mrs. Murphy pushed through the animal doors, followed by Pewter.

Pewter got straight to the point. *"Are they eating anything? I don't smell anything."*

"No," the dog replied.

*"Can't you beg?"* Pewter encouraged the dog.

"No." Tucker was in no mood to humor the cat, whom she considered a conceited pest.

Mrs. Murphy leapt onto the kitchen counter to tap at a cabinet. *"This will work."*

As the steam spiraled out of the teapot snout, Harry opened the cabinet, tossed down some dried treats. "How about some cookies?" she asked Cooper.

The police officer considered this. "What kind of cookies?"

"Picky, picky. Shortbread cookies? The real kind."

"I would love a cookie."

With cookies on the plate and fresh cups of tea, they returned to discussing Professor McConnell.

"Did he enjoy retirement?" Cooper asked.

Harry immediately replied, "He never truly retired. The university, as a mark of esteem and gratitude, allowed him to keep his office, and he did have office hours. He didn't teach anymore, but he would confer with students, help them with studies, and he would give a special lecture if asked. Trudy always said, 'Thank God.' He'd have driven her mad underfoot."

"Wives always say that, don't they?"

"Sure seems to be the case." Harry smiled. "Ginger's old students like Paul Huber, Nelson Yarbrough, and Marshall Reese would drop in on him, as well as other professors. He was constantly busy. No, Ginger really didn't retire."

"I guess the worst thing you can do is to stop working, if you love your work, that is." Cooper bit into a delicious thick shortbread cookie. "I love these things. Okay, do you know what he was working on when he died?"

"At Reverend Jones's dinner, Ginger mentioned renewing his study of The Albemarle Barracks, reviewing old church records, land acquisitions, and agricultural growth. He thought of it as a peek into everyday life. He also tried to find old family Bibles."

"Why family Bibles?"

"We didn't have a census in this country until 1790. Anything you want to know before that, you need family Bibles or maybe court records if someone had a suit brought against them or was arrested. That's it." She thought for a moment. "Church records, baptisms, burials, and marriages. Many a priest and pastor kept records, and, I almost forgot, enlistment records for militias. Remember, we didn't have a standing army."

"I knew about the standing army but not about the census. I can see that he'd need to visit people and places. Isn't a lot of this on the Internet by now?"

"The public record, not family Bibles or church records. And Virginia still carries the mark of 1865. Thousands and thousands of records, family or public, were burned all across the state after Appomattox."

"Why?"

"People feared that after losing the war the men who fought for the Confederacy could be hanged as traitors. I don't think we can ever truly appreciate the chaos experienced then, and it would be even more chaotic if one had been a slave. Now you are free. Free to do what? Run, stay? Where could a man or woman hope to make a life for themselves, a life free of threat? But most of the records earlier than that were saved. Too far back to cause harm in 1865, 1866."

"Weren't soldiers also in fear of being branded traitors to the Crown during the Revolutionary War?"

"Coop, sure. If we'd lost, the trees would have been filled with hanged men. As it was, if you were a Continental soldier caught carrying a message, you were hanged. We returned the favor. You know, Coop, we've become narcotized by violence. Two huge World Wars, endless violence on television and in films, we forget that the Revolutionary War was no sure thing and it could be brutal."

"War. Going on, as we speak, in other places."

"I'm beginning to think that to kill is to be human," said Harry. "Not a happy thought," she paused, "especially when I think of Ginger."

Cooper glanced at the large clock on the wall. "Well, I am awake. I don't know if I've learned anything that can help me find who killed Ginger McConnell, but I've learned a lot." The lean woman smiled at her neighbor and friend.

"You're just starting in this. Murder is usually easy, at least that's what you've told me, because it generally signals someone losing their self-control. Drugs and drink may help there, or if they're standing over the corpse with a gun, a knife, or a brickbat."

"That's what worries me about this one," said Cooper. "Premeditated murders are a lot harder to solve. This is premeditated."

Harry walked Cooper to the screened-in porch door.

"Thought of one more thing," said Harry. "It isn't much, but Mother once told me that Ginger had to break up a romance between his daughter and a football player. Lots of emotion."

"Name?"

"I don't know."

"Thanks again for the tea." Cooper made a mental note to ask some of the old football players if they remembered.

As Cooper drove off, Harry said out loud, "Maybe it's better to die a swift death than to linger with some horrible malady." Then she caught herself. "How can I even think that about Ginger?"

"*Needless suffering is cruel,*" Tucker remarked. "*Think of those deer and bear who are wounded, and it takes them days or weeks to die. That's cruel. You've got to finish off your game.*"

"*I hardly think a professor emeritus of history is fair game,*" Mrs. Murphy drily noted.

# 5

*E*ach day at march's end or when the prisoners were allowed a brief respite from marching, Lieutenant Charles West would pull out a notebook and draw a farmhouse, a meandering creek, rock outcroppings, the roll of a hill or the shape of a tree. These things interested him, but he also wanted to forever remember this march. Over the last year many captured soldiers had made this journey. Leaving a week ago, West's group of veterans from the Battle of Saratoga was one of the last to leave Cambridge, Massachusetts. Outranked in his group by a Captain Graves from the Royal Irish Artillery as well as by a Hessian dragoon captain, West thought Graves a prophetic name for a dragoon.

Charles marched with his surviving four marksmen, and by the time they reached a large camp, a palisade thrown up west of the King's Highway, he was grateful to stop. How far west? He guessed a day's march. Merely a young lieutenant, and not of an elite unit, Charles was quiet and cooperative. The other captured officers outranked him, and quickly established their chain of command.

As the second son of an impoverished baron, Charles had been lucky his father had prevailed upon old friends to push his career forward. His father had borrowed to scrape together £450 to purchase Charles's lieutenancy. A good education and this army commission were his inheritance. His other paternal gift, the expensive flintlock pistol, remained in Captain John Schuyler's belt. Whatever Charles got in this life he would have to get on his own after his paternal send-off. He would rise through competence and bravery—if he survived this ordeal.

The young man's talents lay in drawing, possibly in architecture, but the army it was, and he did as he was told. Charles had found he liked the non-officers. He also liked a few of the junior officers, young men like himself or older men who had made a name for themselves in the Colonies in the recent French and Indian Wars. Men who had proven themselves in battle were worth more to him than a rich scion colonel. He wound up in Fraser's regiment with the marksmen because of his good, artistic eye. Charles could read terrain, and terrain in this New World proved demanding.

On a good day, the marching prisoners might cover fifteen miles. Usually it was ten, slowed by wagons and pack animals and those who, from fatigue or wounds, needed to be left in whatever care could be found. Piglet tacked along besides Charles, an indefatigable companion. He noted that they were moving southwest. Sometimes directly south, sometimes west, but ultimately southwest. Since the British, as far as he knew, still held New York Port, this made sense.

The Continentals followed streams and wagon roads moving away from the coast. To the west lay greater security. Conditions improved inland. Once they were even able to bathe in a deep creek while being guarded. The cold and clear water invigorated the well-built lieutenant. Other prisoners and even the guards laughed when Piglet took a flying leap into the creek to be with Charles, who then bathed him too.

As the prisoners pieced together their experiences at Bemis Heights, a few facts asserted themselves. The colonial Loyalist population did not rise up to help them, nor did they sabotage the

Continentals. And they fought blind. For whatever reason, the British invading force had lost its eyes, their Indian allies. None of the British on the march knew how many of their countrymen had died, but their losses were heavy enough. Those in the infantry on the field and on the rises said when they withdrew, the dead had covered the ground. Splashes of Redcoats and blood, blood everywhere.

Those captured on the day following Charles's capture, October 8, verified that General Burgoyne had retreated east of Saratoga, but they did not know where he'd gone. Some assumed he had kept going, others that he had returned to camp, others that he awaited reinforcements to again give battle.

Captain Graves growled that the general should have retreated to Albany, where the lines to Canada would be better. From that direction help might yet arrive. The Irishman made it no secret that he thought good men had been badly led. Higher ranking men ignored Graves. He was Irish, and they held that against him too.

Charles thought to himself that if the Canadian commander had wished to send troops, he would have done so before Saratoga, but he kept his mouth shut. That was a lesson he had learned early. Better to wait to be asked. And who would ask a nineteen-year-old lieutenant?

The sun was setting. Dappled light shone in meadows, and long slanting rays shafted through the endless forests bordering the rutted wagon trail. The frosts seemed to arrive the instant the sun set. If not in a camp, they slept on the ground without blankets. No man there had been able to retrieve gear, and the Continentals didn't have enough for themselves. Many of the marchers actually looked forward to being in a prison camp, for they would finally have a roof over their heads or at least some cover, and probably better food than they had on the march. Still, they were treated decently.

Hoofbeats alerted them. Calls came from behind. A messenger rode alongside and then surged forward to Captain Schuyler. The column stopped, men dropped to sit by the side of the road, glad for a breather. Charles noted that the messenger was a major and wore a full Continental uniform. He was on his way to becoming a ranking officer; deportment mattered. After a few words with Schuyler, the major trotted off. Charles noted that the horse was fit. Forage in this land was easy to find and good for the rebels.

Back on the road, the silver evening star rose large and luminous. With relief, they marched into a fort. Temporary but not badly built huts would provide shelter from the frost. As the prisoners were directed into the dwellings, each exhausted man dropped onto a bed, ropes sagging underneath straw mattresses.

Fresh bread and cheese appeared. The farmers and carters were eager for money. The prisoners as well as the men normally assigned to this small makeshift camp pumped a bit of money into local pockets.

Captain John Schuyler walked into Charles's hut, and Charles noted that his captor always wore the flintlock he'd taken from him. While it might be the fortune of war to Schuyler, Charles wanted it back. "You learned while imprisoned at Cambridge that General Burgoyne surrendered his army to General Gates October seventeenth, shortly after the Battle of Saratoga," Schuyler informed the British soldiers. "The terms of the surrender were that troops will be sent back to Europe after parole if each man promises not to again fight here."

A silence greeted this announcement until a Hessian corporal, Karl Ix, asked, "Us too, right?"

"Those of you from Hesse will be exchanged for our men. I think, gentlemen, those are favorable terms. However, the major just told me your king is dragging his feet. He doesn't want to negotiate with those he considers traitors. It's all still dragging on."

With that, Schuyler left. The twelve men in the hut waited until they no longer heard Schuyler's footfalls, then all spoke at once. Though the Battle of Saratoga was nearly two years before, the prisoners were still putting together the pieces as more information became known.

Karl's English was good, although he spoke with a pronounced accent. He boomed, "The whole army! The king can't ignore the loss of one of his armies."

"Burgoyne couldn't surrender it piecemeal," declared Samuel MacLeish, one of Charles's men. "Six thousand men."

"Not after the battle," Edward Thimble remarked. "The rebels gave Burgoyne good terms. The king and his counselors sit in luxury in London. The people may be rebels, but they whipped us. Honor the deal."

"Aye," a few others agreed.

Another chimed in. "The rebel bastards can fight."

"If Clinton had reinforced us, we'd have won," said Thomas Parsons, another Ranger and the oldest man among this group at thirty-five. His voice stuttered with conviction and regret.

"I expect there is abundant blame to be apportioned," Charles wryly said as the men laughed.

Too tired to talk more, they soon fell asleep. Piglet snuggled next to his human, each appreciating the other's warmth. As Charles drifted off, he felt this war would go on. The Colonials were organized, fighting for a belief.

He believed in king and country. How could these people dream of political success without a king or queen? But then, how could they dream of ultimate military victory with raggle-taggle militias? Yet those same militias had defeated an army.

These provocative thoughts floated through his mind as he closed his eyes. He promised himself he would record as much as he could.

# 6

*M*arshall Reese's business was located on Pantops Mountain and was filled with six of his former teammates. The UVA alumni had gathered in short order to discuss a proper memorial to the professor they loved.

Pantops Mountain, on the eastern edge of Charlottesville, was once home to just one large, pleasant home, then a private school, and was now filled with modern buildings. The upscale location of his office was as important for Marshall, a real estate developer, as it was for some doctors, lawyers, or investment firms. Part of success is appearing successful.

Marshall's personal office easily accommodated the assembled alumni, which, given the time during which they had matriculated at the University of Virginia, were all white and male. Behind the partner's desk, specially imported from England, a Fry-Jefferson map hung on the wall. Showing the roads in 1755, the facsimile gave the viewer a good idea of roads still in use. Back then, coach travel was uncomfortable but had to be endured. Rivers offered better transport, but usually heading only toward the Atlantic Ocean. In order to move up and down the coast, or due west, one had to go by coach, on horseback, or on foot.

"Would anyone care for a drink?" offered Marshall, still plenty fit despite the passing years.

"I know where it is. I'll tend bar." Lionel Gardner took a few drink orders. He was class of 1961 and had flown in from Los Angeles after hearing the horrible news about Professor McConnell's death.

A large leather couch and leather club chairs bore testimony to Marshall's success, just in case you'd missed his name on signs in front of numerous high-end developments, all with a historical theme. Finally settled, Nelson Yarbrough's distinctive gravelly voice opened the gathering. Once a quarterback, always a quarterback. "Marshall, thank you for allowing us to use your office, and Lionel, thank you for flying in from the coast." The two men nodded to the acknowledgment. "I'll get right to the point: What can we do to honor a good man and a great professor?"

A brief silence followed this, then Lionel said, "To start, we should send a wreath from the team."

"Does Trudy want flowers?" asked Rudolph Putnam, fullback 1960, now a rich paving contractor.

"She and the kids," said Marshall, "felt this was more important to the giver than to them, but Olivia wishes we will distribute to the hospitals afterward." The McConnells had two children, one now in her late fifties and another in her early fifties. He then added, "They're worried there isn't room for all the people who will attend the service."

"Hadn't thought of that." Paul frowned, picturing the small chapel.

"Can they mic the service for those standing outside?" Lionel had picked up a few media terms in L.A.

"Yes," Marshall simply said.

Nelson added, "We also have the use of the lawn and Pavilion Seven after the service. It's all arranged."

Recently, there had been an uproar over the university president being ousted in 2012. She was then reinstated, thanks to a revolt of students and faculty, prompting Willis's question, "Is the president going to attend?"

"Not only is Teresa Sullivan going to attend, most of the Board of Visitors, past and present, will be there; former university presidents; both Virginia senators; the governor; a smattering of representatives, as well as state officials. David Toscano is leading the state group, as you would expect. Everyone will be there. Larry Sabato, just everyone." Marshall beamed. "The *Richmond Times Dispatch*, of course, already printed a fulsome obituary, but a reporter will also be at the service and at the Pavilion."

"If we could announce at the Pavilion that we are endowing a chair in the history department in his name, I can't think of any more fitting tribute." Nelson's voice carried conviction and emotion.

Paul Huber gasped. "We'll need millions."

"Tim Jardine, class of '72, made a great deal of money in Wall Street. He's pledged one million to get us started," Nelson informed them. "And Tim also pledges to lead the drive."

All of a sudden, everyone was talking at once.

"I pledge another million." Marshall's voice rose. "Ginger is one of the main reasons for my success." Indicating the Fry-Jefferson map on the wall, he said, "I constantly study that map, which was a gift from Ginger. In my work, I've always studied the early landowners, tried to keep a bit of the history with the demand for new housing, new people. I put up a marker at the entrance to each development, giving the history of the place. It's the least I could do."

They all knew this, but Marshall was proud, ever reminding people.

Nelson smiled. "Gentlemen, you can see how important this is, and few of us can give millions. I know I can't, but Sandra and I will do our best to be generous. I will work with Tim in the drive for funds, but I will need your help—"

Marshall interrupted. "Tim Jardine says he will also take care of the endowment once we have the monies."

"Well, what do we need? I mean, do we need, say, twelve million dollars all at once?" Willis, an artist, made a decent living, but he earned nothing like the others. He did, however, live an exciting and full life. This was a man not suited for business or compromise.

Marshall spoke again. "Endowing a chair essentially means providing a high salary to attract a leading professor to the school. A star professor in the sciences or medical research might command a million dollars with additional benefits, research assistants, et cetera. For a nationally significant history professor, we have to compete with Yale, Harvard, Stanford, Princeton, you name it. I would like the salary to be commensurate with those in medicine or scientific research, to announce our steadfast belief in the humanities. Mr. Jefferson certainly believed in them."

Although most of these men had made careers in medicine, law, or business, their educational underpinning in the humanities had served them well. They had a long view of human affairs, thanks to Ginger McConnell.

Lionel threw in his lot. "Nelson, I think Jennifer and I can scrape up fifty thousand dollars. That might pay for the phone bills, the trips to talk to people personally."

"Hear, hear!" the others cheered.

"I assume the history department will be the ones hiring this person. Why can't we save money by hiring a young man or woman," Lionel said, adding hastily, "one on the way up, with salary escalators?"

"That's part of a discussion with the university," Rudolph remarked. "We can't do anything without their being on board."

"I doubt they would pass on such a generous offer," Lionel wryly commented.

"Well, we know the university can't endow a chair. Chairs are always endowed by individuals. Then, too, the budget is approved by the legislature." Willis sourly added, "That's the damned trouble with state schools."

"So it is, but state school or not, this is one of the leading universities in America," Marshall proudly stated.

Rudolph waved his hand dismissively. "Yes, but it's so difficult for a state school to compete with a private institution like Yale or Stanford."

"That's a discussion for another day." Nelson guided the conversation back to the topic at hand. "Are we all together on this? The goal is to raise initially ten million, and we've already got two."

"I'm in." Willis nodded. "I always do what the quarterback tells me." Willis was a good fullback in 1959, a position somewhat in flux today with the various offensive formations.

The rest of the meeting was taken up with each man agreeing to fund-raise from a list of names given to him, all known to him. As the meeting was breaking up, Paul said to Nelson, "What about Ginger's publisher? He won award after award, so he had to have made them money."

"He did, but a history bestseller isn't like *Fifty Shades of Grey*."

Marshall, overhearing the query, stepped in. "Given some of the punishment out there on the field, I think we could write *Fifty Shades of Black and Blue*."

Nelson smiled slowly.

Marshall smiled back. "With Trudy's permission, I did contact his publisher. They will give us one hundred thousand dollars, a goodly sum for them."

Paul shook his head. "Strange business. I don't understand it."

"I'm not sure the people in it understand it. Probably what makes it exciting. Building a high-end home is fulfilling, some creativity is involved, but pretty much, it's cut and dried. I prefer more of a sure thing," Marshall remarked.

"Well, you sure hit it," Paul replied.

As the men filed out, Nelson began to clean up the glasses, not many.

"Nelson, the cleaning service will take care of that," Marshall said, then changed the subject. "I thought that went very well, did you?"

"I did. I just want to make sure that everyone feels included even if they can't write a check."

"You thinking about Frank Cresey?" Marshall mentioned a spectacular failure from the seventies, now a homeless resident of the Downtown Mall. "You know, Frank wouldn't give us money even if he had it. He always blamed Ginger for his flameout."

Nelson quietly agreed. "No, he wouldn't."

"If Olivia had been my daughter, I would have done the same thing."

"Yes, I think most of us would. Frank drank too much, even when he played football."

"Drank, hell! He had FUTURE ALCOHOLIC tattooed on his forehead. But he was handsome. All-American. A fun party boy. Olivia thought he was a knight in shining armor."

As Marshall closed the door to the office, he flicked off the lights, one of which shone directly on the Fry-Jefferson 1755 map. "On today's date, Lincoln was assassinated."

Nelson murmured, "You always remember historical dates, but I suppose we should all remember that one."

"Ginger's murder doesn't have the repercussions of a presidential assassination, but it's terrible. Can't get it out of my mind."

Walking with Marshall to their cars, Nelson agreed that he couldn't get it out of his mind either. What he didn't say was that one of the things he had learned in Ginger's history class was that violence is like a firecracker. One pop sets off explosions. He truly hoped that was not the case now.

# 7

*S*hort and wiry, uneducated but intelligent, Edward Thimble packed mixed mud and straw between the open spaces separating the fir trees used as sides for barracks. His hands were raw from the wet mud.

Charles, next to him, also shoved mud between the spaces. "Poor stuff. Still, we have to try something."

The marksmen stuck together. Those captured from other units gravitated toward these men, and the guards thought that was fine. Charles West was a natural leader and kept his men working. They loved him. Few other British officers cared to work along-side their men or share their hardships; he was a rarity. As it was, most captured British officers were being housed in individual homes in the area, while others had remained in Cambridge. Their hosts, although aware that these men were the enemy, were also aware that they were well born and sophisticated. And, like all Colonials, they aped their "betters" even as they wished to form their own country. Hosting a British or Hessian officer carried social cachet.

"*A storm is coming.*" Piglet lifted his handsome head, sniffing toward the north.

"These people need crofters," Sam MacLeish grumbled. "Not

one house in eight hundred miles was thatched. If we could do that, we'd be warm enough."

"So you think they have the right kind of reeds?" Edward asked.

"Nah, but we can use straw. If we can find some straw or convince the guards to give us some, I can get up there on that worthless roof. Tree trunks with split fir trees overlap. Do not these outlaws know how to build?"

"You saw the brick homes." Charles remembered some large, handsome houses between Saratoga and Charlottesville, Virginia—now their home, more or less.

The Albemarle Barracks—tossed together west of Charlottesville and northwest of Scottsville, the local gathering center on the James River—afforded an inspiring view of the Blue Ridge Mountains, but little else.

Farmers, cobblers, and tailors from Charlottesville and Scottsville began to frequent The Barracks, as they called the prisoner-of-war camp. It was not heavily fortified; there was no need to do so in winter, as most of the captured had sense enough to know they wouldn't survive long in these winters. Not that a vicious wind and snow could knock the Scottish lowlands or northern England, but the weather here seemed wilder somehow. As for the captured Scots from the Highlands, they could endure anything. They planned their escape for spring.

The Barracks had been thrown up in haste; more were under construction.

The American Captain Schuyler walked by. "Chinking."

"I beg your pardon, Sir?" said Charles, on the north side of the long twenty-four-foot wall. He raised his blonde eyebrows.

"That's what we call filling in the spaces between logs. Unfortunately, what you have isn't the best, but it's a beginning."

Sam MacLeish called down to Charles, "Sir, might you ask the captain about some straw or reeds?"

Charles looked directly into John Schuyler's eyes, as was his habit. "Might we have some, Captain? To help with the roof? Begging your pardon, but these barracks are . . ."

Edward finished the sentence, ". . . windy."

Captain Schuyler did not commit himself. Instead, he changed the subject, turning to Charles. "Your drawing book, where did you learn to draw? You drew as we marched. And you draw now."

"My father allowed me a tutor when I was young, before he sent me off to Harrow."

"Your pictures are true to life. If you would draw one of me, I would send it to my mother."

"I haven't many materials, but if you could bring me some good paper, pencils, and perhaps even paints, yes, I could do it."

Schuyler hedged a bit. "No telling when mails will arrive from England, Scotland, or Hesse. I'm sure your father will send money and the enlisted men, perhaps a bit."

Charles smiled. "Ah, Sir, my father is a baron, but he is not a wealthy man. He won't be sending me anything. Perhaps you would make me a loan against my pistol, which you could give me, after I'm released, of course."

Schuyler smiled in return. "I will purchase supplies, and I will keep your pistol. For a poor fellow, this is a fine weapon."

"Indeed it is. Our harvests had been bad, and even though my father owns large acreages, the bills outrun the means to pay them."

"Perhaps when you are exchanged, you will return home and amend that situation."

"I'm a younger son."

"Ah!" Schuyler simply replied. He knew, given England's laws of primogeniture, that this young, energetic man would inherit little, if anything at all.

However, West remained ever motivated. "But if you bring me

paper and drawing charcoal or pencils, I will gladly draw you. When your mother receives your portrait, she will feel you are in the room."

The young captain's eyes flickered. He greatly loved his mother. "I'll see to the straw."

# 8

April 15, 2015

Just west of Farmington Country Club on Route 250, on the north side of the road, Ivy Nurseries was doing a robust business. The beautiful day drew in everyone who wanted to try new plantings. On such a day, everyone thinks they can garden.

Over the holidays, Susan Tucker often filled in at the nursery. Formerly, she worked full-time, but as Ned's career took up more time and energy for both partners, Susan had cut back on her work hours. Both she and Ned realized that public service, not an easy road, was surely an exciting and expensive one.

Susan and Harry strolled through rows of boxwoods. "They have English boxwoods," said Susan. Two lovely rows of old, tight English boxwoods lined the McConnell driveway just down the road at Ednam Forest. This well-established high-end development was exceeded in desirability only by Farmington Country Club, itself on the west end, and the up-and-coming Keswick Club on the east.

Three things were necessary to live in any of these places: money, affability, and taste. Naturally, the taste was always questionable. What one person finds beautiful, another finds too tried and true, which means everyone else does it.

"Why don't we try two dwarf crepe myrtles?" suggested Susan.

"If we get them in now, they'll bloom mid-July, provide a bright note. Trudy likes color."

Harry walked with Susan to where the bushes were in pots, ready to go. "You never suggested dwarf crepe myrtles to me."

"You have enough to take care of: the quarter acre of grapes, the sunflowers, the corn. You don't have time to garden, and I don't have time to do it for you."

"Depresses me," grumbled Harry.

"Why?"

"Her gardens meant so much to my mother."

"Harry, your mother didn't have as much to do as you do."

As they bickered over what color to purchase, Olivia Gaston, the older daughter of Ginger and Trudy McConnell, came into view across the lot. As she meandered—a stop here, a stop there—Harry spotted her first. "Let's ask Olivia."

They greeted her.

"I had to get away," Olivia explained. "I couldn't take one more guest. Rennie is with Mom. I don't know how she does it."

Rennie, Renata, was Olivia's younger sister.

"She's outgoing," Susan said. "All the visitors don't make her tired. You're more sensible."

Olivia smiled. "How diplomatic."

"I'm so sorry about your father," Harry said sincerely.

"Thank you."

Susan reassuringly touched Olivia's arm. "You've heard from so many people. It's got to be overwhelming, which is why we're here."

"Here?"

"We wanted to plant two dwarf crepe myrtles for your mother. They'll bloom in mid-summer, giving color at an off time, just before the zinnias and mums take off."

"What a good idea!" said Olivia. "Well, I'll buy two, one from

Rennie and one from me, so we can sort of mass them, you know?" When Olivia smiled, it was her father's generous smile.

"What color should we get your mother?" asked Susan.

"She will like the hot pink. If she could, she'd wear hot pink to the funeral. I think I'm awash in beige because of her. You know how, when you're young, you swear you'll never grow up to be like your mother?"

"We know," both women said in unison.

"Let me go fetch Nathan," said Susan, naming the man in charge of moving larger plants and trees.

Harry and Olivia waited, observing the springtime planters: sniffing this, buying that.

"Is that Elizabeth Taliaferro?" Olivia inquired. "I haven't seen her in years. Well, that's what happens when you move away. She's held up rather well. Let her hair go gray. Looks good." She lowered her voice. "Daddy so loved my strawberry-blonde hair that I colored it just for him. I suppose I always will color my hair even if I look ridiculous. And I suppose my husband is accustomed to it."

"Olivia, you could never look ridiculous," Harry complimented her.

They purchased the four crepe myrtles, and Nathan loaded them onto Harry's truck. The three women leaned against the truck for a moment.

"Olivia, we'll come by tomorrow to plant them. What, say noon? You pick the spot."

"I wish we could do it now! Mother will be happy. However, I don't know where she keeps the gardening tools. So doing it tomorrow instead will give me a little time to get things together. Actually, once Mom reached eighty, she hired a gardener. That was my first clue that Mom and Dad are, were, growing old." Olivia's eyes misted. "You never really think these things will happen, and now this."

"It's a terrible shock," Susan consoled her.

Olivia looked at Harry. "The sheriff and your neighbor came by. They asked a lot of questions. They must, I suppose. One that took me by surprise is that they asked about Frank Cresey. I haven't thought about him for decades. Oh, I was so in love with him when I was eighteen! He made All-American . . . 1975? Yes, it was '75, and Dad broke it up. Wouldn't let me see him. Dad actually told the coach of the football team to give Frank an ultimatum. If he kept trying to contact me, he'd be off the team. The coach demurred, but Dad insisted and finally got his way, I suppose, because Frank never contacted me again. And I learned that football was more important for Frank than I was. Thank God, Dad did break it up. I'd have never been happy."

"Once a UVA player, always." Susan smiled. "That's what Ned says, but remember Ned treads carefully. He's William and Mary, but heard that teammates tried to help Frank over the years. Once a Wahoo, forever a Wahoo," she said, using UVA's nickname. "After all, Frank was an All-American. The older players established by the time of Frank's glory especially tried. Gave him a job when he was down on his luck. Stuff like that."

"What did happen to him?" asked Olivia. "Mom said he failed at business. At everything. He wrote Dad hateful letters. I didn't know any of this until the nineties. Mom said Frank's marriage blew up. He blamed Dad, always blamed Dad."

"Olivia"—Susan paused—"Frank lives on the Downtown Mall." "What!"

"He does. Ned has the sheriff's department pick him up and put him in the Salvation Army shelter during the winters. He's a total drunk."

"My God!" Olivia's hand flew to her heart. "He was beautiful, you know. He could have gone into the pros. I had no idea."

That was obvious.

"I don't think your mother knows how far he has fallen," Harry said.

"I swear some people are born self-destructive," said Susan. "Frank is one of them. Ned does what he can. His fear is one of those damned reality shows will dig him up. From All-American to Bowery Bum, or something like that. Frank will start raving. People would eat that up. How the mighty have fallen. That sort of thing." Susan's lip curled.

"On the mall?" Olivia half whispered, horrified as it sunk in.

Harry frowned as she recalled. "The only two times that anyone could cite where your father endured people's anger was during the revival of the Jefferson-Hemings controversy and Frank's bitter lost love, I guess that's what you'd call it. But Fair says that Frank even drank back when he was on the team. He heard it from older football players."

"Yes, Officer Cooper brought up the Hemings affair," said Olivia. "All water over the dam. No one even then threatened to kill Dad."

"Do you think Frank might've threatened your father?"

Her blue eyes widened. "Daddy never told me." She paused. "But then he never told me anything. He thought he was protecting me, and he was. Once I got over hating him for breaking us up, I realized that."

Driving to Susan's to drop her off, Harry inquired, "You don't think Olivia will do anything stupid, do you?"

"Like what?"

"Like go down to the mall and see Frank."

Susan gasped. "Harry, don't even think that!"

# 9

*D*ebating what to do, Harry pulled her old truck into Susan's driveway. After they unloaded the four dwarf crepe myrtles next to the garage, Harry opened the front door and called for Tucker, who had been left behind at Susan's to play with her brother.

"*Where are we going?*" Tucker asked, happy to be outside.

"In the truck, kid." She lifted the solid corgi onto Susan's lap. "I'll get Owen."

Driving out the curving driveway, Tucker sat between the two women while her brother Owen sat in Susan's lap.

"You make me crazy," said Susan.

"Ditto."

"Well, why did you have to say anything about Olivia going to the mall?"

"It popped into my head, Susan. I've explained myself all the way down Route Two-fifty. I'm not going to explain myself all the way back. It just popped into my head, and I got a funny feeling."

"Well, now I do too. She was shocked, and, well . . ."

"She has diminished judgment. Death, divorce, even losing your job causes such turmoil. Diminished judgment can last as long as the loss or sorrow. At least that's what I've observed."

"Yes," Susan tersely replied.

Neither spoke until they reached the Charlottesville Downtown Mall. Once the hub of economic activity, Main Street was blocked off to through traffic in 1976, creating a walking mall. Harry's mother had a fit because, she declared, they could walk just fine when there were cars and sidewalks. When the anchor to this scheme—the large department store, Miller & Rhoads—left, activity sagged, and with it, profits. Over time, nice restaurants took over old spaces, the Paramount Theater was restored, specialty shops opened. Much had improved, but like all those revitalization ideas, the city planners rarely took into account how people really shop. At least there was still a large hotel at the western end, the Omni.

Harry pulled her truck into the parking garage at the eastern end, circling upward until she found a space big enough to park the 1978 Ford F-150. She and Susan hopped out, lifted out their corgis, snapped on the dogs' leashes. The concrete stairwell's heavy walls amplified their steps.

"I don't know why I do things with you," said Susan. "All you do is get me into trouble."

"Oh, spare me, Sissy Tolerance! You get me in as much trouble as I get you. Now, where do you think the drunks are on this beautiful spring day?"

"Down by the Paramount, I guess."

They headed to what people thought of as the center of the mall, passing storefront shops, displays in the large windows. As they reached the Paramount, they heard a scream.

"Don't touch me!" they heard Olivia's voice holler, then saw her backing away from a man at one of the large planters filled with blooms.

"Let's go!" Tucker gave a hard yank on her leash. She flew across the brick walkway.

"Tucker!" Harry yelled.

Owen also broke free from Susan. The two dogs and two women ran toward Olivia. Tucker reached her first and spun around, facing the man advancing on her. *"Touch her and you die!"*

Bloodshot eyes looked down at the corgi as Owen reached the scene. He bared his fangs. Olivia, startled by the shocked reaction of Frank Cresey when he saw her, was now startled and gratified by her two protectors. Harry and Susan reached Olivia as a small crowd of people gathered around.

"What are you doing here?" growled Frank. He wore tattered clothing, had long, unkempt hair. His beautiful body was now wasted and thin.

"Come on, Olivia, let's go." Harry put her arm through Olivia's.

Susan was trying not to breathe, as Frank reeked of sweat, alcohol, and urine. She inserted herself between Olivia and Frank, as did the two dogs. "Frank, she has as much right to the mall as anyone."

First mistake. Never try to reason with a drunk.

Frank took a step toward Susan, who held her ground, as Harry pulled the transfixed woman away. That fast, both dogs latched on to a leg. He was so loaded with alcohol, he barely felt it.

"Owen, leave him!"

With jaws clamped tightly around a thin lower leg, the corgi, not yet willing to release Frank, looked up at his human.

"I'm glad he's dead, you know!" Frank screamed, so the retreating Olivia could hear him. "Ruined my life. I hope he died in fear and pain! You came here to pity me. I don't want your pity. I don't want to ever see you again. And you'll never see your father again!"

Susan backtracked and again ordered, "Owen, Tucker, come on!"

The two dogs released Frank. Trotting to Susan, they were still looking backward, fangs bared.

A man attempted to help Frank, bleeding heavily now, to a bench on the mall. Frank backhanded the Good Samaritan. Two police of-

ficers appeared from different directions, both running. Frank howled, no words, just howled.

Harry half pulled, half dragged Olivia to Fourth Street. When she reached the corner, she pulled Olivia into Daedalus Used Books. The proprietor, Sandy McAdams, looked up just as Susan, Tucker, and Owen crossed the threshold.

"Ladies, dogs, is it literature that created such flushed cheeks?" The bearded book lover smiled.

"Oh, Sandy." Harry caught her breath. "You don't know how good you look!"

Before he could respond, Susan filled him in on the uproar on the mall.

"Frank Cresey," said Sandy. "Well, well, I'm not surprised. Some days he walks into the store, sits down, and picks up a book. I give it to him just to get him out because customers can't stand the smell. Other days when he's clean, I let him stay. He says he was the star halfback on the 1975 UVA football team. Hard to believe."

"He was," Olivia quietly affirmed.

"Oh, sorry, Sandy," said Harry. "This is Olivia Gaston, Ginger McConnell's daughter. She lives in New Orleans with a brilliantly industrious husband."

"Your father was a wonderful man, and a good customer," said Sandy. "Please accept my sympathies."

"Thank you." Flustered, Olivia glanced from Sandy to Harry to Susan, then down to the corgis. "This is all my fault."

"You are not responsible for a drunk," Susan firmly told her.

"He screamed he'd recognize me anywhere, which after forty years amazes me." She turned to Sandy. "I was wildly in love with him when I was eighteen, and Daddy broke it up. I haven't seen him since."

"Your father was a wise man." Sandy took a deep breath. "Those poor devils have killed so many of their brain cells, even if they could once think rationally, they've forgotten how. But—he recognized you. How extraordinary."

"Olivia hasn't aged much." Susan smiled.

"Susan, that's a fib." Olivia was calming down. "I've changed, my hair color hasn't." She half laughed.

*"Any good books on dogs?"* Tucker inquired.

Sandy reached under his desk, twirling two pungent treats, which he tossed to the dogs.

*"Better than a book."* Owen swallowed.

"We'll get out of your hair, Sandy," Susan apologized. "But we knew we'd be safe here."

"Thank you. If you need anything, let me know. More books coming in every day." He smiled, then turned to Olivia. "Your father would call once a week to ask if I had found anything from 1775 to 1820. Occasionally I come upon valuable old books, or I hear of a family Bible that's turned up. He was diligent. He wanted old maps, old anything. He'd go down to Richmond, up to D.C., to Atlanta. I remember, one time, he drove to Guilford, North Carolina, as some wonderful old Revolutionary War maps turned up. Big battle there, you know."

"I know. We lost that one." Olivia smiled. "Daddy would talk about that time as though remembering old friends."

"I guess to him they were," Sandy said kindly. "We owe who and what we are to those who came before. Now, please, let me help you with anything, anything at all."

As the group left, they walked toward the parking lot, where Olivia had also parked. Her car—well, her mother's car—was on the second level, so they entered the stairwell. It was always dark, a source of complaint, but Olivia was glad because she burst into tears.

"I am so stupid."

At the second-floor landing, Susan put her arms around the slender woman. "You've had a terrible shock and you've lost one of the mainstays of your life. A girl only gets one father."

"I don't know what possessed me. I . . ." The group entered the garage's second level.

Harry, ever logical, said, "We shouldn't have told you where Frank lives, so to speak. Curiosity would drive any of us to take a peek."

"Forty years. Why would I want to look at him? I guess I couldn't believe he'd fallen so low." She wiped away the tears with a handkerchief supplied by Susan, always ready for flat tires, tears, headaches, anything and everything.

"Everything is a jumble when someone you love dies." Harry knelt down to pet Tucker and then Owen. "At least it was for me when Mom and Dad died."

Olivia stood up straighter. "Here I was acting as though I'm the only person to ever lose a father, and I had mine so much longer than you had yours, Harry. I don't know what's wrong with me."

Susan said, "Nothing is wrong with you. It's just right now, and for the next few months, it's best not to make major decisions."

When Olivia looked puzzled, Harry succinctly said, "Diminished judgment."

"Yes." Olivia walked to her car. She pushed the unlock button on her key ring but didn't open the car door. "I can't sleep. I keep turning over in my mind who would want to harm my father, the kindest of men. I even rummaged through his desk at home, the file cabinets, looked through his checkbook. I was sure I'd find a clue, but no. His piles of research were, as they always were, neat stacks all over his desk and some on the floor."

"Did he use a computer?" Harry wondered.

"Daddy? He did. He was slow. Of course he had all those research assistants at UVA. All he had to do was tell them to look up something, or send a message to a colleague who used email. Dad was hands-on. Even if one of his 'kids,' as he called them, handed him research papers, if he could, he'd drive to examine the original sources. He was fanatical about that."

Although seeing that Olivia was more composed, Susan suggested, just in case, "How about if I drive you home? Harry can follow. Good plan, I think."

Olivia hesitated for a moment. "Yes. Yes, I think it is." She scanned both of their faces. "Please don't say anything to Mother or Rennie. No reason to upset them over my mistake. My curiosity got the better of me."

"Of course not." Susan took the keys from Olivia's hand and slid behind the wheel as Olivia walked to the passenger door.

Five minutes later and two levels up, Harry opened the truck door. A little creak reminded her: Time for more grease. She lifted the dogs onto the bench seat, swung herself up, and then followed Susan and Olivia home.

"I wonder if Frank is even strong enough to kill someone," she mused aloud.

"Best not to find out," warned Tucker, still angry at the man.

# 10

December 25, 1779

*S*now squalls swirled through the camp, promising heavier snows
soon. From each barracks, a tendril of smoke attempted to escape
from the log fireplaces—only to be flattened by the low pressure.
Brick would have been far better for the fireplaces, but logs, charred,
cost nothing. Central Virginia's red clay made excellent bricks, but
brick, practical and beautiful as it was, proved expensive. An all-
brick home shouted *Money!* Many lovely clapboard homes splurged
on brick fireplaces. However, not the primitive log barracks now
housing the British prisoners. And worse, from time to time, a
downdraft pushed the smoke back into the rectangular interiors.

Sergeant Edward Thimble's thatching of the roof helped keep in
the warmth. When the needles died on the cross-laid firs, and the
rain, sleet, and snow filtered inside, accentuating the gloom, the
sergeant was suddenly much in demand to thatch other barracks.
The commandant of the prison camp secured extra funds from the
colony's legislature for straw. His appeal was met with grumblings
from the governor of Virginia about how wickedly the colonists
who were imprisoned by the British were being treated. Many
rebel prisoners were held in the holds of ships anchored in the
harbors of coastal cities occupied by the British. And for helping
the Continental soldiers, many civilians were also suffering in mis-

erable conditions. The accepted rules on the treatment of prisoners of war were ignored by the British, although the standards were known throughout the Western world. As far as the Crown was concerned, these rebellious people were criminals at best, traitors at worst. Since they were not recognized as soldiers, they could not be exchanged, and were subject to deplorable conditions. Many died of disease. The terms of surrender at Saratoga had now been emphatically denied by the Crown, creating uncertainty for all.

In contrast, the Continental commanders behaved with decency toward their captives.

General Washington was distressed by the suffering of men he considered patriots, men he considered under his care, but his entreaties and letters to Britain's General Howe and others were ignored. Clearly, the king and his ministers meant to teach the upstarts a painful lesson. And so they did. They also hardened the colonists' resolve.

The war that the British had thought to win quickly dragged on and on.

As the small number of captives from Captain Alexander Fraser's regiment sat around the fire, smoking clay pipes, they wondered how long they would be imprisoned. Edward Thimble groaned, "I can count on the fingers of one hand the number of women I have seen since I was brought here!"

"Oh, Edward, 'tis not that bad!" Samuel teased. "The sutlers' wives come along, and some have daughters."

"Not enough. I'm tired of looking at your ugly faces." Then Edward laughed and quickly glanced at Charles West. "Not yours, Lieutenant!"

At that moment, they heard the men in the next barracks singing, men from the Braunschweiger Regiment. "They keep their customs," Edward remarked of the Hessians.

Charles simply noted, "As do we."

Sam lowered his voice, although no one other than his mates was near enough to hear him. "When spring comes, we have got to put ourselves forward to work on the farms. Better than being cooped up here."

Thomas counseled, "Do your job for the family that takes you. Who's to say, Samuel, they won't have a beautiful daughter! Falling in love with a woman isn't a crime now, is it?"

A silence followed this observation, then Sam piped up: "With my face?"

They laughed. Thomas said, "'Tis different for you, isn't it, Sir?"

Charles nodded. "As an officer, I do not know if I would be allowed to go out for farm work. But I would not mind. Along the way on our long march here, Americans could have spit on us, thrown rocks, but they did not."

"They wanted our money," Edward caustically observed.

"And why not?" Thomas challenged him. "There's no harm in making a shilling, now, is there? If we marched on London, people would sell food for a price. People have to make out as best they can, and 'tis no crime to feed a man."

"No," Charles quietly spoke. "But I fear we are here for a long time."

"They cannot win," Edward said of the war, his voice carrying belief. "They have had some luck, and they can fight. I thought they would run the first time they saw Redcoats drawn in a line, but they did not. Still, they cannot win."

"Their rifles are better than our muskets." Thomas admired their firearms. "Their gunsmiths are good, very good."

"Cannons not as good as ours," Samuel observed without emotion.

"What good does that do unless you're on flat ground?" Edward asked. "We couldn't get our cannon proper set at Saratoga. That's what Howard said." Howard Wilson, 53rd Regiment, had gotten separated from his unit in the smoke, but he had seen the problems with the cannon and the hard push by the Continentals. He was assigned to another barracks.

"What do you think, Lieutenant?" Thomas asked.

"We underestimated them, but for how long can they hold on?" Charles shook his head. "War costs thousands and thousands of pounds. The Crown can afford it. I doubt the colonists can. But I will wager it will not be over soon."

"And more of us will be coming here, I think." Thomas reckoned they were building more barracks for a reason.

"Lieutenant, you can do anything with a pen and paper. We saw the drawing you did for Captain Schuyler." Sam folded his large, rough hands together. "To the life! And your handwriting is like your drawing, wonderful to see. Would you write a letter for me? For my little brother?"

"Of course. I will write for any man who cannot write."

Edward admired Charles's skill. "I can write, but not with flourishes."

"I want clear papers," a corporal said. "Papers that state where I served. We will all need them to collect our pensions."

"You will never see a ha'penny," puffed Edward.

Thomas sat quite still for a moment. "A man could make a good life here. Why go back to England to fight and wait for what's owed? I'm here. I will stay here."

Quiet enveloped them. No one protested. Then Sam said, "A man could make a good life here with the right woman!"

They all laughed. They laughed even harder when Piglet scratched at the door. Charles opened it and the intrepid dog burst through with a string of wurst. Charles brushed off what had to have been part of the Hessian Christmas celebration, gave one to Piglet, and all the men took one.

"Happy Christmas, Piglet!" Edward cheered.

Later, Charles lay back, his head next to Piglet's own. He thought how strange life was. The certainties vanish. What takes their place is resourcefulness and thanking God for life.

# 11

"Will you get back in the cart!" Susan ordered Harry, who, with the cats trailing her, rummaged in the rough.

The lean woman trotted toward the cart, cats following on their own sweet time. "I'm coming. I'm coming."

"*Susan's a crab today,*" Pewter noted.

Since the fat gray cat could outcrab any human, Mrs. Murphy wisely kept her mouth shut. The human and two cats hopped into the golf cart. Susan floored it, jerking them all backward, as she sped to her ball on the tenth green.

Stepping out, Susan saw her ball shimmering on the green. "Ha!"

Harry walked up and handed Susan her putter. Out on the course late after planting the dwarf crepe myrtles for Trudy McConnell, the two passed golfers rolling back in, carts chugging. Few were headed in their direction. Late-afternoon Thursdays, except in summer, didn't have as many people on the course as the mornings or mid-afternoons.

Except for her caddy, Harry, Susan felt as though she had the course to herself. As a woman who could read greens, terrain of any sort, she knelt down, looked at the hole, which had been set on a slight, deceptive rise. Miss your putt and the ball would roll back if you lacked force, or roll beyond it if you hit too hard. Susan loved these challenges. Harry thought she was nuts, but then this was an old argument. With a light grip and a sharp eye, relaxed, Susan nailed the eight-foot putt.

"I am going to be ready this year!" she vowed. "You just wait."

"Susan, you can do it. You can be club champion."

Bending over, plucking out her golf ball, Susan beamed, half skipping back to her cart.

*"Takes so little to make her happy,"* Pewter remarked.

Mrs. Murphy always appreciated any rolling object and had been known to push around a soccer ball. *"It was a good putt,"* she declared.

The next hole would punish a player who got lazy. With a slanted fairway and hidden sand traps, it called for a well-hit but not terribly long ball. A curve in the fairway meant that if you hit big and straight, you'd sail off into one of those damn traps. On the right side, a particular rough awaited.

Using the club handed to her by Harry, Susan popped a high ball that dropped just to the right, not far into the rough, but far enough that Susan knew she'd have a devil of a time with her second shot. Through intelligence rather than power, she was working hard this season to shave a stroke here, a stroke there. *Touch:* Sometimes she could just feel the shot in her hands. For example, she had known the minute she hit the ball that it would veer to the right, not a lot, but enough to make trouble.

"Damn. Damn. Damn!" She strode back to the cart, tossed her wood into the bag next to the alarmed cats. As she started to speed off, she realized that Harry was still back there. She stopped as Harry came toward her.

"Better you figure this out now than when you start playing this summer," said Harry.

Susan agreed. "Yeah. But I know this hole, and I also know if there's even the slightest wind, it cuts through the fairway. You'd better hit into, as opposed to away from, it. So what did I do? No wind, so I didn't pay attention."

"Susan, it is possible to hit a less-than-perfect shot. No matter what."

"How would you know? You swung a golf club once, in tenth grade. I tried to get you to play with me." Susan directed some of her ire toward Harry, who had become accustomed to this on the course.

"What are friends for?" Harry patiently let her friend vent her frustration. "I remember. I also remember that you had no patience with me."

Susan lurched to a stop, hopped out. "I was very patient."

Harry joined her in the rough, as did the cats. Good pickings in the roughs if you liked field mice and voles. Harry found the ball, not too far into the rough but hard next to a tree stump that had been neatly sawed years ago. Susan came over, looking down in disgust at the traitorous ball.

"Oh, bother!"

Harry looked through the rough and back onto the fairway where Ginger McConnell had been shot. "Clear view," she said.

"No, it isn't. A limb hangs low."

"Susan, look here. Clear view."

"I don't care about that. I need to get my ball out of here without racking up the strokes. This is a real pisser, excuse my French!"

Pewter hopped up on the tree stump. *"Owee! Susan rarely cusses."*

*"Golf brings out her emotions."* Mrs. Murphy smiled. *"You and I should be grateful that Mom didn't take it up."*

*"Think she'd swear?"* Pewter said, as she was joined by Mrs. Murphy on the tree stump. Good view from up here. She kept an eye out for unsuspecting mice.

*"Remember when the vacuum cleaner broke?"* Mrs. Murphy said.

"You're right."

The gray cat leaned on the tiger cat. "*The air was blue. Mom would cuss her way through all eighteen holes. Ha!*"

Worrying about which club she should use, Harry ignored Susan, walked back to the cart, and pulled out a seven iron.

Susan took it from her hand, looked at it. "Oh, I don't know. Hand me the five."

"Just do it, Susan. Wait a minute. Let me move the cats off this stump, just in case."

"I am not going to hit Mrs. Murphy or Pewter!"

"No, but they could jump down just as you are swinging. Let's not take the chance." Harry picked up Mrs. Murphy with both hands, put her down. When she reached for Pewter, the gray cat jumped down. *No mice around here, with all these noisy humans tramping about!*

Susan waited for a moment for the cats to get far enough out of the way. Then, as she stood over her ball as best she could, Harry suddenly exclaimed, "Spikes!"

"What now?" Susan exhaled, her patience depleted and utterly put out.

"Look at this." Harry pointed to the top of the stump. "Spike marks."

Susan peered down. "So what?"

"A clear view, a good angle to height, an easy shot, and it's thick in here. Whoever did it could just walk out, casually carrying a ball they supposedly hit into the rough."

Susan finally realized Harry was talking about Ginger's murder. "Oh, now, let's not get carried away. People are in here all the time looking for lost balls."

"Was not Ginger killed in the middle of that fairway?" Harry pointed.

"Yes, but we don't know the exact location."

"Stand still." Harry walked behind Susan, lifted her up so her feet hung at the same level as the stump. "Now look."

"Well?"

"Do you have a long, clear view?"

Susan wasn't ready to agree. "Possibly."

Harry, strong as an ox, put her down.

"I could have just stood on the stump," said Susan.

"And put your spike marks there to cover up the ones already there? I'm going to show this to Coop."

"Harry, don't get carried away. It never leads to"—she paused, thinking of the right word—"safety. Now, how am I going to take this shot?"

Harry, Mrs. Murphy, and Pewter moved back onto the fairway, where they could see Susan, who hit it just right, taking a piece of bark with the ball. The ball didn't make it all the way to the green, but landed perhaps thirty yards from it. Not bad. With a careful third shot, Susan would get up there close to the pin. The hole might not be the disaster she'd imagined.

Once back in the cart, Harry took over the wheel. She was tired of being jerked about, but now smiled. "Good shot. How'd you do it?"

Susan smiled back. "Thought of what Mary Pat would do."

"Funny, isn't it, how we miss some people? Even though they're gone, they're not. They are still teaching us."

"It's true. I bet those people who took Ginger's classes still remember many of the things he said, or they look up passages in one of his books." She turned to Harry. "Can you still hear your mother's voice?"

"Yes."

They rode in silence to the ball. From there, Susan lifted it right up onto the green. She missed her putt by inches so she was one stroke over par. Given the mess it could have been, she grumbled only a little. Driving back, they bumped over a little crack in the paved path. Harry stopped the cart. A foursome played ahead.

"Getting cool," Susan remarked.

"We'll make two more holes. Won't get that cold."

"You know, yesterday haunts me. I can't get Frank Cresey out of my mind. To see someone hit the skids like that man has. Ever notice it's often the football players or the other team sport players who take a nosedive? Not so much golf or tennis."

"I don't know. Maybe they just hide it better. It's got to be a huge adjustment to go from that kind of adoration and money to being over the hill."

"The good thing about yesterday was that it took our minds off of tax day."

Harry laughed. "Every cloud has a silver lining." She looked ahead at the foursome. "They're moving on."

"Good." Susan bounded out. "Maybe it's better to forget a lot of things. Focus on the present."

"Maybe," answered Harry, but she didn't sound like she believed it, not that Susan noticed. She was impatiently waiting for Harry to give her a club.

# 12

"Purest blue," Harry said to the two cats and Tucker as they walked around the house, inspecting her flower beds and the sky above. "Those huge cumulus clouds, so white, set off the blue."

Tucker tagged right behind her human, the faint scent of a rabbit somewhere nearby enticing her. Mrs. Murphy picked up the odor too. *"That bunny better not nip off the daffodils."*

Daffodils, four inches above the ground, bulbs swelling, promised color soon to come along with the jonquils. The snowdrops had passed, crocuses still bloomed here and there, but the riot of color was only a week away, if that, that first burst of spring. Three weeks would pass until the redbuds, the yellow willows, and finally the dogwoods would explode on lawns and on the mountainsides. High spring brought with it spring fever to animals. Calves frolicked, horses chased one another, while deer observed from the distance, amused. Birds opened the sunrise with a chorus that ended only at twilight, which then filled with whip-poor-wills' calls. Other night creatures also sang or croaked. Spring in the Blue Ridge Mountains so intoxicated people that only the most insensitive or overly burdened could keep their minds on practical matters.

Harry ran her hands over the top of the boxwoods along her

walkway. The quiet *whoosh*, the snapping back of the branches, satisfied her that those dark green shrubs would grow a lot this year. Not that English boxwoods ever enjoyed the annual growth of American boxwoods, but the density and shape of the English boxwood couldn't be duplicated by any other bush.

"*Let's go to the barn,*" Pewter urged Harry. "*I'd like to check the mouse holes.*"

Tucker, walking next to the gray cat, replied, "*You'd like to see if there's any kibble in the tack room bowl.*"

Pewter ran ahead before Tucker could bump her. "*What's it there for, Bubblebutt?*"

Mrs. Murphy ran to catch up with Pewter. This morning was a morning for running. The tiger cat drew alongside Pewter, passed her, then bolted in front of her. She stopped, then leapt over the other cat, landing behind her. "*Whoopee!*"

Tucker trotted up to the cats. "*You're too fat for acrobatics.*"

"*Peon!*" The gray cannonball jumped and soared over the corgi with surprising grace.

The show made Harry laugh. She joined the dash, ran up to them, passed them. Harry ran to the tractor shed and back to the barn, the three animals frolicking with her. Sheer exhilarating silliness—what could be better? Breathlessly, they all dashed into the barn, first squeezing through the small opening in the large double doors. As winter receded, Harry would open the barn doors at both ends of the aisle for more air circulation.

The cats proceeded to play tag. Mrs. Murphy reached the ladder built on the wall up to the hayloft. Nimbly, the cat clawed her way up, Pewter in pursuit. They chased each other around the square hay bales, on the bales, between the bales, their speed increasing. Down in the main aisle, Harry listened to the thumps overhead.

She looked at the stoic corgi. "Oh, Tucker, to be a cat for a day."

Tucker had many occasions to question the intelligence of the human she loved. This was one of them. *"Better to be a corgi."*

*"Don't touch me!"* Pewter cried from up in the loft. She had her back to a hay bale, standing on her hind legs, claws unsheathed, as Mrs. Murphy crouched, ready to pounce.

Behind the plump puss emerged another, decidedly different form. Matilda, the huge blacksnake, out of hibernation but still groggy, flicked her tongue. What was this fatty doing at the entrance to her home? *Egad.*

Matilda had used the same hay bale for years, and Harry gave her a wide berth, plus a few treats in the spring before she revved herself up for hunting. Matilda hunted a radius around the barn, sheds, and house from which she never varied. You could tell the time of spring or summer by where Matilda was. High summer she lived in the gorgeous old tree by the back screen door. Occasionally she would hang from a branch and swing, which sent Pewter into orbit.

Another rocket launch was about to happen, because Matilda, eyes now wide open, drew herself up, large body curled underneath her, and let out a loud *"Ssssst!"*

Pewter shot straight up, fur puffed out, turned in midair to reach the top of Matilda's hay bale. This further irritated the snake, who now stuck her head out.

The drama queen screamed, *"A dragon! I'm going to die!"*

Prudently backing up, Mrs. Murphy hollered, *"Calm down. It's just Matilda."*

Those glittering snake eyes now focused on the tiger cat. However, Matilda, half in, half out of her hay bale, twisted around to give Pewter the full effect.

*"Save me!"* cried Pewter.

"What the hell is going on up there?" Harry climbed the ladder, passed the hay bale where Simon the opossum hid, way in the back.

Discretion seemed the better part of valor for the opossum. Although half a pet after all these years, he mostly stayed out of view.

Seeing Harry, Pewter wailed more piteously. *"The biggest snake in the world. She's as long as the barn."*

Pewter and Matilda regarded each other. Harry, who quite liked this snake, spoke in a low voice. "I'm going to reach over you and lift off this terrified cat."

Matilda turned around to fold herself back into her cozy quarters, although in fairness to Pewter's frazzled nerves, it did take quite a bit of time for the serpent to whirl around her hind end. At last she was back in the rear of the bale, comfortable in her home.

Harry leaned over to lift up the cat, who put her arms around Harry's neck. "She is huge, Pewts. I'll give you that." Walking to the ladder, Harry put the cat down. Mrs. Murphy already sat nearby, her expression bemused.

*"You could have tried to help me."* Pewter swatted at Mrs. Murphy, who deftly avoided the slap.

*"I give Matilda a wide berth,"* the tiger cat admitted. *"She's okay, but still ..."*

Most of the expensive alfalfa and orchard grass/clover mix hay had been used up, and the hayloft was almost empty. Harry was reminded to clean the rafters. Cobwebs in summer catch flies, but by this time of the year, those cobwebs hung in dark clumps and strings. Time to take the leaf blower, bring them down, and sweep up the debris. The next generation of spiders would build silky new webs to catch the next generation of flies.

Climbing down, Harry walked into her tack room, sat down at her desk, and made a note to clean. Under it, she added the need to purchase more square alfalfa hay bales. Harry ran a tight ship. She grew her own orchard-grass hay, round-baled it, and if the hay was exceptionally good, when she needed square bales, she'd unroll a round bale and square-bale it. All this took expensive equipment. When he died, her father left hay equipment behind. Harry used the same equipment today as had her father, who had kept things in the best order. Sooner or later some of it would wear out. However, if well cared for, farm equipment from good manufacturers could last decades and decades.

Scribbling on a notepad designed by Gustave Eiffel, she whistled. The day was beautiful. She actually loved making lists and planning. She'd like to think it was in part due to her efficiency that her crops had brought in enough money last fall so she now had a little cushion. Purchasing alfalfa wasn't going to crack her budget. Harry counted her blessings.

The phone rang. Susan's voice sounded as if she was in the next room. "Hey, I called the house. No answer, so I'm calling the barn."

"What's up?"

"Frank Cresey tried to kill himself."

Harry thought for a moment. "What did he have to live for? Poor devil, he even failed at suicide?"

Knowing how Harry's mind worked, Susan was not put off by this response. "I don't know what he's got to live for, but maybe if he makes it, he'll find something."

"How'd you find out?"

"Olivia called me. Sobbing. Feels this is her fault."

"How could it be her fault? He started his love affair with the bottle a long, long time ago." Harry marveled at the human capacity to feel guilt. And then there were those who felt no guilt at all, regardless of what they'd done. Did Ginger's killer feel guilt?

Susan stated the obvious. "Olivia's a very emotional woman."

"Trudy's not. Where did she get that?"

"Harry, it doesn't matter. She just is, and she's upset. She didn't tell her mother or Rennie about the scene on the mall. She called me because, well, you know, it's obvious."

"I guess," said Harry, to whom it wasn't obvious at all. "Is there anything I can do, or we can do?"

"Yes, meet me at the McConnell house. We'll take Olivia for a drive or something. Her mother and sister know she's upset. They don't know much more."

"All right. I'll be over there shortly. Right now I'm in my work clothes. And I have to put the animals in the house. I don't think Olivia would mind them, but it'd just be us."

"That's fine."

Harry reached the house in Ednam Forest in twenty-five minutes. In the driveway, she stepped out of her truck and into the backseat of Susan's Audi station wagon. Olivia sat in the front seat.

As Susan backed out, Harry reached forward, putting her hand on Olivia's shoulder. Olivia covered Harry's hand with her own.

The women talked in the car as Susan drove all the way to Sugar Hollow.

"I set him off," Olivia cried. "I never imagined he would recognize me."

"You've changed very little," Susan remarked, observing from the road here that this part of Albemarle County was about one week behind the rest with its spring flowers and such.

"How did you find out, Olivia?" asked Harry.

"Sheriff Shaw."

"What!" Both Harry and Susan exclaimed.

Olivia stared straight ahead, but didn't seem to see the road. "When Frank was picked up on the mall after a nine-one-one call, he was writhing, retching, screaming in pain. So the ambulance driver obviously took him immediately to UVA Hospital, which is close by. They stabilized him, washed him, cleaned him up, and put him in a room by himself. He was unconscious by then, plus the doctor had given him something to calm him down."

"Poor devil!" Susan exclaimed, checking in the rearview mirror to see Harry's expression.

Olivia composed herself. "Well, when he became conscious, he asked for the sheriff. Sheriff Shaw and Deputy Cooper came to the hospital. Frank confessed to killing Daddy."

"What!" Both Harry and Susan exclaimed again in unison. They were a regular Greek chorus.

"Frank said he shot Daddy with a .45."

Harry's keen mind was like a blade being sharpened. "Frank yelled on the mall that he wished he'd killed your father. Now he says he did."

"Yes, I told the sheriff that, too."

"And?" Harry's voice lifted.

Olivia turned all the way around in the seat and looked Harry in the eye. "He pointed out that Daddy was killed by a .45. But Frank says he walked up, faced him at a distance, called out his name, and shot him. Obviously, he didn't. Brinsley Sims said no one was on the fairway when Dad was shot." Brinsley Sims, a longtime friend of Ginger's, had been playing golf with him that horrible day.

"I've read where people confess to crimes they haven't committed," Susan thoughtfully mentioned as she slowed for a curve on the old gravel two-lane road.

Olivia's tears slowed. "Why? To save someone else?"

"That, or for attention," and Susan. "And then there are always those who are crazy, flat-out crazy," she added.

"Frank would seem to fit the bill," Olivia softly replied.

"Being a drunk makes someone deceitful, shrewd even, but not necessarily crazy," Harry said.

"Alcohol kills brain cells. Sooner or later, the mind unravels." Olivia stared out the window. "Frank had a good mind. He remembered all those complicated football plays. How he could run, how he could run and fly through tackles as though they weren't there." She sighed at the memory. "And he was a good history student. Daddy liked him until we started dating."

"Somehow, seeing someone with a good mind, with athletic talent, ruin themselves with alcohol, it seems worse than if they were average." Susan pulled to the side of the road.

"Doesn't mean he wouldn't have become a drunk. Think of all the brilliant people who destroy themselves and everyone around them by drinking," Harry replied.

A flash of humor enlivened Olivia. "Harry, you sound like Carrie Nation!"

"I'll bring my hatchet next time." Harry was glad to see Olivia bouncing back just a touch. "She wasn't really wrong, but Prohibition was. You can't legislate human behavior. Murder. Right! The Ten Commandments: 'Thou Shalt Not Steal,' but we've been fleecing one another for thousands of years. And how does one circumvent 'Thou Shalt Not Kill'?"

"Nations always come up with a reason. Daddy used to say there are times when the only answer is war. Without that, some problems will never be settled."

Harry's curiosity rose up. "Did he mention murder?"

"Funny you ask that, because I was trying to remember if he talked about that, and I don't think he did. Oh, if there was something in the news, he would discuss it, but other than something like that, no. Dad concentrated on the grand sweep of history, on the lives of our ancestors. Sometimes he might talk about the crime rate, such as after the Revolutionary War."

Susan turned around to head back toward town. "There is a difference between murder and war. At least I think there is."

"Volume, for one thing." Harry tossed that off.

"There is that," Olivia agreed.

"For whatever reason, Frank's confession is peculiar," said Susan. "Peculiar, unbelievable, some weird fantasy."

Harry turned sideways to put her right leg up on the rear seat. "Did Sheriff Shaw say how Frank tried to kill himself?"

"Rat poison, but he didn't take enough. He also said that all that retching only brought up alcohol. Frank hadn't eaten for days, and that seems not to have been unusual."

"Forgive me for asking this, but it could be important." Harry leaned forward. "Did you ever sleep with Frank?"

"Oh, my God, no! Not back then. I mean, if I had, and Daddy had found out, he would have killed Frank." Harry looked into the rearview mirror and saw Susan looking back at her.

Harry changed the subject. "Ginger, as always, was hard at work on something. He said that he was returning to the Revolutionary War and immediately after. He also said that he had to have lived this long to ask the right questions."

Olivia smiled, remembering her father's enthusiasm. It was like a kid's. "Oh, Daddy would say to me when we talked on the phone, 'Before now, I never wondered how those who secretly thought we were wrong to separate from England accepted the new order. The really passionate ones fled to Canada or returned to England.'"

Harry knew something about early history. "It is interesting, but apart from the Whiskey Rebellion, people did accept the new ways. Trying to figure out how to run a new country, how to make money, no doubt took up everyone's time," she mused.

"Your father really was enthusiastic," said Susan. "He bubbled over. When I was in school, they'd focus on the wars only, and you had to memorize the dates. But the periods leading up to war and then their aftermath are critical. If you don't get it right, boom!, another war, or at least some form of collapse." Susan smiled. "That's what Ned says. He's the reader, not me."

"Maybe we all need to go back and read about that time," Harry suggested, although she couldn't understand what had set off Ginger's killer. Sometimes, nearly anything sets off a new idea or radical course of action.

# 13

*N*elson Yarbrough, Marshall Reese, Paul Huber, and Rudy Putnam sat in Frank's hospital room.

When the admitting doctor had asked Frank his next of kin, he had given Nelson Yarbrough's name. Despite being no relation, Frank put Nelson's name down, as he'd always looked up to the quarterback. As a kid, he had worshipped him. Nelson, shocked to receive the call from the hospital physician, called the alumni in town. With the exception of Willis Fugate, who was in D.C. that day, they all showed up at the hospital in support—of Nelson Yarbrough rather than Frank Cresey.

Gasping for breath, hooked up to an IV, Frank couldn't believe his bloodshot eyes as he looked at this gathering of football players: his childhood heroes, all of whom had tried to help him over the years. "Will you all bury me?"

Nelson answered simply, "Frank, you're going to live."

Frank flinched. "Why? I've made a mess of it, and I killed Professor McConnell."

Paul took a chair beside the hospital bed. "That doesn't seem possible."

But Frank just nodded.

His four visitors exchanged glances.

Paul Huber said, "Frank, what you did was swallow rat poison, but not enough. You'll come through this. This is a blessing in disguise. You can come back. I know you can."

"He's right." Nelson seconded the idea.

"Better I die. I don't want to go on trial."

Not one of the men thought Frank had killed Ginger McConnell. Too many gaping holes in that scenario.

Marshall grinned, trying to jolly Frank along. "You drank too much, buddy. We all know a Wahoo can drink, but you are in a class by yourself."

Frank smiled weakly. "Not this time." Then, suddenly animated, he sat up and spoke louder. "I saw her. I saw her, and she was beautiful."

They all knew who, even though they didn't know of the incident with Olivia on the mall. The four stayed another half an hour. At last Frank, wearied, fell asleep.

The men stepped outside into the hall.

A nurse walked by.

Marshall whispered, for they were in a hospital. "No way in hell he could have killed Professor McConnell. Christ, he couldn't hold a gun without it shaking. He's delusional. Do you think he really saw Olivia?"

"He thinks he did," Nelson noted.

"Complicates things. If he pulls through, where does he go? Back on the mall?" Paul hated seeing a former All-American in this condition.

Rudy folded his arms across his chest. "No. We'll think of something."

"He might come up with something," said Marshall. "I'll call Lionel."

Lionel had returned to L.A., but was coming back to Charlottesville for the professor's funeral. Good thing he was successful, as those coast-to-coast flights cost a bundle.

"There's a halfway house, city owned, on the east side of the mall," said Paul, who volunteered, "I'll check into it."

"I don't think he'll live with other people." Marshall gratefully sank onto the bench along the wall. The others took seats as well.

"Everything at once." Rudy's shoulders sagged. "But the endowed chair seems to be coming along."

"Tim Jardine knows money better than anyone," said Nelson. "I think we should each give Frank's physician and the nurses on this floor our cell numbers. If he does anything foolish, tries to leave, makes a scene, one of us might be reached. I also think we could make a schedule so that one of us visits him every day until he's discharged. With luck, by then the police should know more about who shot Ginger."

"God, what a mess!" Rudy dropped his head for a moment.

"Yes, it is, but it's gotten us back together, working as a team." Nelson stood up, slapped Rudy on the back. He looked for the head nurse to give her his cell number.

# 14

Trudy stepped out through her front door as Harry and Susan set the last dwarf crepe myrtle in a hole. "Girls, come on in and have some lemonade."

"Wonderful idea," Susan enthused. "Be another ten minutes at the most," she called to Trudy. "Don't you think planting these four balances the ones we put in earlier? It bothered me that you'd have all this color on the right side of the house. Needs balance."

"You're right, but then, Susan, you're the gardener," said Trudy. "Don't bother to knock. Just come in." She closed the door.

The two friends finished up, watered the crepe myrtles, washed their hands under the hose, checked their shoes. Had they tracked dirt in the house, Trudy wouldn't have minded, but Susan would have pitched a fit. Harry, not so much.

Tucker and Owen, who had accompanied Harry and Susan, got their paws wiped before entering the house. Tucker wiggled with happiness—in part because she could go home and lord it over Pewter, expressly not invited.

As they entered the front door, Trudy called out, "In the kitchen."

The four creatures walked down a wide center aisle to the rest of the house. The kitchen sparkled. Ginger and Trudy had lavished attention and money on a colonial kitchen with a walk-in fireplace on the western wall. Fieldstone covered that entire wall. The one non-colonial element they had insisted on when they were building the house was a wall of windows. She hated a dark house. So the kitchen, apart from the windows overlooking the backyard, also had two large French doors with paned glass. The kitchen glowed with light at two o'clock in the afternoon.

Trudy put the finishing touches on a tray, on which was a large lemonade pitcher, glasses with polka dots, a china plate filled with peanut-butter cookies, and a smaller plate loaded with dog biscuits.

"Oh, Trudy, you're the best." Harry filched a cookie before they even sat down. "The Devil made me do it!"

Susan carried the tray to the kitchen table. Too hot outside. Glad for the company, Trudy chattered about the weather, the ongoing struggles over a proposed bypass, the state's response to federal guidelines for schools. Trudy's passion had always been education, and when she and Ginger first married, she had taught at an elementary school until her children were born.

Tucker and Owen sat on either side of Trudy, who fed them a treat now and then. The reward was a love-drenched look.

"Did I tell you the girls drove to Richmond to pick up Adrian?"

Susan bit into a fat-filled cookie. "No. I wondered where they were."

"Adrian will be here through the next week. He apologized over and over for not coming with Olivia, but I told him I understood. Running a big company has to be both exciting and frustrating." Adrian Gaston made a fortune by perfecting a special plastic packaging. Starting with two other workers, his factory had expanded to 650. His product was used by almost every food service, shipper, and supermarket in the eastern United States.

"An amazing man." Harry admired anyone who started their

own business, whether it was an artisan cabinetmaker or someone who made it big like Adrian.

"Olivia." Trudy paused. "So many gentlemen callers, as my mother would say. That girl would walk into a room and men would trail her like ducklings." She smiled. "Rennie wasn't a wallflower by a long shot, but Olivia has that magnetic personality. Well, Ginger had it."

"In spades." Susan smiled.

Trudy was solemn for a moment. "Thank you for the crepe myrtles, for spending some time with Olivia, and most of all for not coming around here with long faces just oozing sympathy."

"It was terrible," said Susan. "It's still terrible, but, well—" She considered her words carefully. "People think that's the right thing to do. And really, how does one express sympathy? You're such a positive and strong woman, but others need all the props. Maybe I shouldn't say *props*?"

Trudy waved her hand, Tucker and Owen intently focusing on every move just in case any food fell. "For some people, it's the one time they get to be the center of attention. Their marriage, the birth of their children, and then passing. Personally, I don't want to be the center of attention." She stopped then, and with clarity and some volume, said, "What I want is an answer!"

"Yes. Everyone who loved Ginger wants that." Susan sank in her chair a bit, tired from the physical labor and everything else.

"The sheriff and that nice deputy, your neighbor, Harry, were very sensitive. They asked questions the day he was killed, and they've come back. You don't realize how good a public servant is until you need him or her."

"True," Harry simply agreed. "Did they ask you anything that surprised you?"

"Yes, quite a few things surprised me." Clearly, Trudy wanted to talk about this. "I know they also talked to the girls, but as both of them no longer live in central Virginia, they knew so little about current affairs. Olivia is the more emotional of the two. I've kept things to myself and, well, Rennie, too. I suppose parents always seek to protect their children."

"What was it that surprised you?" Harry's antenna vibrated, and she didn't want to push, but she sure wanted to know.

"Oh. Well, they asked about Ginger's investments. I said his retirement plan, a few stocks. Nothing, just enough to keep us through our old age. God, I hate the twilight years, don't you?"

They both laughed and nodded in affirmation.

Trudy continued. "They asked had he suffered large losses? Well, no. Then they asked about anyone from years back, during the Sally Hemings blowup, what about those people? Had any of those hotheads from that time reappeared?" Her hand stroked her throat briefly. "They never left. Really, except for the far-flung family members, most are still here, some still teaching. And, of course, Monticello has gone from strength to strength. Water under the bridge."

"Seems to be."

Harry realized that Trudy knew nothing about Frank Cresey seeing Olivia. Nor had she been informed of Frank's confession. Sheriff Shaw and Coop, both shrewd law enforcement people, probably decided to wait a bit on that news.

Susan ate another cookie. "These are divine."

"I've been baking to keep my sanity."

Susan took another. "Trudy, we're all supposed to bring you food."

"People did, and do. It's gobbled up rather quickly, but cooking and baking have always settled my mind." She looked at Harry. "For your mother, it was gardening." Then she looked at Susan. "For yours, I guess it was tennis. I never asked you why you took up golf instead of tennis."

"Because Mom always beat me. I hated it!" Susan's eyes widened. "Even when I was supposed to be in my prime, Mom could wipe the court up with me."

Trudy reached over, touched Susan's hand. "Honey, you're still in your prime."

The clock struck three.

Harry dabbed her lips with a napkin. "Here we are taking up your afternoon."

"No, you're not. I enjoy your company."

"*I enjoy yours,*" Tucker politely said, and was instantly rewarded with a treat.

Owen, no fool, imitated his sister. "*Trudy, you are the best,*" the corgi cooed. A treat, miniature lamb-chop shape, color and all, was handed down to him.

"Here, let us clear the table," Susan offered.

"Don't you dare." Trudy needed things to do. "Oh, one thing I didn't mention which surprised me. The sheriff and deputy wanted to see Ginger's office. They couldn't believe the books on the shelves, the piles of books on the floor, and his brand-new desktop computer."

"When did he buy a new computer?" Harry asked.

"Come on. I'll show you. Cost as much as a used Toyota." She led them down the cross hall, off the main hall, to Ginger's bright office. Lots of windows here too. Trudy, with trepidation, had let him decorate it himself. Apart from the flintlock rifle over the fireplace and the flintlock pistols used as paperweights, he did okay.

"I've never been in Ginger's office." From the doorway, Harry took in the hand-tinted old maps, the famous reproduction of Washington on horseback in a gold frame.

"Wait until you see this." Trudy walked behind his desk. Everyone followed, dogs too, to stand behind Trudy. She turned on a super-expensive Mac with an enormous screen. "His baby."

Always interested in anything mechanical or technical, Harry let out a gasp. "This did cost as much as a used Toyota! Maybe even a new one!"

Trudy sat down, punched in a password, and a crude drawing of The Albemarle Barracks popped up. "Drove him wild that everything at this site was destroyed or built over. He swore if we could dig there, we would find so much useful information. Funny, he was coming full circle. When he graduated from Yale, he became fascinated with two things: slavery in the North, and prisoners of war during the Revolutionary War. Then he moved away from that, focused on what we called 'the common man.' But Ginger's curiosity, relentless, pulled him down many a byway. Can you believe one time he had to learn everything about marriage customs in seventeenth-century Poland?" She threw up her hands. "I have no idea why, and I don't think he did either."

They laughed. She clicked on an icon and opened another file.

Harry exclaimed, "This screen is fabulous. The detail." She leaned over to peer at the text.

Susan did too, and read aloud, "*A Memoir of the Exploits of Captain Alexander Fraser and His Company of British Marksmen, 1776 to 1777.*"

Trudy said, "Ginger would still drive to read diaries and letters in private collections, or in small college and university libraries. But was he thrilled with how much information he could get using his monster machine." Trudy turned the computer off, looked around the office. "I miss him. I miss his conversation. I knew when I married him that he was a remarkable man. The years only confirmed that."

Harry smiled. "You could learn more from Ginger in a half hour than an entire semester's course with someone else."

They walked out of the office. Harry paused for a moment to

study the Fry-Jefferson map framed on the wall. Trudy noticed. "I think half the old places in Virginia have that map on the wall. Can you imagine travel back then?"

"Sometimes," Harry replied.

"I can't," Susan quipped. "Nor can I imagine what you endured if you had a toothache. And bleeding people. Probably hastened Washington's death, all the bleeding."

"We've come so far in some ways, and yet remain primitive in others," Trudy thoughtfully said, then added, "I think the sheriff and the deputy were amazed at the little they saw of Ginger's research. Sheriff Shaw asked if Brinsley Sims could read through what Ginger was working on because he would be able to put it into some kind of perspective. I said of course, as long as he does it in the house. I quite like Brinsley. Lord! He's got to be close to retirement. Where does the time go?"

"I don't know, but if you find out, let's go bring some back," said Harry.

After laughing at Harry's idea, Trudy said, "I asked the sheriff, 'Was Ginger's research important to the case?' They were very honest and said they didn't know. They had to explore many avenues. Which I understand." She took a breath as they walked to the front door. "Ginger's refrain was 'The past is always with us.' Much as I believe that, it can't have anything to do with his murder."

Driving back to Harry's in her truck, the dogs, satisfied, slept.

Susan turned to Harry, who hadn't spoken a word since they left Trudy's. "All right. What's whirring through your overheated pea brain?"

"Oh, I don't know. Thinking about the past."

"Go on." Sometimes Susan had to wheedle.

"What if Ginger's murder has to do with a buried treasure? You know, maybe a robbed pay wagon."

"Harry!" Susan's voice registered disbelief.

"Well, you never know." Harry shrugged. She was headed in the right direction, but on the wrong track.

# 15

April 20, 2015

Snoop was perched on a large planter of colored concrete, on the Downtown Mall. Half in the bag this morning, he was nevertheless alert and observant, watching the world go by.

Harry never could tell what those enormous planters were made of, although the plants filling them reflected the season. In this one were daffodils, unfurling ferns for a background, along with small white teardrops. The gardeners serving the city could do only so much in the changing season. Had they filled these big pots with tulips, or many early colorful blooms, one hard frost would kill them off.

As it was on her mind, killing propelled her to the mall, not a place Harry normally patronized. If Harry were going shopping, a dreaded chore, it would be at Southern States Feed or AutoZone. If money were to leave her hands, it would be for something useful. This is why her friends, twice a year, would throw her in a car, drive her to Short Pump, and force her to buy new clothes at Nordstrom. They thought of it as a benevolent fashion intervention. She thought of it as kidnapping.

Snoop smiled when he saw the corgi and the attractive woman wearing jeans and cowboy boots approaching him. At his feet was a small bucket filled with hardwood letter openers he carved. Tucker, at her heels, added to the vision. Few women approached Snoop, once a successful and good-looking cabinetmaker. He had lost his battle with the bottle. It seemed doubtful he could ever fight his way back.

Harry didn't understand addictions, nor did she evidence much sympathy for them. But, raised to respect people, she tried not to sit in judgment. Mostly she sidestepped the whole issue, but she didn't want to sidestep Snoop. She had noticed him standing nearby the day Frank blew up at Olivia.

Holding out her hand, she said, "Hello, Sir. I'm Harriet Haristeen. Harry, for short."

Fortunately for Snoop, he still had all his teeth, so when he smiled he looked fine. "I saw you before, you and the dog."

The handshake was firm, and Harry then disengaged. "May I ask you a few questions?"

"You're not from the Salvation Army, are you?"

"No, Sir."

"Snoop, my name is Snoop." He placed his hands on the edge of the planter, slightly tilting forward. "There's room to sit if you like."

Harry smiled, pleased somehow that he hadn't forgotten his manners to a lady. "No, thank you. I won't take much of your time."

"Miss Harry, time is all I got." He said this without rancor, just a fact.

"I see. Well, let me get to the point. So you saw me the other day, when Frank Cresey screamed at my friend, the lady with the blonde hair?"

"I remember."

"Did you ever see Frank act that way before?"

"No."

"Actually, I should back up. Do you know him well?"

Snoop drawled, "Well enough. We all live down here on the mall. Sometimes we sleep under the railroad bridge in bad weather. Winter, sometimes at the Salvation Army. Sometimes we tough it out. Best I can remember, Frank's been here off and on for ten years, maybe more."

"Does he ever pick up work?"

Snoop thought for a bit. "He does cleanup for construction, gardening. He works for old buddies. They slip him a few bucks. He gets them to hire some of us too. He's good about that."

"Ever talk about his past?"

"Nope."

"Did you know he was a star halfback for the UVA football team in '75? Made All-American."

"Some of the other guys told me. Frank never mentioned it. Not much of a talker."

"Ever talk about lost love?"

Snoop laughed low. "Hell, no!"

"Do you like him?"

"I do." He rocked back and forth a little on the planter. "How come you're asking?"

"I'm wondering if Frank knows reality from fantasy. I've heard the alcohol kills brain cells. People have hallucinations."

"Screamers."

"Beg pardon?"

"Usually they see things, they start screaming. Frank never screamed. Like I said, he was never much of a talker. Why would hallucinations matter? He knew who that woman was."

Harry realized that Snoop was no dummy and, for now anyway, he thought clearly. "Well, first answer me one more question, then I can answer yours. Was Frank on the mall April eleventh?"

Snoop had no calendar, but counted days backward. "Don't think he was. So what's this about?"

"You've noticed he hasn't been here for a couple of days?"

"Right. Figured he made enough for a bottle and he's still drunk."

"No. He confessed to a crime. He says he killed Professor McConnell, the father of the blonde woman he was yelling at. The professor was killed April eleventh on Farmington's golf course."

Snoop burst out laughing. "Old Frank couldn't set foot on that golf course. Someone would throw him off. No bums allowed, except rich ones!"

Harry wryly smiled. "But he says he did it. Says he shot Professor McConnell, and he did get the location correct where the murder occurred."

"Ma'am, why listen to a drunk?" Snoop stopped for a moment. "'Cept for me, of course."

She couldn't help but like the man. "Thank you. I didn't mean to bother you."

"You didn't bother me. You talked to me like I'm a human being."

This hit her. "Snoop, you are. Look, I don't know you from a hot rock. Of course, I'm sad that you are in this state because you are intelligent and respectful." She blurted out, "You're a nice person."

Snoop, dark brown eyes searching her face, replied in a hoarse voice, "I . . . Thank you."

She reached into her pocket to hand him a ten-dollar bill. He put his hand over hers.

"Couldn't you use a hot meal?" she asked.

"I will not take money from you. I'm afraid I'd go buy a bottle."

Thrown for a loop, Harry paused for a moment, shoved the money back into her front pocket, reached into her back pocket, and pulled out her farm business card. "Here. If you need something, or you think of something that might help Frank, call me."

He read the card in his hand. "Sunflowers. Bet your farm is something."

"It is to me. Please, keep the card. And I mean it, you call me."

As she walked away, Snoop watched. He pulled out the card, read it again. He wouldn't lose it, no matter what.

Patiently accompanying Harry, Tucker said to her, *"He's telling the truth."*

"We're almost at the car, Sweetie," she said to the corgi.

*"I can smell things. When humans lie or they are afraid, there's a scent. That's one of the ways I know how to protect you. Wrong scent, I get between you and that person. That Snoop, he's okay, even if he does need a bath."*

Miracle of miracles, Harry had found a parking space big enough for the truck in front of David Wheeler's office right by Jackson Square. A wooden door to the small front yard creaked as she pushed it open. David was Harry's accountant and a good friend. She was bringing him documents she'd filled out for the U.S. Department of Agriculture. The copies would be useful when she itemized her fertilizer and seed expenses.

After climbing a small series of wooden steps, she opened the office and found Marshall Reese and Paul Huber standing with David in the corridor outside his office.

"Well, hello." Marshall beamed as the other two men also rushed to greet her and the corgi trailing her.

"Tucker and I just wanted to say hello. This looks like a UVA versus Tech standoff." She knew David loved his alma mater and gloried in Virginia Tech's football prowess.

David was never averse to expressing his opinion. "No standoff. The Cavaliers aren't going to do squat."

"I'm telling you, London is turning things around," Marshall said, citing the UVA coach. "Look at the recruitment of outstanding high school players, and it takes a good two years to work those kids into any system."

David grinned. "Marshall, we're going to kick your butts into next week."

"No way!" Paul protested.

"Fellas, I don't have a dog in this fight," Harry smiled. "I went to Smith, remember."

They laughed, then with a glint in his eye, David said, "Given the transgender people at Smith now, I expect you'll have your own football team."

That set the men off and running at the mouth. "Do you let transsexuals compete with the sex they changed to? Do you keep them out of the locker room or let them in?" None of the males were shy about their feelings on this.

Harry held up her hands, surrendering. "Hey, I'm not responsible for my alma mater."

"You haven't said a word," said Marshall. "Would you want to be in the locker room with a girl who was becoming a guy?" he queried.

"I don't much care," she answered. "I just think it's incredible that we live in a time when someone can make a choice. I mean, think about it! Choosing your gender. If you have the money, the inner you can match the outer you."

"I don't get it." Paul really didn't.

"Well, Paul, you don't have to." Harry punched him in the arm, and they all laughed. "Hey, I just spoke with one of the homeless men on the mall. Really nice guy, Snoop. I wanted to know if Frank was on the mall the day Ginger was killed. Snoop said he wasn't."

"Could have been anywhere." Paul slipped his right hand into his pocket.

"This is such an unfortunate situation," Marshall noted. "Obviously, Sheriff Shaw has to consider Frank no matter how unlikely a suspect. Rick put Frank in a halfway house. He's pretty fragile right now."

"He's getting three meals a day," David sensibly noted. "That's something."

"Might put on some weight," said Marshall. "Look, like I said, this is such an unfortunate situation, and Trudy doesn't need to be dragged into it." He sounded adamant.

"True," both Paul and David chimed in.

Harry had full confidence in Sheriff Shaw. "I'm sure Rick and Coop will do the right thing by police procedure as well as by Trudy."

"While you're here, Harry, Paul and I were talking about an endowed chair for Professor McConnell that we wanted to announce at the gathering at the lawn after the service. Would you and Fair care to contribute?"

"Of course we will. He'll be home from the conference tomorrow. I'll call you then. You know we can only do but so much, but this is the best tribute possible."

Marshall and Paul thanked her as Harry bid the three men goodbye. She walked down the few outside steps, the wood reverberating.

Tucker always stuck close to Harry in crowded areas and by roads. Once in the truck, the tough little dog stared at Harry. "Something's not right."

"We'll be home soon." She half-fibbed.

"Pay attention, Mom!"

# 16

April 7, 1780

*T*wo miles east of the prisoner-of-war camp, Charles West, Thomas Parsons, Edward Thimble, Samuel MacLeish, Macabee Reed, Karl Ix, and Hans Wistan worked under the eye of Captain Schuyler at Ewing Garth's ever-growing estate. Before the men rode off toward the farm, Captain John Schuyler had been given strict instructions to keep Old Man Garth happy. Ewing Garth, a shrewd businessman, owned land throughout Virginia, much of it south of his showplace estate, which sat above Ivy Creek. He grew tobacco on the southern acres, hemp near Williamsburg, more tobacco on his lands in North Carolina. Ewing Garth owned hundreds of slaves scattered among his holdings, but he needed more hands for his dreams, and the few available prisoners at The Barracks were manna from heaven. Free labor. Ewing Garth didn't have to feed them, clothe them, see to their health, or house them. Granted, he did feed them when they were on his land, and he did pay special courtesy to the imprisoned British Captain Graves due to his rank.

In exchange for the prisoners, Ewing Garth offered foods and other necessities to the camp for sale at reduced rates. Well, his idea of reduced rates. Neither brutal nor devoid of feeling, money still came first for the medium-sized man in his fifties.

The eight prisoners possessed useful skills. Corporal Ix, a Hessian, had engineering abilities. He and Charles West studied a steep incline ending at Ivy Creek, and an equally steep incline on the other side. A dirt road was the only path east to Charlottesville, or heading west toward the Blue Ridge Mountains, Staunton miles on the other side. The steep grade, difficult enough in good weather, was impossible in bad. Many a carter had turned over, tangling traces, sometimes even breaking up the cart, and there went the money from hauling goods.

Ewing Garth rightly surmised that an improved road would increase his profits; he could then sell surplus from his farm in both directions. The tobacco and hemp farms made the large profits, but he was determined to show he could make money here as well. His eye was on apples. This area's elevation, soils, and temperature were perfect for apples, and two years ago he had planted his first orchard from bare root. So far, so good, but the trees needed more years to produce a larger amount of fruit. That first orchard on the hillsides evidenced the earliest sign of green buds.

"Corporal." Captain Schuyler stared out at the problem. "A higher bridge?"

The sturdy Hessian shook his head. "Nein. No." Descending sideways for a better foothold, he made it halfway down the grade, pointing to the left of the existing dirt track. "Come to here, then to there." Leaning, he walked at a right angle to where he had been standing.

Captain Schuyler couldn't grasp what Karl intended.

Charles brought forth and opened a thin, light wooden case. Small chains held the lid upright. He pulled out paper, a thin, round piece of charcoal, and sketched what he thought the Hessian meant. Then he too crabbed sideways down to Ix.

Karl looked, nodded, then took the charcoal from Charles's hand and drew over the base idea. "See?"

"I think so." Charles flipped over the paper, too expensive to waste, and drew to the corporal's instructions. The precise drawing began to make sense.

Karl pointed to the spot on the creek. "Bridge here, raised up. *Verstehen sie, ja?*"

Charles drew a wide bridge with a grade to make entering and exiting it easier, especially for a carter with a heavy load. Both men then climbed up to the captain.

Taking the case from Charles, the Continental officer studied the drawing. Looking about for a place to sit, to really look at this, he moved over to a large log. With a prisoner on each side of him, he settled in to examine the drawing.

Karl Ix traced his new route, which incorporated parts of the old road. "If a wagon slides, it slides to here." He marked a small landing. "Better this way."

"Yes, yes, I see that." Captain Schuyler squinted, looking at the old roadway. "What do you think, Ix? Looks like almost a forty-five-degree angle."

"We can lessen the grade."

"And build a new bridge?" Schuyler asked.

When the Hessian nodded, the handsome young captain looked to Charles. The two of them, nearly equal in height and broad-shouldered, were handsome men. They liked each other, despite their separate stations.

Charles agreed. "What's down there must get swept away every time the water rises. Raise the bridge, and only the most severe of storms will destroy it." He looked across Schuyler to Karl. "Yes?"

"Yes," Karl replied, but with his accent his "yes" lacked the sibilant ending.

"All right. I will take this up to Mr. Garth." He handed the case to Charles, who folded it down. "Both of you, come with me. Karl, you might need to explain. He will have questions, and I am sure the first one will be how much will it cost." A wry smile crossed the captain's lips.

They walked to a large brick house built in the Georgian manner, very modern and very expensive. At the stables, Captain Graves and the other prisoners were fixing broken stable doors. A fractious horse cursed inside.

Piglet, always at Charles's heels, murmured, *"Hot temper."*

At the grand house, a large brass pineapple knocker rested in the center of the wide wooden door painted glossy navy blue. The woodwork trim around the door and windows was white, but the shutters matched the door. Charles wondered how these raw people managed to ape European fashions. Well, some Americans had traveled abroad before the war. They learned quickly.

The door opened to an impeccably turned-out butler, Roger. A proud light-skinned man in middle years, he smiled and bowed slightly to usher them into the huge center hall. He had obviously been told that the officer in charge was welcome.

"The Master will be with you in a moment, gentlemen." The butler, Roger, then turned, walking down the long hall to fetch Ewing Garth.

Charles sensed that both the Continental captain and the Hessian corporal were uneasy. Ewing Garth approached from the opposite end of the hall, walking toward them. Charles swept off his hat, tucking it under his arm. *"Pssst."* He hissed the sound through his teeth. Awkwardly, John Schuyler did the same while Karl Ix pulled off his own tattered cap.

"Ah. My good Captain, what can I do for you?" Ewing Garth inclined his head slightly.

"We have studied your road, Sir, and would like to show you a possible solution."

Charles quickly opened his drawing case.

"Here, here." Interest high, Garth took the box in his own hands and placed it on a long, exquisitely graceful hall table, a large display of dried flowers in the center flanked by a small marble bust of Apollo on one side, Artemis on the other. "A new bridge? What's this?" Garth noted the landings.

"Sir, if Corporal Ix might explain. He studied as an engineer before the war." Captain Schuyler smiled, nodding to the Hessian, who stepped forward.

"The road is too steep." The man's accent was noticeable, but he spoke good English. "Change the grade with a catch point on the other side."

"Yes." Ewing Garth was listening intently.

"Bad weather, failed brakes, the landing can catch them. That is why the road goes at an angle and emerges at an angle. Safer."

"Yes, I see."

"This way, one moves heavier loads, fewer wagons, fewer men off the farm," said Captain Schuyler, and as an afterthought, "It could accommodate cannons as well. We will widen the road."

"Yes, yes. I see." Ewing Garth's bright brown eyes lit up. "Costly."

"With your permission, Mr. Garth, I can supply men such as Corporal Ix, who have had to build all manner of things, pontoon bridges, palisades, during their service. And if you are willing, you have hardwoods which we could use to construct a sturdier, higher bridge." As these words left John Schuyler's mouth, he knew he would have to convince the commandant he had done the right thing, and that such efforts would certainly also benefit the commandant. Captain Schuyler was learning politics.

The key would be to convince his superior that he had to strike while the iron was hot. To bring this up the chain to the commandant's superiors would take a flock of letters and waste time. To just go ahead, then alert the various colonels and generals to the speedier transport route, would be a feather in the commandant's cap.

He would appear far more decisive than subordinate. Ewing Garth could be useful to all. Captain John Schuyler, born and raised in rural western Massachusetts, was not a political creature, but the war was teaching him a great deal about how the world really worked.

"Who did this sketch?"

"I did, Mr. Garth." Charles smiled.

"H-m-m." The wheels were turning, but Garth said nothing for a moment as he studied the road. "Captain, this is an excellent idea, and a benefit to commerce as well as military matters, as you noted. I will visit your commandant myself in a few days to fully discuss the matter. Of course, I am at his service in the prosecution of the war."

He walked them to the front door, Roger hovering, in case of need. As the door opened, a tremendous uproar from the stable area caused them all to fly down the stairs.

Piglet, who had been left outside, rose from his curled-up position, alarmed, as a horse, a young woman on sidesaddle, bolted toward them. The out-of-control animal charged while its rider gamely stayed on, trying to check and release the reins. Running on foot behind were two grooms from the stable, as well as Captain Graves and Samuel MacLeish. Captain Schuyler dashed across the yard toward the enraged animal. Handing his case to Karl, Charles, too, ran forward.

A lovely young woman, perhaps fifteen or sixteen, ran from the barn on foot, with plainly no hope of catching up. Landowner Garth, clearly not built for speed, moved toward the horse, which now attempted a terrific buck. Still, the rider stayed on. Coming out of the buck, the big bay leapt up, straight for Captain Schuyler. Without flinching, the American soldier stood in front of the horse. Just as its front hooves reached forward, Schuyler nimbly stepped to the side, jumped up, and grabbed the bridle. With all his might and weight, he pulled the horse's head downward and forced it to stop. As he did so, Charles grabbed the bit on the other side.

"I have him!" Charles yelled.

Releasing the bridle, Captain Schuyler put his large hands around the rider's waist and lifted her off the horse. He held her tight for a moment, her arms circling his neck.

Catherine Garth had never been so close to any man other than her father. Even through the sleeves of his coat, she could feel huge, powerful muscles.

The fearless man set her down and found himself looking into the eyes of a goddess. John Schuyler had never beheld so beautiful a woman in his life. Thunderstruck, he said nothing.

As one of the grooms reached the horse, Charles came around the other side, saw the two, paralyzed by the sight of each other. With good humor, he swept off his tricorn in a flourish, bowed low. After rising, he removed Captain Schuyler's hat from his head, handing it to the man. Finding his voice, Captain Schuyler rasped, "At your service, Madam. I hope you are unharmed."

Face flushed, her father finally reached the scene. Grasping her hands, kissing her cheeks, Ewing Garth was nearly undone with terror. "Oh, my darling, my angel! Come into the house. You must rest," he babbled.

"Father, it was my fault," she coolly said. Turning, she called over her shoulder. "Jeddie, don't punish him. It was my fault."

"Yes, Miss," the groom called back.

Rachel Garth, obviously Catherine's younger sister by the strong resemblance, was now also by her side. The teenage girl smiled up at the captain. "I thank you, good Sir."

The American officer was awestruck at Catherine's equestrian skills. "You rode him like, like . . ." He struggled.

Charles said, "A Valkyrie."

Captain Schuyler swallowed, grateful to the Englishman.

Catherine laughed. "You flatter me, Sir. I so hope none of us wind up in Valhalla soon."

Ewing Garth patted her hand. "My dear, my dear, please come into the house!"

"Father, I am quite fine. I was a fool. Had I been hurt, I would have deserved it."

Rachel, eyes wide, remained silent.

Regaining some possession of his emotions, Ewing Garth smiled. "Gentlemen, my elder daughter, Catherine, much like her late mother, and my younger daughter, Rachel, also a reflection of my wife." He paused, looked at his elder child, high color in her face. "Headstrong, my dear, headstrong."

With a tilt of her head and a mischievous grin, she said, "And, Father, the apple does not fall far from the tree."

Charles quipped, "So many apples," as he swept his hand toward the new orchards. At this, they all laughed.

"My angel, please, don't get on that beast again."

"Father, all the work and noise at the stable has unsettled him, and when I mounted, I was a bit lazy, and hit the poor dear hard in the ribs. It really was all my fault."

"Yes, yes, yes," Garth said, not at all convinced. "Well, gentlemen, I must return to my labors, and you to yours."

Catherine cast her warm, luminous brown eyes up at the tall captain. "I do so hope I shall have the pleasure of repaying your courage and kindness."

"I . . ."

Charles, half bowing, said, "What he means to say, Mistress Garth, what we all say, is that just to look upon you is repayment enough."

At this, Rachel giggled. Catherine playfully swatted her sister. The two made their curtseys and walked toward the house.

As Schuyler, West, and Ix headed toward the stables where the other prisoners were working, Charles exclaimed, "A woman like that in England would be the mistress of a king."

"Then I would kill the king!" blurted out Captain Schuyler.

"Well, you would anyway, would you not?" Charles could not help but tease.

Some of his emotion calmed, Schuyler replied, "Ah, Lieutenant, you are too quick for me."

Karl Ix had been amused by the drama, and happy the gorgeous woman hadn't been injured. "Smooth, our lieutenant. Ah, well, he is high born, you know."

"I could not think of anything to say," bemoaned Captain Schuyler. "I stood there like a dumb beast myself. She must think me a fool!"

A silence followed this outburst. Karl Ix left to join the barn crew. Jeddie could be seen nearby, hot-walking the horse, now untacked.

"Captain, if you help me, I will help you," said Charles. As the love-struck man looked at him, he continued, "I can show you the small and varied courtesies you need properly to address Mistress Garth. In return, I ask for more straw to bolster our roof. The winter was hard. And I will need other small things from time to time. I must look out for my men, and"—he looked down at Piglet— "my best friend."

"I'll look out for you, too," Piglet vowed.

John Schuyler stopped, looking straight into Charles West's eyes. "You can make a gentleman out of a farmer's son?"

"Yes."

"You shall have whatever you and Private Piglet require."

"Good." Charles put out his hand, and the two clasped hands. "Here is your first lesson. You must be as gallant toward the father as the daughter. An admiring word here or there, constant deference to his wisdom. I will show you. And for God's sake, Captain, learn how to sweep your hat off your head with a graceful arc, just"—he paused—"not when she is riding. Then a small tip will do."

"I have never seen a woman ride like that!" Captain Schuyler inhaled, overwhelmed by Catherine's skill and tremendous poise.

"Yes. Well, it is not uncommon for English ladies to ride well enough that the Devil himself would sweat chasing them."

"I will learn, Lieutenant. I will learn!"

# 17

*P*eople stood outside the chapel at the University of Virginia, down the walkway, onto the front lawn. The crush was so great that even the roadside of the Rotunda was filled. Those of all ages stood to bid goodbye to an exciting teacher, an intellectual ornament to the state of Virginia, and a good man.

Every living governor was there, as was every living president of the university. Paying homage were the two United States senators, the representative to the United States congress, as well as their counterparts to the state General Assembly.

Those current students who had read his books and chatted with him during his office hours also attended. The males wore coats and ties. This was UVA, after all.

Sunshine flooded through the chapel windows. The eulogies, succinct and touching, befitted Ginger. Together with her surviving family and Ginger's, Trudy sat in the front pew. And while some institutions would have paraded the governor first, not so here. Ginger's former colleagues, the UVA presidents, sat just behind the family.

The football team of 1959 was in the rear, as were Harry, Fair, Susan, and the Very Reverend Herbert Jones with Miranda Hogendobber. Those who had loved Ginger in life came to bid him farewell. It was a mix of sorrow and loss, as well as joy and admiration.

After the dignified service, the crowd moved behind the chapel, then around the Rotunda and down the undulating lawn to the statue of Homer before Old Cabell Hall. The reception was at Pavilion VII. The lawn of this most beautiful of American universities was filled with people.

Caterer Warren Chiles, who had catered the Reverend Jones's small dinner party, had prudently hired twenty extra servers to carry trays onto the lawn. There was no way all those folks would fit into the Pavilion, even if they kept circulating, which they did not. Four bars served those inside and those outside, with students under twenty-one not drinking. On their own, at their own parties, they could drain the James River, but in a situation such as this, students knew what was expected of them.

Harry—separated from Fair, who was trying to get drinks— found herself with Nelson and the old boys from the football team.

"Harry, let me get you something to drink," Marshall quickly offered.

"Thank you, but Fair is at the bar."

Looking at the mob, Paul Huber remarked, "Fair has the advantage of height." Then he spoke to Nelson, "Ever wish Fair had played when we did?"

"All the time," Nelson replied. "But Fair's an Auburn man, through and through."

Talking to Sandra Yarbrough, Harry fell silent for a moment.

Sandra whispered, "Let's hope there's no one from Alabama within earshot." This brought a grin to Harry. The two universities had not quite reached the level of hostility of the nations in the Middle East, but sometimes they hovered close to that.

Back from UCLA, Lionel Gardner walked toward Fair to help

him carry the drinks. Counting the glasses, Willis Fugate left the group, saying to Marshall as he did so, "I'm almost as tall as Fair. I can complete this mission."

Handed libations first, the ladies gratefully took sips, for this felt like the first day of high spring. A light breeze, low seventies, sunshine.

Rudolph Putnam asked, "What did you all think?"

Marshall cleared his throat. "Fitting. Teresa Sullivan"—he named the president of the university—"and her staff organized a wonderful service. But even knowing there would be a crowd, I don't think anyone could have anticipated this." He swept his arm to indicate the numbers.

Paul checked his watch. "You've got about fifteen minutes before announcing the endowed chair, and I think it will take fifteen minutes to get in there."

Marshall straightened his tie. "Right."

Accompanied by Nelson, Lionel, Paul, and Rudy, Marshall made his way to the open front door. Willis, hands full of glasses, passing them, hurried additional libations to the ladies. "Girls"—he was of a generation that would use this term without any hint of offense—"I've got to go block for the boys."

Sandra laughed. "People will think we're lushes."

"Could think worse." Harry smiled.

Susan gratefully sipped another vodka tonic. "This is overwhelming."

"Yes, it is," Harry observed. "I don't know where Herb and Miranda are."

"Maybe Herb is with Trudy and the girls," Susan murmured. "He would be a great support."

"He would," Sandra agreed. "He always knows just what to do and what to say."

The 1959 men made it through the Pavilion's crowd. When Marshall made his announcement, only those in the room could hear, but the news rapidly spread to the outside.

"The boys" as they would probably always be known, even if they all lived to be one hundred, had to date raised six million dollars for an endowed chair in Ginger's name: "The Professor Greg McConnell Chair in Early American History!" Cheers rippled outward like waves, and when Marshall and the boys tried to get back to their wives and friends, they moved at a snail's pace. Everyone wanted to shake their hands and slap their backs, and a few ladies kissed them. Everyone said "Thank you" or "How wonderful." The money engine, Tim Jardine, had called everyone he knew. Walking with the old football players, he was also feted by those who recognized his success in the business world.

One former governor was overheard saying to another, "Ah, imagine if Jardine had been our campaign treasurer!"

While not happy, if a funeral can be said to be positive, Ginger's was. People, giddy with spring, thrilled at the endowed chair, talked, mixed, cried, and laughed. Those without the money to make handsome contributions pledged one another to various activities memorializing Ginger. Knowing this, Marshall worked the crowd, as did the others, urging people to help: any amount, even five dollars, would benefit the fund for the new chair.

Fair finally caught up with his wife, who was walking toward the arcade to get out of the sun.

She had just noticed a furtive figure lurking nearby.

Stopping, she studied the lone man hiding as best he could behind one of the Rotunda's large pillars. "Fair, get Marshall or any of the boys, will you?"

"What?"

"Never mind. Come with me." She hurriedly made her way

through the throng to Marshall, who turned from another hand-shake. Harry put both her hands on his shoulders, stood on her toes, and whispered in his ear.

"Marshall, Frank Cresey is on the Rotunda behind a pillar. If Olivia comes out." She left it at that.

Marshall turned to Paul. "Get the boys, will you?"

Within a few minutes, Marshall, Willis, Lionel, Paul, and Rudy were walking under the arcade toward the Rotunda. Harry watched with apprehension, as did Susan, now beside her. Fair, given his size, had left them to trail the other men, just in case.

"God, I hope he doesn't make a scene," said Harry.

Frank froze as he saw the other men walking toward him.

In a gentle voice, Lionel called out, "Frank, good of you to come."

At this, Frank burst into tears, ran down the Rotunda steps away from the crowd, away from his past.

Paul began to follow when Marshall called out, "Let him go, Paul."

Nelson also said, "Let him go. We need to rejoin the mourners." Then he said to the others, "Does anyone have a cellphone with them?"

Willis pulled his out from his inside coat pocket, as did Marshall. "Whoever knows Sheriff Shaw's number, call and alert him," said Nelson. "I doubt Frank will do any harm, but we don't want any-thing to upset Trudy, the girls."

Marshall quickly dialed the sheriff's number, as Willis did not know it by heart. Marshall was always good with numbers. He made the call. There were already university security people all around, as well as sheriff's cars, with lights flashing, to eventually lead people to the grave site.

Trudy, Olivia, and Rennie had decided to have the reception immediately following the service. Then family members, dear friends, colleagues, and his students could follow to the grave site if they wished. Otherwise, it would have been a snarl to leave UVA grounds, then try to return.

Two hours after the chapel service, they reached the grave site.

Out of the corner of her eye, at least one hundred yards away from the grave, Harry again spied Frank. How he had gotten there was anybody's guess, but the burial details had been printed in *The Daily Progress*. Perhaps he'd hitched a ride with someone. Frank's eyes never left Olivia, but he kept his distance.

After the interment, Harry said to Fair, "Frank's here."

"Where?"

She looked again at the spot. "He was over there."

Fair unobtrusively, or as unobtrusively as a six-foot-five-inch man could, moved toward Olivia.

But Frank did not show himself again or harass Olivia. Their good luck held. Frank's good luck was running out.

# 18

*F*oot traffic on the Downtown Mall filled the brick sidewalk going in both directions. The lovely weather brought out residents living in the area. Other people drove downtown for an outdoor lunch.

Relaxed in a director's chair, Snoop sat under the overhang of the small crook of buildings next to the Paramount Theater. The shade felt wonderful. At his feet rested a colorful painted bucket. He'd made wooden letter openers with a sharp point, priced at two dollars each. People would walk by, notice how smooth and graceful they were, and figure for two dollars, how could they go wrong? Some folks were even nice enough to forgo making change, giving him a few extra dollars. With business this brisk, the night ahead looked promising, for Snoop would be able to buy a bottle of real liquor, not wine. He hated wine, although he'd drink anything if he had to do so. Even Listerine contained alcohol.

Half dozing, the shuffle of feet opened his eyes.

"Hey, man," said Frank.

"Hey." Snoop smiled at him.

Frank dropped next to Snoop, sitting on the ground. The bricks were hard beneath him, but he didn't seem to care. "Heard some of the bastard's funeral."

"Who?"

124

"The Professor. Greg McConnell."

Snoop said, "Why go, if you don't like him?"

Frank grunted. "To make sure he's dead." He paused. "Taught me a lot about history, though. I'll give him that. Taught me it all comes down to history."

They both laughed.

A middle-aged woman stopped, picked up a letter opener, noticing the veining in the wood. "Red oak," she said.

"Yes, Ma'am."

"I can never resist red oak." She fished two one-dollar bills out of her cloth shoulder bag, handing them to him.

"Thank you and hope you only open happy mail," said Snoop.

Frank plucked a letter opener out of the painted bucket. "Downed tree?"

"One blew over near the railroad track. I stashed what I could. Been busy ever since."

The railroad line ran parallel just south of the mall. The small old C&O station at the northern end was no longer in use. Another brick station farther away handled passenger traffic. All across the United States, tidy small stations had been abandoned. Many towns no longer had passenger service. Those that did had nothing near the standard of the old days. Still, anything was better than getting ensnarled in Washington, D.C.'s traffic a hundred miles north. A pity the nation's capital wasn't on the Buffalo border, close enough to Canada's capital. Many a resident in these parts, Virginia, Maryland, a sliver of West Virginia and southern Pennsylvania, would have thrown a joyous going-away party, thrilled to shift the congestion to upstate New York. Of course, those who made their living in the maw of endless traffic might feel otherwise. Once just to feel truly free again, Snoop and Frank hopped a freight boxcar, rode to Culpeper, Virginia, then hopped one back.

Despite their drunken dreams of escape, the Downtown Mall

and its surroundings was their home. The other alcoholics, the shopkeepers, the sheriff's people, and even some of the patrons of those shops knew them.

The two men sat next to each other for another fifteen minutes, then Snoop said, "You gonna stay sober?"

A long sigh. "No."

"The man's dead. Seems like you should be happy."

"I'm glad he's dead. I wish I'd killed him. Wish I'd had the guts when I was young but then Olivia would have hated me. No win. Know what I mean?"

Snoop nodded. Frank had some sense, but then so did most of the guys down here. The lights might flicker upstairs, but they could think clearly enough between power outages. It wasn't lack of brainpower that drove them to hide in the bottle. He was never really sure why he or anyone else sought refuge there. Maybe the inciting pain receded, but the drinking had become a habit. Once one was a bona fide drunk, those first deep pulls on the bottle felt like rapture.

"So?"

Frank shrugged. "Dunno. I walked out of the halfway house. Didn't check out."

Snoop nodded. "They'll be looking for you."

"Yeah, they will. I hid at the old man's reception, but some of the guys from '59 saw me."

"Fifty-nine what?"

"Football team. Good year. Those were the guys who gave us jobs, off and on. I let them down." Frank stared off. "Didn't mean to."

Snoop nodded. "Maybe you should go back to the halfway house. Then check out."

"Aw, Snoop, I don't have to learn a skill. I already got a skill: I can drink you under the table."

They laughed.

"Got that right." Snoop smiled broadly.

"And I have to be 'reviewed.'" He tapped his head. "I'm not crazy. I might do crazy things, but I'm not crazy."

Snoop poked at Frank with the letter opener he was holding on his lap. "What's the craziest thing you ever done?"

"Hanging out with you!" Frank picked up a letter opener from the bucket and poked Snoop back.

"Thank you. Come on, what else?"

"Marrying three women. Man, one's bad enough."

Snoop roared and nearly tipped over in his chair. He knew Frank had no children, despite the wives. The men on the mall didn't talk about the kids they'd left behind. Many had been in jail for missing child-support payments. That multiplied their feelings of worth-lessness so the denials escalated, as did the drinking.

Snoop had four children, two grown now. He hadn't seen them or the mother in five years. Couldn't face them. Told himself she turned the kids against him, but truth was she hadn't. He did.

The pair sat for a little longer. Snoop noticed a Charlottesville police car parking in the lot just above the Paramount, catty-corner from the main library, once the main post office.

He tipped his head. "Frank."

Frank followed Snoop's gaze, stood up. "I don't want to go back. I belong here."

"You gotta place to hide?"

"Yeah. Down by the new construction at the hospital. No one will be working tomorrow."

Tomorrow was Sunday.

Snoop shook his head. "Can't stay there forever."

"No, but it will give me time to figure out how to get all these people off my back. Guess I shouldn't have said I killed the professor. Was pretty well lit when I did." He smiled. "Wish fulfillment."

As Frank started to leave, he leaned over to plunk Snoop's opener back into the bucket.

"Take it," said Snoop. "You might need it."

"Maybe I'll write you a letter." Frank nodded his thanks and put it in his pocket. He melted into the crowd as he headed into a side street.

Harry and Fair reached the farm an hour before sunset. Her husband dropped her off, then drove to his clinic, as he had two horses there he wanted to check. On weekends an intern looked over any patients, but Fair liked to check in. He valued his human clients and often loved his equine ones.

Harry got out of her clothes in a hurry, and put on boots, jeans, and an old sweatshirt, then hurried outside to do chores. She blew through the water buckets, threw down hay, swept out the aisle, and then hopped in the old truck, two cats and the dog with her.

Minutes later, she turned onto the dirt road leading to Cooper's place, passing the Jones family graveyard, a huge hickory in the middle of the place for the departed. The blackbirds favored that tree.

Pewter stared out the window. "If only they'd sleep."

"Yeah?" Tucker thought the limbs were thick with birds.

"I could climb right up there and grab one." The gray cat licked her lips.

Not especially motivated by thoughts of dispatching birds, Mrs. Murphy said, "They'd dive-bomb you."

The conversation stopped as Harry stopped, cut the motor. She stepped down from the truck and lifted Tucker down. The cats easily jumped out. Harry reached back for a jar of honey she'd bought on the way back from Ginger's reception.

The lights shone from Coop's kitchen windows as the twilight deepened.

Harry knocked on the policewoman's back door. "Your neighbor."

Coop's voice called out, "Come on in."

The small visiting posse stepped into the clean, bright kitchen, a large butcher-block table in the middle of the room, a small eating alcove under a window.

Harry placed the honey on the butcher block. "You've been busy."

"Had it with those old curtains." Cooper noted a folded pile of curtains by the back door. "They've got to be older than you and I put together."

"Well, there are people in Albemarle County who value antique curtains even if they do have smiling daisies on them." Harry's mouth curled upward, for they were just awful. "Brought you some honey."

"Thanks. Sit down. What will you have?"

Harry looked at the wall clock. "If I drink black tea, I won't go to sleep. Same with Co-Cola."

"White tea? Or beer? Or bourbon?"

"White tea." As Harry selected her bag from the offered box, Cooper put on the kettle, then pulled out two heavy mugs made in Bennington, Vermont.

"How did it go today?"

"A cast of thousands." Harry filled her friend in on events: who was there, the endowed chair, the fund-raising. "Thought you might be there to direct traffic."

"No." Cooper shook her head. "Paperwork. Rick made me go to my desk. Do you know how much I hate paperwork? Harry, you can't turn around without this and that to fill out and how anyone thinks they can actually get anything done is a mystery."

Harry laughed. "It is awful. That's why I make Fair do it."

"Now, there is a good reason to get married." Cooper brought over the teapot, then the cups and a bowl of sugar cubes, white and brown, plus granulated sugar in a bowl.

Neither woman took milk, but both had a weakness for sugar.

"Your choice of sugars."

"M-m-m." Cooper took a sip, raising her eyebrows. "Thanks to you, I'm learning to love tea."

Harry smiled. "Took me years to like white tea, but now I do. Hey, I came to tell you about Frank Cresey lurking behind a pillar on the Rotunda. He slipped away, but wasn't he in custody?"

"*Was* is the operative word." Cooper took another long sip as the three animals prowled the kitchen floor in case any crumbs fell. "Hold on." The tall deputy rose, pulled out a few treats, and tossed them down, as these three were regular visitors.

Large though she was, Pewter snagged hers first.

"So he was released?" asked Harry.

"His stories about the murder"—Cooper twirled her hand upward—"impossible. Once he was sober, checked out by the psychologist, he was sent over to the halfway house. The report was that he was cleaned up, was well behaved, cooperative. Then he walked out. And right now we don't have the manpower to pick him up. He's harmless, basically."

"Offensive but harmless," Harry concurred.

"The Downtown Mall isn't my beat. The Charlottesville police will pick him up, I'm sure."

Harry laughed. "Wouldn't it be funny if Frank stood on the county/city line? You all would come for him, he'd step into the city. And vice versa."

Cooper smiled. "One of these days, I swear it will happen."

In Virginia, cities are incorporated, having their own law enforcement, mayor, city commissioners. Counties had sheriff's departments and a board of county supervisors. Often the towns weren't large enough in the counties to have mayors. Some did, some didn't, but the county courthouse was always the hub. Confusing as the system might be, it worked for Virginians, and Virginians were quick to note they had managed since 1624.

Each of the original thirteen colonies kept their systems. Pennsylvania had townships, for instance. And not one of those former colonies would change its ways. As one moved westward, in theory, those states became easier to govern, or at least more streamlined. This fiction was easily exploded when a state squared off against the federal government. The attorney general of Missouri would fight just as hard as the attorney general of Virginia if he or she felt the clumsy hand of Washington squeezing its citizens or its coffers.

Made life interesting.

Tucker joined them at the alcove, looking up at Cooper with an expression of saintliness. *"Might you have more bones?"* asked the dog.

"Ignore her, Coop."

"Oh, how can I? And it just so happens, now that I think of it, I bought some greenies. Plus I have a tuna bomb for the cats." No sooner did Cooper distribute these treats than the three creatures entered a state of bliss.

Coop sat back down at the kitchen table. "Do you want anything? I actually have deviled eggs."

"Oh, thanks, no. I ate my way through the reception." Harry paused. "I'll miss Ginger. He and Trudy were friends of Mom and Dad. I know you have to be, uh, careful about sharing information, but have you learned anything at all?"

Cooper looked into her teacup. "Not a damn thing."

"I keep thinking it was a mistake," said Harry. "Maybe the bullet was meant for someone else."

"No way."

"Yeah, I'm afraid you're right, but Ginger's death was like a bolt out of a clear blue sky. There's no sense to it." She finished her tea.

"We've investigated the Hemings angle, and then the uproar

over blacks, then women being admitted to UVA in 1972. Yes, Ginger got a few folks angry, but those that signed letters to the editors from that time are mostly dead." She stopped for a moment. "Except for Carroll Kruger, who, about ninety, I figure, held forth on how admitting blacks and women to the University of Virginia has ruined—*ruined*, mind you—that once great institution and he will never give them a dime."

"He's pretty rich." Harry tapped the edge of her cup. "Do you think you ever completely eradicate prejudice?"

"No, but it's only the ancient and the cranks who cling to race and all this sex stuff. I think we're beyond that, most everyone. But, you know, something else will take their place, some new category of outrage."

"Solves nothing and hurts many. And that's what I keep coming back to, Ginger never hurt anyone."

"Frank Cresey."

"Okay, but Frank didn't kill him." Harry leaned back against the cushion on the alcove booth. "The only thing I can think of is it's some form of academic anger, revenge. Far-fetched. His research consumed his life. Maybe he stepped over into someone's territory and Ginger got the credit they thought should have come to them or he wrote about a subject first. I know professors and doctors are incredibly competitive regarding their research."

"We thought of that, Harry." Coop held up her hands, empty.

"When you combed through his desk at home and then at UVA, what was he working on?"

"I'm not a scholar. I don't know what's significant or not. He had old maps. Trudy said he would consult the maps of the time because that was what the people used. She said how Ginger praised those early brave surveyors. Uh." She tapped her forefinger on the table. "There were some first-person memoirs of the Battle of Saratoga and prisoner-of-war camps, and materials on old roads. Professor Brinsley Sims has been a big help. He went through everything and said he didn't find anything incendiary, for lack of a better word."

"When the department is finished, might I look?"

"I'll ask Rick, but why?"

"I'm born and bred here. I might be able to pick something up, you know, from his going through old family Bibles."

"Harry, what could that have to do with Ginger's murder?"

"Maybe an old crime provoked a new one."

"It would have to be a very old crime."

"Maybe, but then again, it kept being brought forward, in ways we don't understand but Ginger did. I can't think of anything else. And I know it's out there, but, okay, think of this. The Constitution says that in order to be president of this country, you must be born here. Ever wonder why?"

"No. I figured it was one more rule, like initially only giving the vote to white male property owners."

"Aha! You do know some history."

Cooper smiled. "Enough to know the fussing and fighting will never end."

"There is that." Harry's animals came over and flopped down, though they were listening. "If the presidency were available to a naturalized citizen, of course that person's early years would have been somewhere else. Our Founding Fathers knew the experience of the New World was just that: A person from another place, from Europe, no matter how brilliant, ought not be trusted with being our chief executive. They can hold any other office, but not that one. You have to be of this soil."

"Never thought of that."

"They did, because they saw how feudal past continued to affect

Europe even in the eighteenth century, and really even today. We were born of the Enlightenment. No feudal past. We truly are significantly different from Europe and Asia."

"Well, okay."

"See, these were the kind of conversations Ginger would have. The man just loved what he did. It spilled over and out of him, and he was never pedantic or boring at it."

"The past is prologue," Cooper repeated the famous axiom.

"The past can kill you."

Cooper looked at Harry, then said, "I'll see what I can do. I have nothing else to go on."

"Good. It will keep me off the streets at night."

Mrs. Murphy said to Pewter and Tucker, "No, it won't. When she gets like this, she—"

Pewter interrupted. "Fools rush in where angels fear to tread."

Mrs. Murphy thought Pewter might be onto something for once. After all, there weren't too many angels in Virginia.

# 19

*G*orgeous early fall weather made up for the work in a sweltering summer. No one complained about the labor. Two Hessian prisoners of war had broken their ankles sliding down as they worked to ease the grade on Ewing Garth's wagon road. Other than that, no injuries.

At three in the afternoon, tired men picked up their tools. The walk back to their barracks would take forty-five minutes. Captain Schuyler pulled his horse out of the stables, where Garth allowed him to put the sturdy fellow.

Captain Schuyler unrolled the light blanket across the horse, then rolled it up, throwing it across the front of the saddle. "Almost done for the day."

As he easily mounted, a figure slid through the barn doors opened for her. Captain Schuyler swept off his hat, bowed as low as he could while on the horse.

"Captain," she greeted him. "Do you read, Captain?"

"I do, Miss Garth."

She smiled again, incandescent. "I have brought you something. I imagine the nights at the barracks can be tedious." She reached under her silk shawl to bring out a small volume wrapped in heavy

135

white paper, tied with raffia. "I have not been able to thank you properly for the assistance you gave me when Renaldo misbehaved." She drew in a deep breath. "Father doesn't like me out of his sight when the prisoners are here, so you and I have enjoyed few conversations. I have not been able to show my gratitude."

"He is quite right to protect you, although I do not think there is a man among the prisoners who would harm you."

"But would they harm you?"

His black eyebrows raised. "Me? I don't think so."

"Should we lose this war, Captain, you will be branded by the British a traitor. My father fears he will lose everything and die a pauper for aiding our great cause. We must win our freedom."

He smiled as his horse stamped a foot, eager to go as he heard the traces on the wagons jingle. "Miss Garth, we will win this war. I have seen the British in battle. They are disciplined but not so well led. Many of their soldiers are paid men from other countries. We are fighting for our land and"—he grinned—"we are paid infrequently."

She had not known about the realities of the army, the haggling with the Continental Congress. "But still you serve?"

"With all my heart. I languish here at the camp, and I hope in time I will be recalled to my regiment so I can fight."

She stared at him, saying nothing.

He blushed under her gaze. He tried to remember what Charles taught him. "Making your acquaintance has sweetened my current situation."

Finally, her cheeks flushing too, she replied in her beguiling alto, "You are a brave man, Captain Schuyler, but I do so hope there is no"—she paused, searching for the right words—"foolish risk." Then she collected herself, turned, and opened the barn doors even though Jeddie was ready to do so. "Might you keep the book's giver to yourself, Sir? Father would be upset."

He tipped his hat again. "Yes. And I am grateful as the nights are endless."

As Captain Schuyler rode away, Catherine pressed three coins into Jeddie's palm. The fourteen-year-old slave looked up at her.

"Miss Catherine."

He didn't get to finish his sentence because she whispered in his ear, "Jeddie, if you will keep your own counsel and occasionally assist me, I promise more." She paused significantly. "You know how my father can be." A gap-toothed grin revealed that Jeddie knew Garth's ways only too well.

Catherine hurried back to the house, slipped into the kitchen, threw off her shawl. Rachel tiptoed down the back stairway.

Catherine shot her sister a look. "Better view from the top windows, Rachel?"

Ignoring her sister's tone, the younger girl giggled. "He's so handsome."

Catherine shrugged. Sounding nonchalant, she said, "I suppose he is, in a rough way. I owed him something for his pains. This is the first time since Renaldo's theatrics that I've been able to see the good captain by himself. I can't stand the thought of an audience— like you, for example."

"Oh, Cat, don't be a toad. I'm not spying."

"I'm not a toad. But there's always someone around, watching, listening." Catherine yanked her shawl off the table, wrapped it over her sister's head, and slapped her bottom.

Laughing, they both walked down the hallway to their reading room, where the fire would ward off the coming night's chill. Catherine kept thinking about how it felt to have Captain Schuyler's arms around her. She'd never felt anything like that shot of heat.

How powerful he was. Not for the first time, the young beauty wished she had her mother to talk to, to ask questions. Her mother had been both wise and uncommonly sweet.

Some men rode in the wagon, but most walked, the movement keeping them warmer. Captain Schuyler rode up next to Charles West. "You take your gloves off when you draw. I doubt I could hold a quill, a piece of charcoal, or anything in heat or cold. I can hold a sword or an ax handle, but nothing so narrow."

"I have to work fast. Then I go back to add more details. As to the road to the bridge, I keep reviewing with Corporal Ix. I am not sure of the proper grades."

"Can't be that far off."

Charles half smiled. "I hope not. And as to gloves." He pulled his gloves from his breeches' pocket, many of the fingers were now missing. "You know, Captain, I had hoped to add to my slender purse with some bounty from victories, but as you see. . ." He held up his open palm.

"No bounty for you, and I have your fine pistol." Schuyler touched the handsome flintlock gun.

"Indeed." Charles glanced down at Piglet, happily trotting beside him. He scooped up the dog, carrying him for a while.

Captain Schuyler nodded and rode forward.

Once back at the camp, his horse untacked, brushed out, a light blanket over him, fresh water in his bucket, John Schuyler opened the wrapped book. It was *Aesop's Fables*, with illustrations. An inscription in French was written in a flowing, artistic hand.

Slipping it back into his tunic, he saved the paper and raffia, for he wanted everything her hand had touched. He briskly walked to Charles's barracks, twilight enhancing even those rude structures.

Opening the door, he felt a bit of warmth from the fire. The men stood up as he entered.

"Lieutenant West, would you step outside for a moment?"

Grabbing his outer coat, Piglet at his heels, Charles followed John Schuyler outside.

"Will you read this for me? I cannot read French."

Charles gingerly took the book. "Ah, I remember this."

He opened the cover, looked at the beautiful hand, did not comment, and translated, "'How true these are. Catherine.'" He handed the book back.

"Thank you."

"I quite like 'The Fox and the Grapes.'" He waited for a moment. "A gentleman would read this, then write back a thank-you, perhaps with something witty or amusing regarding one of the fables."

"I can write, but it's a scrawl." His face registered disappointment.

"My hand is good."

"She doesn't want her father to know she gave me this." Captain Schuyler slipped the book back into his coat.

"Ah, well, that changes things." Before the Continental soldier took his leave, Charles inhaled the cold air. "Let me think on this, and"—he inclined his head slightly—"if you can learn anything of our fates, that would be most kind."

As they parted, Charles returning to his makeshift cot, he thought that while he was a captive, he was not nearly so much a captive as John Schuyler. Odd? Fate? He had no idea. Piglet jumped up, in answer, snuggled next to him, and they fell asleep fatigued by the long day's work.

# 20

*April 28, 2015*

*H*arry spent the morning in Ginger's office. Trudy was delighted to have her there, as both Olivia and Rennie had returned home: Olivia to New Orleans, and Rennie to Virginia Beach. They chatted a little, but Trudy was busy, doing her best to set things in order and send thank-you notes regarding the service at UVA for her husband. Having been given permission by Sheriff Shaw, once in Ginger's office, Harry read everything on his desk.

Ginger had maps in a neat pile, in an editor's cabinet, maps from Revolutionary times, maps drawn twenty years after the conflict ended, and current maps. He'd marked some large estates, but Harry wasn't certain why. One or two of the properties remained in family hands throughout the centuries. Most were broken up, divided among children or sold for profit by some—especially once the magnets of the great, growing cities beckoned, and along with them, riches, if one was shrewd. Men like Thomas Fortune Ryan, who left central Virginia to become one of the five richest men in America in the early twentieth century. But even before that man's phenomenal rise due to equally phenomenal intelligence, men and women left Albemarle County for the cities or for the West. Many who had prospered during the Revolutionary War shrank into self-satisfaction. The energy moved away from the state that created a nation, the state on which Europeans managed finally to live in 1607. Lulled by good living, glutted with blood snobbery, the old Virginia names had little to really brag about now other than their old names.

Sitting at Ginger's desk and looking at the changes on the maps made her think. It was only now, in the early twenty-first century, that Virginia was again open to and rewarding of new thinkers, innovation in business and science. These days the flood of new people irritated many, but they were a bright hope in saving this gorgeous state from becoming a museum.

Back home, looking out at those mountains, her touchstone, Harry could almost see the past, present, and future. She wasn't one of the bright ones, the entrepreneurs, the scientists. She was the product of an old line, but she was open to new ideas. In her own way, she could feel the excitement, and wondered what it had been like back in the eighteenth century. Once we'd kicked out the British, anything was possible.

At the desk she pulled a piece of paper from underneath Pewter, a born paperweight. "Pewter, a little decorum, please." Harry rubbed the gray cat's ears. The other two grumbled but moved closer to Pewter for a rub.

Harry copied a rough drawing from 1789 of The Albemarle Barracks, by then empty of prisoners. All those log barracks, each with a log chimney, made her realize how much activity flourished at the prison camp. Outbuildings, horses, crop patches were visible on this drawing, and not one palisade. Clearly no one was much worried about escapes . . . or maybe the guards welcomed them.

She'd read in Ginger's papers about how the farmers and blacksmiths, coopers, et cetera, used the free labor, much of it highly skilled. The Barracks was a gold mine. Needing to see for herself, she hopped in her truck, animals in tow, and headed toward The Barracks. Her farm lay eight miles west of the turnoff to The Barracks.

From the entrance to Barracks Stud, a driveway forked to the left. The drive down to the stables and indoor riding arena gently curved right. Harry peered at the lay of the land.

In the distance on this early Tuesday afternoon, the Blue Ridge Mountains stood to the west as a line of defense. In the early days, that defense held against western tribes, today it continues to somewhat defang high winds from Canada and the West. The mountains couldn't protect anyone against the winter of 2014, when storm after undiminished snowstorm soared over the mountains, covering all below.

Closer to the mountains, Harry's farm afforded her a more dramatic view, but The Barracks Stud view was longer, and today the mountains dazzled, almost royal blue against a robin's-egg-blue sky. She climbed back in the truck, where her three friends patiently waited. Well, two patiently waited.

Pewter had much on her mind. *"If she lets us out, we can run into the indoor arena. Sometimes there are birds in there."* Her lips parted slightly.

Barracks Stud and The Barracks were owned and run by Tom and Claiborne Bishop. The Stud, a small breeding operation, blended nicely with what was now called The Barracks, referring to a large indoor arena, stalls next to same.

Pastures, fencing, and outbuildings completed the well-run equine operation, all of it on the former prisoner-of-war camp. The camp had been dismantled more than one hundred and fifty years ago.

The historical buildings, grave sites, and service building were long gone by the time Tom and Claiborne purchased the rolling meadows in the 1970s.

Driving down to the office attached to the stable and the indoor arena, she parked the truck, jumped out, and opened the door for her friends. Tucker, lifted down, scampered after the two cats, who shot for the arena.

"Harry."

"Claiborne, thanks for letting me come over and poke around."

Claiborne smiled. "Well, you're not the first, you're just the one I know best."

"Before going through Ginger McConnell's papers, I had no idea how big this place was when it was a prisoner-of-war camp."

"Not a trace of it left, really. Ginger would come here a lot. I can't believe he's gone. He would point things out to me and Tom"—she mentioned her husband—"and he'd make it all come to life. Me, I look out and see a pasture that needs overseeding, yearlings that need to be brought in, potholes in the driveway." She laughed.

"That's why you're the best at what you do." Harry had known Claiborne for years, and her late mother as well, a lady of graciousness.

"If you need anything, holler," the tall, good-looking Claiborne offered. Claiborne was one of those women confident enough that when her black hair turned gray she didn't color it. The gray actually was stunning.

"I will. Thank you again."

While liking history, Harry missed much, as did most people when only the highlights and battles were taught. It occurred to her even then that whoever wins a war writes the history books. But the battle at Saratoga was critical, not just for the colonists' victory, but for lifting their spirits. The mighty British war machine, its powerful ships in our harbors, had landed its troops without issue. We'd lost New York and Philadelphia, severe blows. Again, Ginger had returned to this battle and its aftermath, a period he wrote about when he was young.

She had no idea that about four thousand prisoners shifted to

Charlottesville in 1779, marching all the way from Boston. They'd been held in Cambridge since the Battle of Saratoga. Prisoners of war were not usually studied in high school, nor in college, but how those men were treated says a great deal about the capturing army. As she read, she felt sorry for the British and Hessians. The terms of their surrender, called the Terms of Convention, had fizzled. Instead of being paroled or sent back to England, Scotland, Wales, and Ireland, the poor fellows were stranded in America. King George would not ratify the arrangement.

When the attitude of the Crown became unpleasantly clear, the congress—sitting in York, Pennsylvania, as it was far safer there than elsewhere—revoked the terms of the Saratoga surrender, the Convention. More or less tit for tat, but, to the congressmen's credit, they made their position as clear as the Crown's. It was not a happy situation.

The Albemarle Barracks found itself overwhelmed even as the county's population realized profit. She'd read personal journals; there were quite a few. The number of prisoners was so great the British had had to be divided. More than a thousand men marched up to York itself in 1781 to live in Camp Security, as a boon to the merchants in that beautiful area. Possibly congress pushed this along as a reward for York's hosting the congress. Should the war be lost, the residents of York and York County would pay dearly for this, as would the residents of Albemarle County.

A fat gray cat thundered past, followed by Mrs. Murphy and Tucker. Pewter made a U-turn, blew by them, and dashed into the stables again, turning left toward the arena where she had begun her race.

"Harry, if that cat gets any bigger, throw some tack on her," Claiborne suggested.

Harry threw up her hands, laughed with her, and decided it best to follow her pet. She hurried into the stables. One of the stable girls just pointed like a traffic cop. Harry trotted in that direction. Stepping into the huge indoor arena, Harry couldn't see the cats and dog, but she heard them thundering on the raised viewing section, the lower arena to her right.

"*You'll never catch me!*" Pewter squealed.

Tucker didn't answer, trying to catch up.

Mrs. Murphy, now next to Pewter, said, "*Let's jump over her head. Turn around.*"

"*Yeah!*" Pewter agreed.

The two cats skidded to a halt. Tucker was now three steps behind and moving forward. They hunched down, wiggled their bottoms to fly right over the dog's head, then raced to the other end of the building, where the doors were slightly open to allow horses inside.

The air, still cool, flowed through that opening. Harry, foot on the steps, nearly fell over as the cats shot between her legs and Tucker blew by her. Out the cats ran, now turning toward the cars parked by the arena and from there into the pasture. Once in the pasture, across from the large structure, they cut left, ran for all they were worth, crossed the driveway, and halted in another smaller southern pasture. Tucker caught up with them. The three sat there, breathing heavily, thrilled with themselves.

Harry trotted alongside the road to reach them. She didn't climb into the pasture, didn't want to disturb the horses who didn't know her. Her animals laughed a bit more.

"*Two legs,*" Pewter simply noted.

"*Makes them unbalanced,*" Mrs. Murphy added.

Harry reached the black board fencing, leaned over on the top board. "You all are crazy. Luckily you didn't scare the horses in the arena, but they could hear you. I think your screaming and hissing could be heard down to the Rotunda." No one said anything. They stared at her, wondering if she was going to climb over the fence. She stood where the drive to the buildings curved and a little speed bump was perhaps twenty yards away. A new three-trunk river birch had been planted there in the line of long-established trees. Harry thought the tree lovely. The older dead tree had been removed, so this was truly brand-new. She wondered who had selected this type of tree, for birches didn't grow well in Virginia. Being more of a northern species, they died off, especially the white-bark ones called paper birches by country people. But these dark river birches were different. The peeling bark created interesting color gradations. Harry stepped closer, keeping her feet on the edge of the mulch. Fingering a peeling piece of bark, she marveled at its texture.

Turning back to the three still sitting there, she said, "Come on."

"Not yet." Pewter sauntered in the other direction.

"Pewter. Pewter, I could wring your neck." Harry climbed over the fence.

"Ha! You could never catch me, slowpoke." Pewter ran a few steps, waited for Harry to get close, then ran again.

"I really will kill her!" Harry muttered as Tucker and Mrs. Murphy fell into step behind her.

"La-de-da!" Pewter continued her taunting with a few steps forward, then sat, then took a few steps running.

"Pewts, don't get her in a bad mood," Mrs. Murphy counseled.

"She's already in a bad mood," Pewter meowed. "It's a good idea to remind her every now and then how limited she is compared to me. But then everyone is limited compared to me."

Mrs. Murphy looked at Tucker, who returned the look with a resigned countenance. Pewter was going to milk this for all it was worth.

Harry trudged out to the middle of the pasture, stopped, and looked northward toward the refined brick house in the distance.

Speaking to Mrs. Murphy and Tucker, she said, "A couple of hundred acres, filled with prisoners of war. I bet if we were standing here at that time, 1779, 1780, there were barracks as far as the eye could see. Funny how their blood is still here. Those that stayed." She sighed. "Well, human bloodlines aren't as clear as animals', I think. When I was a kid, Heron's Plume lived in this pasture. About as perfect a conformation as you'd ever see." She smiled, remembering the horse. "My mother would come and visit Mrs. Smith, Claiborne's mother, and I remember Heron's Plume because he'd come over to the fence and I could feed him apples. Oh, I must be getting old, taking a trip down Memory Lane." She turned, walking back toward the fence.

Pewter watched, then called out, *"Hey. Hey, I'm still here."*

Harry, a few tricks up her sleeve, ignored the meow.

Tucker lifted her head. "M-m-m."

*"Where are you going?"* Mrs. Murphy stuck to Harry.

*"A most enticing fragrance."* With that, Tucker loped to the newly planted tree.

Harry didn't pay much attention to her dog, as Tucker frequently investigated things that were of no interest to Harry. The tiger cat and human walked toward the buildings.

*"You're giving up. Lazy!"* Pewter yelled, louder now.

Harry kept walking. In front of her, Tucker was digging furiously at the base of the river birch.

*"Hey."* Pewter emitted a shriek, the timber of which pleased Harry.

Harry giggled. *"Two more minutes and she'll have a hissy fit."*

*"Make that one."* Mrs. Murphy giggled too.

Reaching the fence, Harry climbed over, then beheld Tucker tearing at the base of the new tree.

"Tucker! Tucker, leave it!"

With attention diverted from her game to Tucker, Pewter ran across the pasture to join the dog.

Now there were two animals determined to dig up Claiborne's new birch tree. Already Harry's mind was calculating what it would cost if they ruined it.

"Dammit." She swore under her breath as she hurried to the spot.

Pewter didn't look up, but, more obedient by nature, Tucker did. She stepped back.

Harry grabbed the dog's collar to pull her back, Tucker's snout covered with mulch and dirt. A sickly odor assailed Harry. It was a foul odor she recognized.

Looking down, she saw part of a worn shoe and a glimpse of an ankle. She let go of the collar, peered intently. With the toe of her boot, she brushed off a bit more mulch and soft earth.

No mistake, this was the foot of a sufficiently dead human.

# 21

Sheriff Shaw, Deputy Cooper, and a forensic team of three stood over the emptied makeshift grave. The body, after being placed in a bag, had already been taken away. The police photographer had reached the scene just as Rick and Cooper did, and had been able to document the unearthing, paying particular attention to the positioning of the corpse. The dead person had been folded up, knees to chin, arms tied to torso, and placed on its side under the tree. It wasn't clear if the corpse was put there as the tree was planted or later.

When Harry discovered the foot and ran to Claiborne's office, they both hurried back to the grisly find. Shocked, but clearheaded, Claiborne pulled out her cellphone from her jacket and called the sheriff. Harry had left her cellphone in the truck. Claiborne, a quick thinker, then called her husband, Tom, instructing him to pull and copy the records for the purchase of the river birch as well as the date it was planted.

She and Harry then returned to the stables, where they asked everyone to remain on the premises until further instruction. As is often the case, some took this news better than others, especially those mothers who kept a tight schedule. Claiborne calmly but with authority told the ladies—it was mostly ladies—that no one could leave The Barracks until Sheriff Shaw released them. Which would likely be soon.

Harry mentioned, "Claiborne, call Tom again and tell him what you've done, then post someone at the drive in. Sheriff Shaw should be here within fifteen or twenty minutes."

"Tom," she hollered, and her blue-eyed husband appeared from the opposite direction, in the stables. "We've got to keep people out until the sheriff allows traffic, and Harry says she thinks he'll be here in twenty minutes. Can you go down and sit at the entrance?"

"Of course." He hurried out to bar the road with his car.

Once he arrived, Rick appreciated the quick thinking. He told Claiborne that everyone could leave and asked if she would mind, with Harry's help, making a list of who was at The Barracks now, including staff. Once the body was transported from the scene, Coop came up to the office.

"*I found it!*" Pewter bellowed from Claiborne's desk, which she'd commandeered.

"*Pewter, shut up,*" Mrs. Murphy ordered.

Tom handed Cooper the paperwork for the transplanted birch. She read the company name aloud: "Huber Landscaping."

"They're landscaping Marshall Reese's development, Continental Estates, over there on the back side of The Barracks. Seemed like a good time for us to replace our tree that died," Tom said.

"Did you select the type of tree?" Coop flipped open her notebook as she asked Claiborne.

"Tom did. Once I saw what he was talking about, I thought it was beautiful." Claiborne caught herself looking out the window at the sheriff's vehicles, then she returned her gaze to the deputy.

"Tom, did you go to the nursery at Huber's to pick out the tree?" Coop asked.

"Did. We've known the Hubers forever. By the time I got to UVA, Paul was no longer a student. I met him when he took over his father's business."

"Was Paul on the site when the tree was planted?" Coop continued.

"No. He came the day before. Checked everything out. Had his supervisor with him, and the next day they arrived with one of those huge machines that easily excavates earth. The tree was in the ground in less than two hours. Most of the time was spent throwing the earth back on, packing it down, and staking the trunks." Tom filled them in. "That bill is a copy for you."

"Thank you." Cooper folded it, placing it inside her front pocket.

"May I ask, do you know who was in that grave?" Claiborne, having seen the ankle, hoped she didn't know to whom it belonged. But she did.

"It's Frank Cresey," answered Coop.

## 22

April 29, 2015
Morning

With her notebook flipped open, Cooper sat in Paul Huber's office. Three of its walls were floor-to-ceiling windows so Paul could observe the activity in the nursery. One of the ways his father had figured out to build a better landscaping business was to manage the company's own nursery. The savings passed on to the customer made for loyal customers over the decades. If Paul Huber said he was going to do something at a certain price, no matter what, storms, floods, acts of God, he did it.

In the distance, Cooper could see a large pond filled with water lilies.

Following her gaze, the still athletic-looking Paul said, "We can do aquatic landscaping. It's a small market, but really a fascinating one. You'd be surprised how a landscaped pond can bring in waterfowl. People enjoy that."

"I think I would." She smiled, then said, "Appreciate your seeing me on short notice."

Sitting opposite her by the coffee table, he replied, "Officer, when you called, I was shocked to hear about Frank. He'd failed spectacularly and . . ." Paul stopped, started again. "Frank was in the grip of something we can't understand unless we've been visited by that demon. No matter what, remember he once achieved greatness. He was an All-American and UVA hasn't had but so many. We're not Nebraska or USC."

"You saw him play?"

"Sure. All of us who lived here did. We still go to games. Only now we go with our wives, children, grandchildren." He smiled slightly.

"Can you think of anyone who would kill Frank?"

Paul folded his hands together. "No."

"When did you last see Frank?"

"At Ginger McConnell's funeral. He was hiding behind the pillars of the Rotunda. He hated Ginger. Frank was never shy about expressing that, but maybe on some level he remembered the classes, remembered the old days." Paul shrugged.

"Olivia mentioned that Frank had studied with her father."

"We all did. Everyone on all the teams tried to take the same classes. It created strong bonds between us, and also we could help each other. I would never have made it through chemistry without Nelson Yarbrough. I graduated long before Frank, but I'm sure many of his teammates were in the same classes as Frank. Tradition, sticking together."

"Did he ever mention to you anything about Professor McConnell's class?"

"After graduation, by the time I had contact with Frank, he was speeding on the way down. Once or twice he did mention a historical date, so I guess he learned something."

"Do you think you had a good relationship with him?"

"Well, we never exchanged harsh words. Frank wasn't capable of friendship. He was self-centered. Other people existed to be his audience. Like I said, we never had harsh words, but I gave him odd jobs. He was an All-American, and that counts for something."

"When the tree was put in, were you there?"

"No. Harley Simpson was the supervisor. He's on the job, but he'll be happy to talk to you. I asked him if anything seemed amiss. He said no, it was a simple planting. Nothing unusual."

She scribbled a few notes, then continued. "You would give Frank work?"

"Yes. As I said, especially in the spring and fall. He used to be able to work a full day digging, planting, weeding. The last few years, Frank worked slowly. He weakened. I'd use him when we were overloaded and whoever was supervising the project could keep an eye on him. Actually, Marshall and Rudy would use him, too, at busy times. He was unskilled labor, but he could use a shovel or his hands."

"Can you tell me what he might have done for Mr. Reese and Mr. Putnam?"

"Marshall used him on construction sites, especially cleanup, and Rudy used him occasionally, but the paving business is different. You can't risk a drunk around hot asphalt, but when Frank was sober, Rudy did use him."

A red oak passed the window, small, being rolled on a heavy dolly.

Paul said, "A useful tree. Even has a nice silhouette in winter. The wood is beautiful."

"You grew up in this business?"

"I did. I always loved it. I like working with living things, like creating vistas or privacy. People are more sophisticated about land-scaping than even twenty years ago, when all anyone wanted was Bradford pears—a lovely tree, mind you, but not particularly sturdy." He smiled.

"I like to see the driveways lined in Bradford pears when they bloom, early bloomers." Cooper knew a little bit about shrubs and trees, but not like Harry, who could rattle on. "Let me get this straight. You, Mr. Reese, and Mr. Putnam often work on the same project, so if any one of you had hired Frank, the others might know or see him on-site?"

"Most times, yes. I wouldn't say there was camaraderie." Paul shrugged. "He could be a surly S.O.B., but when he was younger, stronger, he put in a good day's work. Mostly, we didn't want him to starve."

She looked straight at him. "I believe those former UVA athletes that live in Albemarle County often help one another or throw business to one another?"

"We do. I send new people to Nelson if they need a dentist. We all use him. If he wants some landscaping, he calls me. It's pleasant to do business with teammates, friends."

"Yes. Your business is the biggest of its kind in central Virginia."

He smiled. "We are."

"You've bought additional acreage over the years." He nodded, and she continued. "And, if a teammate, even one who played later, wants land, you might sell it to him?"

"Depends." He shifted in his seat. "I need good soil for a nursery. If I have acreage, say, at one end of a larger tract, not such great soil but good views, I might sell that. Most people aren't going to farm. They want a nice house and views. But mostly, Deputy, I should have told you that in the beginning." She gave a little wave of the hand, and he continued. "I don't sell. The cost of land in this county is out of sight. I need it if for no other reason than I don't have as far to haul equipment. You know that tree we planted at The Barracks? An independent contractor with heavy equipment would charge you three hundred dollars an hour the minute he fired up the engine. We can do these things for less, and one of the reasons is scale, economy of scale."

"Like Walmart." She smiled.

He laughed. "I'm not in that league, but yes, same principle.

That's the reason Marshall and Rudy and I work together. Marshall creates historic subdivisions, upscale. He researches the history. I research the gardens for the time. I do the landscaping. Rudy grades, bulldozes roads, puts in the drainage, and then paves. Rudy doesn't need history." Paul smiled, then continued. "Working as we have over the decades, we rarely miss, or perhaps I should say we rarely get in one another's way. The work is smooth. We get along."

"The homes, the yards and gardens you create together are lovely. I like that there is so much land for each home. They're not jammed up together."

"That's Marshall." He paused. "He's adamant about privacy. Adamant about the provenance, the history. He puts up markers that are more complete than the state ones. Marshall's are easier to read too. I enjoy the history, but Marshall loves it. He was one of Ginger's favorite students." He inhaled. "Frank was too, until he tried to run off with Olivia.

"In a way, it's a sad story. She bounced back, married well, is happy. He hit the skids."

"Everyone has mentioned that to me."

"High drama." Paul leaned back. "High drama as only young love can be. People at that time of their life can't believe anyone has ever felt the way they do. When I met Anita, I couldn't eat, sleep." He grinned. "Lovesick but, you know, she somehow liked me and I asked her to marry me before she came to her senses." He laughed heartily. "This year will be our fiftieth wedding anniversary."

"Congratulations."

"Most of us, the team from 1959, married wonderful women. When I see the divorce rate, I don't know. I felt things begin to unravel in the early seventies, and, well, I just don't know. I was raised that there's no back door to marriage, so choose with care. Maybe we were all lucky. No drugs. Drinking, yes, but no drugs, none of the anger that came later. Well, I'm off the track. Sorry." He inhaled again. "And I'm sorry for Frank. A man given great gifts and he threw them away."

"Yes. It certainly seems that he did." She closed her notebook. "Mr. Huber, can you think of anyone or any reason why someone would kill Frank?"

"I? No, unless they thought they were doing him a kindness."

# 23

"An act of kindness?" said Cooper as she walked Shortro, a young athletic Saddlebred, on a lead rope behind Harry, who was walking another one of the brood mares into a stall.

"Well, maybe it was, Coop. I'm sure other people might feel that way." Harry slipped off the halter, hanging it outside the stall.

Cooper, having done the same, followed Harry into the tack room, where Mrs. Murphy, Pewter, and Tucker slept on fleecy saddle pads. Harry had tried cozy dog and cat beds, which they had ignored. The fleece saddle pads it had to be, so Harry used old ones, washing them once a week. Much as Pewter might complain, the two cats and one dog really were a little spoiled.

Coop sank into the director's chair as Harry sank into hers.

"Tea? Coke? A beer?" Harry offered.

Cooper shook her head. "No, thank you. I was so struck by Paul Huber's comment that I had to stop by on my way home from work. What do you know about Huber?"

"Not but so much. My parents knew him, of course, and his father. Paul Jr., is midway between their age and mine. I like him. He does outstanding work. The company wins landscape design prizes."

"Can you think of any reason he might have to kill Frank? After all, the body was found at his job site."

Pewter, eyes open, crabby, as her nap was being interrupted by chatter, grumbled, *"I found the body."*

Tucker, awakened by the cat muttering, lifted her head. "I did."

An altercation began, hisses and barks rising in decibel level.

"Will you two shut up!" Harry said and glared.

*"She's always taking credit for my work."* Tucker's ears drooped.

*"You! Bubblebutt. Ha! I'm the brains of the outfit. I found the exposed ankle before you did."*

*"I dug his foot up!"* Tucker growled. *"I could smell him under the dirt."*

Harry again glared, this time pointing her finger at the two, who finally shut up. Mrs. Murphy turned her back on the lot of them. She had only so much patience.

Focusing her attention on Cooper, Harry replied, "I don't think Paul Huber could have killed Frank even if it was a mercy killing, which I very much doubt. Granted, you never really know for sure about anyone, but he doesn't seem the type to commit murder, hide the body, and then on top of that be stupid enough to hide it where he'd just planted a river birch."

"Yes, there is that, though the killer could hardly guess some nosybody would be snooping around there."

Harry ignored that. "Frank hardly qualified as one of life's useful or positive people. He aroused pity or disgust—all the more so from those who remembered his glory days. To most people walking along the mall, he was just another reeking drunk."

"Harry, clearly, more than a pain in the ass. He was a threat. Irritating people are rarely killed. Too many of them, and too much trouble cleaning up."

A wry smile played on Harry's lips. "I don't mind cleaning."

Cooper smiled in return. "I've even thought that perhaps someone considered Frank a threat to Olivia."

"The only people who knew about that were Olivia, Susan, and myself. Olivia didn't tell her sister or mother. She was too embarrassed about going to the mall. Oh, and we ran into Sandy McAdams off the mall, so Sandy knew."

"M-m-m." Cooper rose. "I think I will have a beer. Mind?"

"Go ahead." Harry nodded at the tack room's fridge.

"Want one?"

"No."

"I owe you a six-pack, and God knows how many tins of tea I owe you."

"Coop, you don't owe me a thing," Harry said as Cooper sat back down. "Olivia lives in New Orleans. She's safe." She paused. "Is it safe to assume this is connected to Ginger's murder?"

"They knew each other. Had a terrible falling out. Frank hated him. Confessed to a crime he didn't commit."

"Did you go back to the golf course, find the stump I told you about? I wanted to go with you, but I'm not a member and Susan told me not to call you. Said I was seeing things, jumping to wild conclusions," Harry said.

"I did. Late in the day, just enough light to see. Better not to be a presence at Farmington." Cooper took a long pull on the bottle. "I saw the spike marks. I'd say a man's size ten-C. Two feet pointing toward the murder fairway, which is how I now think of it. Could be relevant. Could not, and I haven't had time to catch up with you, especially with this latest murder."

"Frank had to know something, and so did Ginger. These murders don't bear the mark of thrill killings or extreme hatred. The corpses weren't mutilated. It was just two shots. A silencer. Ginger drops. How did Frank die?" Harry asked.

"Stabbed. We've sent the remains to the medical examiner, but the damage was easy to see once we dug him out of there."

Harry grimaced. "You know, I hope he was so drunk he didn't know what was happening."

"Me, too." Cooper put the bottle on the desk after folding her handkerchief under it.

"Let me try something."

Immediately wary, Cooper said, "What?"

"The homeless down on the mall, I spoke to one of them, Snoop, because he was with Frank when Frank screamed at Olivia."

"You didn't tell me that."

"I wasn't sure he knew anything important, but I thought I might go back and talk to him more."

"Harry, that's my job. And neither of us knows the level of danger involved in this investigation."

"Snoop won't talk to you. He'll see the uniform and that will be it."

Cooper considered the wisdom of this, nodding as she pulled out her card from her uniform pocket. "When you're finished with him, give him this. Just in case."

"I will. I've already given him my card. I thought I'd take down a basket of food. The man is rail thin. Actually, I like him."


Just before sunset, long rays of sunshine turned old brick buildings coppery, rooftops glowed; there is no light quite as beautiful as the slanting afternoon rays of spring or fall. Harry carried a wicker basket. At her feet, Tucker wore a little backpack filled with a water bottle for her, and one for Harry.

Seeing Snoop once again sitting on the large planter, she waved. He smiled as she reached him.

"I hope you're hungry," Harry said.

"Is that for me?"

"Is." She flipped up the hinged lid, pulled out a fat ham-and-cheese sandwich.

Peering inside, he smiled. A little cooler took up a corner.

She plucked out a grapefruit fizz drink. "Not booze, but pretty good."

"Thank you."

She sat beside him, and together they ate the sandwiches. Harry gave Tucker small pieces of ham. "Heard about Frank?"

He nodded, mouth full, swallowed, then said, "Killed. That's the word down here."

"Knifed."

Snoop looked across the mall. "He never did anything that bad."

"Someone thought he did."

Snoop shook his head. "Except for that one time he blew up at that lady, you saw it, he never troubled nobody. Didn't even panhandle. If someone tossed money in his jar, fine. If not, he blinked and didn't say anything."

"When was the last time you saw him?"

"The day after the big funeral, he said he ran away from the halfway house and knew the sheriff would be looking for him. The next day, he sort of checked in. Asked if they'd been looking for him. I said no. He figured he still couldn't stay around here. Said he was headed down to the construction site around the hospital."

"Seems like there'd be too many people over there."

Snoop shook his head. "There's no one around at night when they're under construction. You sleep with a roof over your head. Same here in town. After that, I figured he'd eventually get out to one of the county subdivisions—no one around at night. Four walls and a roof. Keep you dry if it rains."

"Think he walked?"

"Could. He was still cleaned up from his stay at the halfway house. Hadn't had anything to drink, so he didn't smell like old booze. Someone might have given him a ride."

"How did he seem?"

"Okay" came the brief reply.

"Did he have any interests?"

The question caught Snoop off guard and he laughed. "Besides drinking?" When Harry nodded yes, he said, "I knew when he was going to read because he'd clean up."

"Why?" Harry couldn't understand what cleanliness had to do with reading.

"The library. He didn't want to get thrown out. He'd go on these jags. Go most every day for a week or two, then pick up an odd job, stop."

"Ever go with him?"

Brownie in hand, Snoop smiled. "Ma'am, I'm not a reader. But Frank was educated. Some of us graduated from high school. Some not, but Frank was, I think, the only college graduate on the mall. Could be wrong. We don't much talk about stuff like that."

"I see. Well, did he ever tell you what he was reading?"

Snoop thought for a minute. "Once he said whoever writes a book isn't dead. Never thought of that. He liked history stuff."

Harry smiled, watching him enjoy the triple-rich brownie. "Ginger was a history professor," she said.

"What's the dog's name?"

"Tucker."

"She's watchful."

Harry grinned. "She is one of my best friends."

"I protect her," Tucker spoke.

Snoop reached down to pat Tucker's glossy head. "What kind of dog is she?"

"A Pembroke corgi. Like the Queen of England has."

His eyes twinkled for a moment. "Good choice."

"Snoop, do you still have my card?"

"Do." He reached in his back pocket, retrieved it.

She reached in hers, handing him Cooper's card. "Here. I know she's a cop, but she's my neighbor and a solid friend. Straight up. If you need her, if there's trouble, call. She isn't going to drag you off."

"What kind of trouble?"

"That's just it. I don't know, but there're two murders close in time, two men who knew each other, even though that connection ended back in 1975."

"Ma'am, the professor was at one end, and Frank was down here. I don't see how they can be connected, and I don't see how it can touch me or any of us." He swept his hand to indicate the others who more or less lived on the mall.

"Snoop, I hope that's true. But if someone is frightened or needs to protect something, that person might think you know more than you do. Be watchful like Tucker." She paused. "Actually, Snoop. Be really careful."

# 24

"One, two, three, heave!" Charles commanded three other men, who helped him pick up one end of a huge log.

The four men on the other end labored to raise it as Charles and his side did. They eased this heavy burden onto a horizontal pile of three logs, staked perpendicular with other narrowed logs. They had no iron nails, and pegs didn't work to secure the sides of a new barracks. Given the lack of tools, chains, or nails, Corporal Ix figured the only possible solution was to drop logs between two stakes. The difficulty was in driving narrow logs that had their ends cut to a point into solid ground. Still, they did it. Hard work helped ward off the cold when lifting or chopping, but once a man stood still, the winds cut to the bone. Better to keep at it.

Each new barracks being built had an outside fire to warm men between tasks. The prisoners would run up, hold their hands to the fire, even lift up their freezing feet.

Every few hours one man from each of the work parties would return to his barracks to feed the fire. When the day's work was finished, at least they would be able to walk into a somewhat warm room.

And the new barracks would ease the overcrowding.

Dark gray clouds bore down on them from the north, having

rolled over the Blue Ridge Mountains. Charles was learning to read the weather. Winter in these climes, harsh as it may be, he could bear. It was the New World summers that tested man and beast.

The log settled on top of the others.

"Sir," Corporal Ix called from the other end of the new side, "we need the pulley and the rope is frayed."

"Damn," Charles muttered under his breath as he walked over to the rudimentary pulley that the Hessian had created.

"It won't last," the engineer predicted.

"Can we finish this side?"

"Lieutenant, maybe one more log, two." He held up two fingers in his torn gloves. "When it breaks, well?" He shrugged.

"All right. Take charge, Corporal. I'll seek out Captain Schuyler. He's here somewhere. Maybe we can find more rope."

He walked toward the main house serving as headquarters as well as the commandant's residence, a point of dissatisfaction on the commandant's side. The soles of his boots gapped in sections, the cold seeping through, and when it snowed his feet were always wet and ice cold. It hurt to walk.

A little wind devil twirled in front of him, debris swirling, and a bit of sleet as the clouds finally reached him.

Squinting, he saw Captain Schuyler striding toward the house, coming from the direction of the stables.

"Captain," Charles called to him, trotting in the tall man's direction, then slowing, as trotting hurt worse than walking.

"Lieutenant." John Schuyler smiled. "Filthy weather."

"I fear frostbite as much as I feared battle."

"Did you fear battle?" Schuyler's eyebrows rose up.

"Yes, until the guns opened. Then I was fine," the blood Englishman honestly replied.

"H-m-m. I miss it." Looking at the shivering lieutenant, Schuyler kindly offered, "Come back to the stables. It's warmer there. The heat from the horses' bodies does help and we'd be out of the wind." He glanced up at the house. "I am not needed there. Just going for news."

"And what have you heard?"

The wind, perhaps fifteen miles an hour, smacked them in the face as they walked to the barn.

"The old-timers say this is the worst winter they remember."

Charles smiled. "What do you say, Captain?"

"Nothing. I can't do anything about it."

Smiling, they ducked into the sturdy barn, privates and corporals tending to the animals, each of whom had a blanket or a rug as well as good hay.

"Ah." Charles breathed relief, stamped his feet lightly.

"What I have heard is everyone is in winter quarters. And the Crown refuses to budge on accepting the prisoner-of-war terms fashioned at Saratoga. Your long march presages a long stay."

Charles nodded. "Hard on some of the men. They truly thought they would be going home so long as they took an oath not to return and fight here. For me, I would have tried to get sent to the Caribbean. Somewhere I could serve but not break my oath here."

"I lay this at Burgoyne's door. He refused to list and describe all officers under his command who had been captured."

Charles considered this. "Yes, we heard that." When Schuyler's black eyebrows rose up, Charles smiled. "Prisoners have big ears."

They both laughed.

"I wouldn't want to be in Gentleman Johnny's shoes." Schuyler called the British general by his nickname. "The loss of Saratoga will weigh on him the rest of his life."

"Yes, it will, and given his position, his flamboyance, he will never rest." Charles felt some sympathy for the general. "I was looking for you. Could you spare my men heavy rope? Corporal Ix has rigged up a pulley so we can build barracks faster, and the rope is about to go."

"Private."

A young man, fifteen, perhaps, stood up straight. "Yes, Sir."

"If there is heavy rope in here or up in the loft, bring it to me."

"Yes, Sir."

"Let's get out of the aisle. A thrown bale of hay is as bad as a cannonball, especially the way these lads toss them around." Schuyler turned and ducked, for the door was low, into a tidy room at the southern end of the barn.

Rows of saddles hung on the wall; the odor of leather was comforting. The bits on the bridles gleamed. Harnesses took up one entire wall.

Noticing all this, Charles said, "The leather work is good."

"Every town has at least one tannery. Competition between the people. The English want to be the best with bridles, tanned leather. The Germans think they are, and in those areas where there are Italians, I must say their work is good—light, though. Better for boots, I think."

A light rap on the door. "Captain."

"Come in."

The slight young man carried a heavy rope that probably weighed as much as he did. "Where shall I put this, Sir?"

"Oh, right here and"—he didn't know the fellow's name— "come to me if you need anything."

Captain John Schuyler really was learning. He would help the young fellow, but the unspoken command was "Keep your mouth shut."

"Thank you, Sir." The boy shut the door, made of planks in a Z shape to hold the wood together.

Charles eagerly picked up the rope.

"It has been some time since we've been at Ewing Garth's. The road, still rough, is an improvement, but there's much to do. I hope we will get there before spring but—" A troubled expression crossed his features. "There's much uncertainty. I asked to return to my old regiment and was refused. I was told that I'm here in Virginia and I will be sent to a Virginia unit in time. Meanwhile, I guard you." He smiled.

"You do, Sir. You do." Charles smiled back.

"I did hear that Colonel Harvey is up at the congress. He's offering us more land to house prisoners. The additional acres are between where we now stand and Peter Ashcombe's land."

Charles threw the heavy rope over his shoulder. "How is it I haven't heard that name before? Ashcombe?"

"Loyalist."

"Did you burn him out?"

Surprised, John answered, "When this broke out I was home in western Massachusetts, but I don't think Virginians burnt him out. The Loyalists seemed to have gotten away. Peter Ashcombe fled to Philadelphia, pledged himself to General Howe as a civilian quartermaster."

"Confusing. When we win he will be richly rewarded. And should we not, will he hang?" asked Charles.

"Ah, Lieutenant," John replied, a broad smile on his face. "That is the first time you have admitted the Crown may lose. Will lose." Then he added, "The Ashcombe tract is an original land grant. It goes back over one hundred years, and Ewing Garth's father bought part of it. It's good land."

"Even if we win, I wonder, will Ashcombe return? He will find himself in difficulty." Charles imagined the fellow's reception despite his wealth.

"And if we win"—John's voice rose a bit—"I say the land is privately owned. It will not revert to the Crown. So Ashcombe can wait until passions cool. He has retainers working the land now. Men who favor us."

"The lawyers will be busy for decades."

"Lieutenant, I suspect you are right."

As they left the tack room, Captain Schuyler paused. "One moment."

He returned to the tack room, came out to hand Charles a heavy cloth. "For your boots."

"Thank you."

"Will you do me a favor?"

"If I can."

"I have read and reread every one of Aesop's Fables. As we won't be going to the Garth farm for some time, I would like to thank Miss Ewing and tell her which ones I enjoyed."

"No."

This surprised the tall, dark man. "Why?"

"A gentleman would not write to a lady, especially a lady of marriageable age, without her father's permission. Of course, love being what it is, it happens more frequently than not. But if you are to show you are a gentleman, you must write her father."

"Blast! What can I say to him?"

"Simple, and I will write it in good hand. You tell him that you and Corporal Ix have been considering his bridge and you'd like to suggest more improvements. Tell him the road will be truly finished come spring but there may be ways to improve the bridge and the traffic thereon. Remember, Captain, he's a man who believes in profit. Then you mention, as a courtesy, that you will be heartened to see him again, and you hope that he and his daughters get through this bitter winter without incident."

A large sigh escaped, then John nodded slightly. "You are very clever."

"I was raised as a gentleman. I don't know how clever I am." A pause, then Charles took the rag and said, "But I rather like thinking of myself as clever." He almost reached out to touch Schuyler on the shoulder but thought better of it. "Thank you for the rope."

# 25

*R*esting across from Lee Park, the main library in downtown Charlottesville was in the old post office at 201 East Market Street. Like all those post offices built from the late nineteenth century through the 1930s, the building was imposing, restrained, and well made. Its white pillars lent the massive shape a bit of lightness. Having been converted to a library, the once lovely interior had been violated to serve a different kind of public. The décor is what passed for efficiency at the time (in the late 1970s and early 1980s) and did indeed serve the reading public well. Ugly though the interior was, the fantastic people who worked there more than made up for it.

Deputy Cooper sat at a computer screen in a cubicle off the center area. Those nearby and reading glanced up from time to time, keeping an eye on the blonde in uniform. A few vagrants walked in, spotted an officer, and walked out. Others, library patrons, searching for information, walked by, frankly stared, but kept walking.

After hearing Harry's latest intelligence from Snoop, Cooper asked the head librarian if she could see what Frank had been reading. The Patriot Act allows law enforcement officials to pry into ordinary citizens' reading habits, thinking they might not be ordinary citizens, but terrorists posing as same. Coop, a county officer, claimed no such privilege, but after speaking to one of the librarians who in fact recognized Frank, she was allowed to scan his records. Fallen though Frank was, a bit of that old masculine magic remained. All the women working in the library knew him, nodded to him, and were recognized in turn.

Now and then, Cooper took a break from the screen, which hurt her eyes. She looked over her notes. Frank preferred nineteenth-century literature, most of it out of fashion now. He'd checked out again and again all of Sir Arthur Conan Doyle's novels, including the non–Sherlock Holmes books. He read the memoirs of any secretary of state who had written of foreign affairs of his or her time in office. He'd twice checked out the books of George Shultz and Madeleine Albright. He read everything Henry Kissinger ever wrote, along with masses of books on the American Revolution, some written from the British point of view. She scribbled down a few of these, scrolled down the screen more. When she saw *Fifty Shades of Grey*, she laughed out loud.

Frank did not incline toward fiction, but she found, after that initial shock, more soft-core books written for women. Poor Frank, late to the game.

She finished up and asked if she might interview a few of the staff who worked the floor. A young lady, perhaps in her mid-twenties, came into the small conference room, closing the door behind her.

"Emma Quayle?"

"Yes, Ma'am, Officer."

"This won't take long. I'd like to ask you a few questions about Frank Cresey. Your boss mentioned that you probably saw him more than anyone, as you often are in charge of the front desk."

"I am."

"How did he behave?"

She blinked, thought for a moment, then replied, "He was quiet, always polite."

"Was he clean?"

"Yes. His clothes were torn and I worried about him in the winter. His jeans were thin, holes in them, and he wore old sweaters. The staff and I found a parka that would fit him and we gave it to him for Christmas."

"So, Miss Quayle, you all liked him?"

"Oh, yes. He was never trouble, and if someone came in here off the mall, drunk or, I don't know, just loud or bizarre, Frank would take them outside. He was protective of us." She folded her hands together. "We were all so sad, upset, when we read what had happened."

"I can imagine. Have you any idea who might have wished him ill? Did he ever mention a problem or a person who was a problem?"

She shook her head. "No. He was quiet. And he read a lot."

"Yes, that I know." Cooper smiled.

After dismissing Miss Quayle, she briefly questioned three other staff members, then spoke to the head librarian, Mrs. Deveraux, in her well-lit office.

"You have good people working here."

"Thank you. Some might think that being a librarian is an easy job, a soft one, but these days, not hardly," the slender lady observed.

"Well, I know, like the sheriff's department, you all are constrained by budget."

"Isn't that the truth?" Mrs. Deveraux smiled. "And like you all, we deal with the public day in, day out. A library is a community resource. There are lectures, meetings, outreach activities. The bookmobile, things like that. And we try to help those who can't read very well. We do a lot of work with the various literacy programs. You would be shocked, Deputy, to know how many illiterate citizens live in Albemarle County, one of the richest counties in this country."

Cooper blinked. She was surprised. "I had no idea. On the issue of serving all, you see a lot of the residents, for lack of a better word, who live on the mall?"

She nodded. "A few. Frank was our true reader. Some of the others come in and pretend to read on those cruelly cold days or when the weather is dreadful. When I first started my career, we had no training to deal with the homeless. We do now." She stopped, then her voice lowered. "I think law enforcement, librarians, and postal workers see more than many others. Those without a home or much hope find us, if for nothing else, a brief touch of security."

"I wish I had an answer," Cooper responded.

"I wish I did, too." Mrs. Deveraux brightened. "For all that, it's a wonderful career, at least it has been for me. We are at the center of the community, we know so many people who are doing things. You learn a lot and you make good friends."

"What was your opinion of Frank Cresey?"

"Lost. Carried a deep sense of failure. He had a curious mind, when it was clear. Like so many people with alcohol damage, he'd killed a lot of brain cells."

"Ever troublesome?"

"Never."

"Any ideas as to who might have wanted him dead?" the deputy asked.

"None." Her mouth straightened, tight. "He'd ruined his life. He was a vagrant and, unfortunately, an alcoholic, but he didn't deserve to be killed and stuck under a tree."

Cooper looked into her eyes. "That's why I am here, Mrs. Deveraux, to find his killer."

———

That afternoon was breezy and warm, promising a wonderful first day of May. Snoop had been canvassed on the mall for labor. Given the good weather, people were landscaping like mad, a pent-up demand after a long, hard winter. Snoop and two other men from the mall were picked up by one of Paul Huber's landscaping trucks, a four-door three-quarter-ton Ford, so they all fit in.

He sat in the backseat, bouncing down Garth Road toward The Barracks, out where a series of expensive houses were being constructed on a few acres. To the people buying these huge houses, ten acres seemed like quite a lot of land. At least they could protect themselves from their neighbors by planting rows of border trees, usually Leyland cypress, since they grew fast. Snoop figured that's what they would be doing today, digging holes, lots of holes, in a straight line.

The truck pulled up to a humongous eight-thousand-square-foot brick, neo-Georgian mansion, nearly finished. Snoop was last out of the truck, and the flapping sole of his shoe became loose. Cursing, he looked down, his duct tape had worn through. Standing next to the truck's open door, he placed the exhausted shoe back up on the stair rail, a shiny chrome tube, to see if he could rewrap the sole, but the tape was shot and not a thread of adhesive was left.

"Dammit." He put his foot back on the brown pea-rock drive, when a familiar shape caught his eye.

Tucked under the truck's front seat was his letter opener, the one Snoop gave to Frank.

Hastily, he pulled it out. Something covered the wooden blade. It looked like dried blood.

# 26

*B*ouncing along on her John Deere, Harry plowed some back acres that she'd fertilized in mid-April. As winter proved long and hard, like other farmers, she waited it out, pushing back chores that normally were accomplished in April.

That glorious morning, clear, in the mid-fifties, seemed to invite celebration. Overhead red-shouldered hawks cried out; regiments of robins inspected what Harry had plowed, knowing worms would turn up. Blackbirds sat in the trees doing what they do best: gossiping. Rabbits, squirrels, foxes, deer, bobcats, and, higher up in the mountains, bear all wandered about, thrilled with the weather.

As she'd started at sunup, Harry rolled toward the barn on the last strip. Looking behind her, satisfied that she'd not missed any ground, she chugged along, just as happy as those creatures playing and chirping around her.

Pulling into the large work shed, she cut the tractor's motor, climbed down.

She looked for Mrs. Murphy and the others, but they were nowhere in sight.

"Lazy bums." She smiled, suspecting they were sprawled in the tack room or kitchen.

Inside the four-bay shed, on the wall, a huge thermometer, a big black hand on a white dial with degrees, told her it was now exactly fifty-six degrees Fahrenheit. Next to that hung an old clock, a Remington advertisement for the face, its electric cord tacked against the wall to an outlet.

Seeing it was 8:20 A.M., she dusted herself off, wiped her hands on an old clean rag, checked the clock again, and headed back to the kitchen in the house.

Since he was up most of the night with a mare foaling, Fair now slept. Pushing open the screen door, then the kitchen door quietly, Harry sat at the table and wrote him a note. Then, taking from the refrigerator a wonderful egg-and-bacon quiche she'd made, she put it in the oven but didn't turn it on. She left her husband directions, not that he couldn't have figured it out. Fair had mastered the basic domestic arts, but still.

Curled up in their beds, each of the cats opened one eye. Tucker, dead to the world, snored.

She washed her hands properly this time, grabbed a paper towel, dried them, and quietly walked out the door. Mrs. Murphy shot out of bed to follow.

Pewter rolled over, lifted her head. Did she want to vacate her cozy bed with her name on it? If she didn't, she might miss something. She, too, roused herself, stretched fore and aft, then scurried after Harry and Mrs. Murphy, who had by now reached the truck.

"Sleeping Beauty." Harry laughed as she opened the door, picking up the gray cat.

"*She doesn't need beauty sleep, she needs a beauty coma.*" Mrs. Murphy giggled.

"*Says you,*" Pewter called from the truck seat. As Mrs. Murphy was placed next to Pewter, the fat gray cat turned her back on the tiger, who didn't mind a bit.

Once in her seat, Harry took a deep breath, turned the key, listened to the glorious rumble of an old V-8 engine, popped her in gear, and drove down the long gravel driveway.

Whistling with happiness, Harry rolled down her window a crack for fresh air. She liked old trucks, no frills, no extra doors, more cargo space. The only time she didn't like her old 1978 F-150 was when she pulled up next to someone on her right side. Then she had to lean over and roll down the passenger window to speak. Also, she had to personally lock each of the two doors. Other than that, fewer things to go wrong and fewer upkeep expenses. Harry, careful with money, hated to waste or overspend.

*"Where are we going?"* Pewter inquired.

One hand on the steering wheel, Harry petted the cat with the other but didn't answer.

*"You'd think after all these years she'd know what I was saying."* Pewter pouted.

*"Pewter, don't sit under an apple tree and beg for a pear,"* Mrs. Murphy wisely said.

Turning onto Cynthia Cooper's drive, Pewter brightened. *"Good, she always has treats."*

Pulling into the place by the back door, Harry spotted Cooper out in her small equipment shed. A pair of feet peeked out from under a smallish tractor, of which one end was raised up on cinder blocks.

Harry walked over. "Cooper, get out from under there."

"I will in a minute. I broke a rod."

"No. Get out now. You should never be under any large piece of equipment jacked up like that. Come on."

Pushing herself out from under, Cooper looked up and blinked. "I'm careful."

"Sure you are, but weird things happen. If that tractorette tipped over for any reason, you'd be pinned, squashed."

"Dammit." Cooper ran her hands over her jeans to get off the dirt.

"Don't cuss me. I want you safe and sound. Who else can I pick on?"

Cooper smiled. "Well, I'm pissed because I know you're right, and I'm pissed at this damned tractor."

Harry knelt down to look under the 20HP small Japanese tractor. While nothing is as well made or as expensive as a John Deere, the Kubota was a good product for considerably less.

"You did break a rod. Know how it happened?"

"I dropped the mower mount, started on the front, weeds high." She pointed to part of the driveway encroached by high grasses; they weren't really weeds. "Everything was fine and then I hit a stone. I heard it, naturally, but I didn't know how bad it was until I rolled off it and the mount hung heavy on one side. Cut the mower, tried to raise the mount, still hung on one side, and I drove back here. Now I'm going to have to pay to have this thing hauled in to the dealer. Damn."

"Which dealer, the one in Staunton or the one in Orange?"

"All the way to Orange. I got such a good deal." She sighed.

"Oh, well, there are worse things. Let's go in and you can tell me why you wanted to see me."

As Harry followed her neighbor, she called to the cats, hovering over a mole hole as if the mole would be stupid enough to come out.

Inside, the cats and Harry sank into the alcove. "I'll come over and mow," said Harry. "Don't fret."

"I'll pay you."

"You will not. Now shut up. I don't want to hear another word. But before I do that, you and I need to walk where you want mowed. All that hard freezing and thawing has pushed up stuff, including tree roots as big as elephant trunks."

"I'm surprised some coffins haven't pushed out of their graves." Cooper put up coffee for herself and boiled water for Harry's tea.

"Make a good horror movie." Harry quickly raised her voice. "Don't you dare!"

"Piffle." Pewter took her paw out of the lower cabinet door, which she'd managed to wedge it into.

Cooper walked over, opened the door, took out a bag of treats bought especially for two spoiled cats, then shook it into two bowls. "There."

*"You are the best human, really the best,"* Pewter meowed before shoving her face into the goodies.

"So what's up?" Harry asked as Cooper poured.

"An odd thing, and I'll need your help with Snoop again."

"Really?"

Cooper told her about Snoop finding the letter opener yesterday. Snoop had informed Paul Huber, and events shot off from there. "Paul Huber drove over to talk to Rick and me. He was not far away from Snoop's work site, as he was working on the huge Continental Estates project."

Paul was doing the landscaping. Rudy had already put in the roads.

"I would imagine Paul was both upset and confused."

"He's certainly organized. He pulled out his tablet, one of those expensive Macs, had the truck usage information in maybe two minutes. As it turned out, that was the same truck used to plant the birch over at Claiborne Bishop's. I asked, Did he check mileage each day? I knew it was a long shot. He said the company checks it once a week for each vehicle."

"Because employees might be using trucks for personal use?" Harry inquired.

"Right, especially one-ton and half-ton trucks. Paul said they hadn't found a good daily mileage program but that once a week had been very helpful. If anyone had a notion to use a company truck a lot, it would show up."

"H-m-m. But the presence of the wooden letter opener doesn't mean he was killed there."

"We crawled over that truck, and we also impounded it. By the time that truck returns to Paul Huber, there won't be a fiber we haven't investigated. He was fine with that. Shocked that Frank's body might have been in his truck, but cooperative."

"What did Snoop say?"

"Not much. He was shaken. He swears that it was a letter opener he gave to Frank. As to what appears to be dried blood, obviously, we have to run that through the lab, but there was a stain on the blade."

"Report on Frank isn't back from the medical examiner's office?"

"Shouldn't be too much longer. Luckily, his body was in decent shape. A couple of days packed in soil is better than weeks or months. We already know the cause of death is stabbing."

"Fundamentally, I'd say the cause of death was alcohol."

A tight smile crossed Cooper's lips. "I figure most alcoholics are committing slow suicide. Frank received extra help." She rose, picked up papers from her kitchen counter, and handed them to Harry, then sat again. "What Frank had been reading just this last year."

Harry scanned the list. "Ginger McConnell's influence is apparent even if Frank hated him. May I copy this?"

"I made that for you. You're the reader. Thought you might recognize some of those books."

"I recognize a lot of them. One thing's for sure, Frank still had an active mind. You don't read books like these unless the lights are on upstairs." She tapped her head.

"I thought about Professor McConnell, too. But I still can't find the crucial connection between the two."

Harry folded her hands together, elbows on the table, rested her head on her hands. "Here are two people, one the student of the other back in the mid-seventies, both dead and both interested in the Revolutionary War, post-Revolutionary America. That isn't a period overrun with novelists, historians—some academicians, sure. But for whatever reason, that war doesn't stir up people like successive wars."

"Eighteen twelve. Who thinks about that?" Cooper knew a little about history, liked it some.

"Every time you sing 'The Star-Spangled Banner,'" Harry said and smiled.

"Who can sing that? Too hard." Cooper leaned over. "What about this book?"

"*The Men Who Lost America*. What about it?"

"Wasn't that in Ginger's office?" Cooper asked.

"He has shelves filled with everything and from every writer since the Revolution, I swear. But this was written by a UVA professor. Probably had extra meaning for Ginger."

"M-m-m," Cooper murmured, then said, "Will you go talk to Snoop again?"

"Of course. What do you want me to ask?"

"What he really thinks. He clammed up when Paul showed up. Of course, that makes sense. It's his and Marshall's companies that hire Snoop and the other mall residents for odd jobs. He has just complicated their lives."

Shrewdly, Harry replied, "Whoever killed Frank complicated their lives. Snoop simply realized Frank's body had been in that truck." She finished her tea. "I'll make up a basket and go down today."

"If tomorrow is better, that's fine. I know the weekends are about the only time you and Fair get to spend together."

"He's worn out. Had to deliver another foal late last night. I'll be back so we can watch a movie tonight. He loves that." She stood up. "Now you've got me all fired up. I'll call you as soon as I get back."

Two hours later, basket in hand, Harry and Tucker found Snoop at his usual post on the large planter. He waved to her as she approached.

"Lunch." She sat next to him, placing the basket in his lap as people strolled by.

Opening one end, he peeked inside. "I smell bacon."

"Bacon, avocado, turkey, and lettuce with Thousand Island dressing, and you get to choose between a Co-Cola, water, or sparkling grapefruit juice."

"Sparkling grapefruit." She handed him a light green ice-cold can, as well as a sandwich.

Tucker watched with soulful eyes as Harry unwrapped her own sandwich.

"Here, beggar." She gave the corgi a tidbit.

They ate in the sunshine, the temperature now in the low sixties.

After a few chocolate-chip cookies, with their debris back in the basket, Harry sat, soaking up the sunshine. A full stomach aids good feelings. Snoop sat wordlessly next to her, watching people go by: the piercings, blue hair, cutoffs, as well as those who sported preppy looks.

She noted the painted bucket by his feet with carved letter openers, little boxes, nice things. "Snoop, heard about your discovery."

"Yeah."

"A shock, right?"

He nodded. "I'm standing there in the middle of people, the driver, some of the other work crew, Mr. Huber, Mr. Reese, the sheriff, the deputy, and I'm thinking, *What if one of these guys killed ol' Frank?* Know what I mean?"

Put that way, she did know what he meant. "Makes a lot of sense. You were smart to shut up."

"I ask myself, *What did Frank know?* He wasn't killed for his money. Maybe somebody stabbed him because they believed his raving about the professor, but I don't think so. But I think Frank knew something."

"I expect you're right, but it is hard to figure out what he might have known that got him killed." She put her feet on the basket, Tucker watching every move.

"Well, as I figure it, he knew someone had killed the professor," said Snoop. "He might even have known who or why. That's one possibility. Another is that whatever Frank knew could cost someone a lot of money. He wasn't killed over drugs, or women, or an argument, or anything like that. I mean, his death was neat, right?"

Harry turned to look at Snoop's profile. His beard, while not long, needed attention; same with his hair. He looked like what he was, a man with no visible means of support who lives rough. It would be easy to discount him. She was glad she hadn't, because Snoop was smart.

"Ever see anyone talking to Frank?" she asked.

"Yeah. People would pass by. Might have a word. Most looked the other way."

"Snoop, anyone who was a repeat offender?" She half smiled.

He folded his arms over his chest, looked at his feet, then looked at her. "Nah. Just us down here. We talk to one another." He breathed in, then added, "The crew bosses who hire us sometimes. That's all I can think of."

"Frank talk about money?"

"Just that he didn't have any." He grew silent, then said with some force, "Mrs. Haristeen, he was found under a tree planted by the landscaping company, he was in that truck dead or alive. Who knows? Whatever Frank knew had to affect those people. I'm not going on any more jobs out there."

This comment made her sit up straight. "You worried? For yourself?"

Harry couldn't steer clear. Her curiosity was getting the better of her.

# 27

*S*tanding where the road splits into two driveways, right to Barracks Stud and Stables, and left to a private residence, Harry studied Google Maps on her phone. One was a larger view of the land, the other was close-up. Also in the truck were the most recent maps printed by the state.

The ground rose up to her right, while on the left it dipped away slightly. Satisfied that she had memorized the topography, she climbed back in the driver's seat and headed to where The Barracks stables' road also forks. The left went to the distant brick house owned by the Bishops, the right to the indoor riding arena and stables. It was on this road, the right, that the river birch had been planted. There was new sod surrounding the tree, rubber-wrapped wires in place to hold it steady for the first year of growth; she could see more land than at the gateway drive-in.

Mrs. Murphy, Pewter, and Tucker watched as Harry pulled her truck to the side again and got out, maps in hand.

The two-hundred-and-fifty-acre development to the north of this, Marshall Reese's Continental Estates, was well screened—first, by the topography, which rose up, but also by a thick line of woods between the two properties. To the west of all this, open farmland abutted The Barracks. Not seen by the eye but clear on the map was a road at the edge of this farmland. This was a back way to the airport where the university trained its rowers on a reservoir. If one turned left, the airport was not far away. Development cut up the land west of this road, in contrast to the pristine farmland abutting The Barracks.

No back roads led into The Barracks. Whoever disposed of Frank's body had to drive onto the property in the same way Harry did, which was to turn right off Garth Road, where two light blue signs announced Barracks activities. The right turn was onto Barracks Farm Road. As a development from the 1980s, Ivy Farms eventually took up some of the old prisoner-of-war land on the right of Barracks Farm Road. A car or truck on this road or in Ivy Farms wouldn't seem out of place. Land Cruisers, BMWs, Mercedes station wagons, Tahoes, and Suburbans rolled down this way, along with trailers filled with horses. In summer, the traffic would be enlivened by Miatas, Jaguar convertibles, and Porsches lovingly garaged over the winter. Once at the Ivy Farms turn, if the driver cut the lights it would be easy to glide into The Barracks. And as no one lived at the arena, who would know? From the Bishops' house, vehicle lights might be visible, so they'd be turned off, the truck and its contents would be hidden, especially if this took place between one and four in the morning.

Harry assumed the vehicle carrying Frank came from Continental Estates or from Huber's fleet parking lot. Once back in her truck, Harry turned around and corrected herself. No. A landscaping truck would be parked at the nursery west of Crozet. It would not be left at the site.

She called Cooper to tell her.

"I've already been to Huber Landscaping," said the deputy. "The trucks log in at night. The keys are locked in the office, and the trucks themselves are locked behind a chain-link fence."

"So, Coop, someone got into the office to get the key?"

"Maybe. But if this was done by a worker, he could have been smart enough to get a key made on his lunch hour. These are simple keys, not like the ones that open doors from a distance. Work trucks. Basic. And someone working at Continental Estates, not for Huber, but a known person, trusted, might have access to a landscaping truck. Anyway, I asked you to question Snoop, but I didn't tell you to go poking around."

"You're right," she quickly agreed. "But it strikes me as odd that Frank was planted, literally, at The Barracks. Frank had been reading a lot about the Revolutionary War, and we know that was Ginger's territory."

A silence fell after that.

"I've been thinking a lot about my lunch with Snoop," Harry continued. "Maybe you and Rick should place him somewhere until you know more about all this. He's exposed down there."

Another silence followed this. "I'll speak to Rick."

Her tacit recognition was enough for Harry.

Driving back to the farm, she kept reviewing the same things over and over. Nothing made sense. Once inside the house, she called Nelson Yarbrough from the kitchen wall phone.

"Harry, how are you?"

"When you took Ginger's classes, or at any time, did he ever discuss who owned the land the prisoner-of-war camp was built upon? Or who owned the land around it?"

The tall former quarterback seemed to consider this, then spoke up. "He mentioned the difficulties with forfeiture after the war. Ginger could make those times come alive, like when he actually gave us recipes of that era, but I do recall that Virginia, once it became a state after the war, wanted to confiscate the land of anyone who had supported the king. And every one of the original thirteen colonies approached the problem differently. Courts were jammed with property disputes. If you owned the land, you owned the land, even if you supported King George during the war. That's the short version. I guess the closest we come to that today is how the various western states deal with water rights."

This reminded Harry, not that she needed reminding, of how curious Nelson's mind was. "I never thought of that."

"Who would? That's what made Ginger such a great professor. What did everyday people face? One of the best classes he ever taught was the class about love, sex, and marriage. Full attendance on that one." Nelson laughed, fondly remembering his favorite professor.

"I can imagine."

"Hey, our forefathers and foremothers felt lust, love, disappointment, dealt with pregnancy before marriage, you name it, and what I especially recall is how sensible much of them were. Sex is part of life. Doesn't mean a man wouldn't duel over it, but everyone understood the power of attraction."

"Today it's the power of advertising." Harry sighed.

Nelson chuckled. "Oh, I think there's more to it than that. Hey, to change the subject, the boys and I took up a collection for Frank's burial once the body is released. I was surprised—dumbfounded, really—at how a few of his teammates, '75, still bore a grudge against the old reprobate and refused to chip in."

"That's depressing."

"Some never forgave him for the showboating, all the press attention from so many years ago. A couple even said that if they hadn't blocked for that S.O.B., he'd never have made all those touchdowns, never made All-American."

"What do you think?" Harry wondered.

"I think in any sport, some are more talented than others, and some are in a class by themselves. Today, people would think of the Manning brothers. I remember their father, and he had it all. For me, it was thrilling to see Frank's great talent. For others, not so much. Anyway, we scraped up enough to do right by him, and Marshall donated a burial plot. You know Marshall, he always goes the extra mile."

"Nelson, I try to go the extra mile, but someone always finds me and brings me back."

They signed off with laughter, Harry replacing the wall phone in its cradle. She sat down at the kitchen table, got up, sat down again.

"*Make up your mind,*" Pewter fussed.

Thinking the gray cat was hungry—she always was—Harry got up again and got everyone treats from the cabinet. Then she grabbed a Co-Cola, put ice in a glass, poured it, and once more sat at the table. She needed the caffeine and sugar.

Having brought the maps in with her, she studied them again, which fortified her belief as to how the Huber Landscaping truck had driven in without notice.

"*She's too quiet,*" Mrs. Murphy observed.

"*Never a good sign,*" Tucker concurred.

Harry then thought about how lucky she was to live in a place where good men could throw in some money to bury another man who had made a shambles of his life.

Albemarle County was a good place with good people, except someone living here was a murderer.

# 28

Mrs. Murphy and Tucker had been right about Harry's silence. Provoked by the loss of an old family friend, surprised at the murder of a washed-up football player, she was convinced she could ferret out important facts.

Taking out the list of books Frank had read in the last year, she called on Trudy. But before knocking on the front door, she examined the dwarf crepe myrtles along the drive. Trudy evidenced no surprise to see Harry watering her new shrubs at noon.

When Trudy politely asked Harry inside for a cool drink, Harry and Tucker happily accepted. Trudy liked company.

"The crepe myrtles are doing great." Harry smiled. "Next year they'll bloom even more. Of course, I selected the ones with heavy plumage. The trick is to get them rooted, secure, before the frosts come."

"Fortunately, there's a long time before that." Trudy sipped a sweetened iced tea.

"True, but time goes so much faster than when I was in high school. Surprises me."

"Wait until you're my age. *Whoosh.*" Trudy drew her hand over her head indicating a jet fighter. "Like a Blue Angel."

"Mom said the same thing about time flying, but now it seems she died young."

Trudy nodded. "Your mother had just turned fifty. Looked thirty." She smiled. "A family trait. Your people never show their age."

"Thank you." Harry dropped her hand to pet Tucker. "Blue Angels reminds me, didn't the government stop the flying during the financial crisis? I don't know why I thought of that, the money, I mean."

"Grandstanding." Trudy grimaced. "I was shocked to hear about Frank Cresey, terrible though he was. But he was a kid spoiled by fame, I guess, and Olivia thought he was the greatest thing since sliced bread. He was handsome. But what a terrible end. Two murders. Why?"

"The sheriff's department has made Ginger's murder their top priority. Frank, well, it's compelling, but . . ." Harry's voice trailed off then she picked up the thread. "Would you mind terribly if I looked at Ginger's office again? Would you go in with me? I'll tell you why." She reached into her jeans' back pocket, retrieving the book list. "Look at this," said Harry, explaining its significance.

Trudy's blue eyes ran down the list. "There are some of Ginger's books on this list. How odd. How very odd."

Leading Harry down the hall, Tucker's claws clicking behind them, Trudy opened the door, turned on the lights.

"May I?" Harry pointed to Ginger's comfortable and expensive office chair.

"Of course."

Harry noted the books on Ginger's desk, the papers from Alexander Fraser, the British captain at Saratoga. She opened the long, flat drawer under the middle of the desk. Clean white papers, pencils, and a flat gray square rubber eraser.

"Where did Ginger keep most of his maps?"

"He was fussy about those." She turned to an editor's bin, long, thin rows of drawers. Most are metal, but Ginger bought a beautiful large, long cabinet in mahogany.

By her side, Harry asked, "The sheriff looked in here, I assume?"

"Did." Trudy opened the top drawer. "Old maps are in this one, new ones are in lower drawers along the aerial photos. The second drawer contains old maps of the King's Highway, which, still in use, runs from Charleston, South Carolina, to Boston. There's one for the Fall Line Road, important to Virginia, as was the Great Valley Road. He's also got the Pennsylvania Road and Braddock's Road. The oldest one, used in 1651, was King's Highway. The others were in use beginning in 1700, some mid-century. Travel was hard— punishing, really. The government used to take survey photos, oh, about every decade. Ginger liked to see the development over former battlefields, old homes. Now that people are more interested in preservation, it's not so bad, but if you compare these maps, it's disturbing. Here, I'll show you." Trudy bent down, opened a lower drawer to lift out a series of large maps, black-and-white photographs. "Look at this."

The first aerial map of The Barracks and Barracks Farm Road was taken in 1920 by a private concern, not a government survey map.

"No Ivy Farms back then, no indoor arena at The Barracks. The brick house is there. Look how open things were. Then, just twenty years later." Trudy laid out an aerial map of that. "Still pretty clean."

"The country club is here on the right, across Garth Road," said Harry. "Well, it was always there, but not as a country club, but now you can see the golf course. Wow, this is something." She pulled the earlier map over this one again. "Even though it's clean, you can't see any remains of buildings or outlines on the fields."

"They'd been cultivated for too long, I think." Trudy returned those maps, moved up a drawer. "Now look at this. Nineteen eighty."

"Well, I guess people need to live and they want to live grandly, but this is so sad. We've lost so much of our history. I mean, even the lovely old houses were torn down. Remember Rustling Oaks?" Harry inquired.

"I remember all of Berta Jones's properties and those of her children. Everyone dead now, and most of the land chopped up. The sorrowful thing about the people that inherited most of the old estates is that they couldn't run them. They cherished the country, but they didn't know how to make money. Their forebears generated the money. My father always said, 'The first generation makes the money. The second tries to keep it, and the third loses it.' Simplistic, but there's a lot of truth to it."

"Yes." Harry studied the 1980 aerial photo. "I suppose that's a form of revitalization."

"It is, but Ginger decried the loss of historical places. Then again, the new people had some money, but not enough. To run a place like the old Jones property or even The Barracks before it became what it is now takes a fortune and labor costs rose, always do. The price of everything shot up. The wars intervened, World War One and Two."

"Don't forget the big one before that." Harry's mouth turned up slightly, a wry smile.

"Oh, Ginger could be quite wicked about the Yankees coming down after 1865. He used to say, 'Before we condemn, we have to remember that carpetbaggers saved Keswick.'" Trudy cited a gorgeous part of Albemarle County that had held fast to the large estates better than the western part of the county.

"Trudy, I think those now living in Keswick would have a fit if they heard the Yankees getting credit." Harry burst out laughing, as did Trudy.

Trudy put the aerial photos away, opened another drawer. "Here's an interesting view."

Harry laid the aerial map on the desk, peering intently at it. "I don't remember this."

"Camp Security, York, Pennsylvania. It was under threat of development and a wonderful woman, Carol Tanzola, fought hard to save it. Took her twelve years with the help of others who understood her reasons for preservation."

"I've never been to York," Harry confessed. "I know a little bit about Hanover."

"You would. All those horses. Oh, Harry, you must go. Old York, the square, the homes on those old colonial streets. It's beautiful, and the York Historical Society is quite good. Ginger was impressed, and I know I am bragging, but he just fell in love with Carol. Quite a beauty, I might add, and he did what he could to help, would hector historians at the University of Pennsylvania, Penn State, Villanova, oh, so many schools."

"What was his interest? I mean, what motivated him?"

"Apart from Carol?" She winked. "Like The Barracks, it was another prisoner-of-war camp. In fact, when the four-thousand-plus wound up at The Barracks, many had to move, a thousand or so, went up to York. But at that time, you see, the campaign in South Carolina was moving up into Virginia. What a dramatic and frightening time."

"Trudy, you could teach classes." Harry put her arm around her shoulders.

"Ginger loved it so. You can't spend all those decades with a man without eventually learning something."

"And he learned from you."

A peal of laughter shook Trudy for a moment. "What he learned was, after you shave, wash the whiskers down the bowl! Harry, it took me the first year of our marriage to get that through his head."

"With Fair, it was dropping his clothes on the floor as he took them off."

"My mother said you had to housebreak a man, and, boy, was she right." Trudy laughed again, then her eyes misted over. "I'd do it all over again. Every second. Every minute. I had the best husband ever."

Harry hugged her again. "I think you did. You were a matched pair."

As she drove home with Tucker's head on her thigh, tears silently spilled over Harry's cheeks. A good marriage teaches everyone around the couple. Trudy could say that Ginger fell in love with the York lady, and she meant that he was enthusiastic about the woman, had a crush, and Trudy trusted him. Loved him and wanted him to have those experiences. And Ginger, in turn, supported her interests, embraced her friends even if he didn't always like a few.

A wave of rage supplanted the sorrow. How dare someone kill Ginger McConnell? She focused on the road.

"Tucker."

The sweet dog raised her head. "Yes, Mom."

"I am going to find who killed Ginger, so help me God! And why was he fascinated with prisoner-of-war camps at the end of his life, camps connected by the prisoners themselves? Was there some kind of illicit trade between Virginia and Pennsylvania?" She thought about that, and decided no.

Although it would be possible to haul the best-quality Virginia moonshine up there, people in the Keystone State were perfectly capable of making hard liquor. They evidenced a real knack for beer, with all those German immigrants. What could tie those two together, and why was Ginger gathering photographs, old maps, reading and rereading battle reports that he already knew so well?

She remembered once that he mentioned to her, if you truly wanted to know about a period of history, any period of history, get your hands on diaries and letters. Well, he had read those all his life.

She spoke aloud again to Tucker. "Buddybud, I don't know why, but all this has to do with The Barracks."

# 29

*E*wing Garth rode a Welsh cob, a sturdy horse, to the bridge being rebuilt over Ivy Creek. Spring brought the workers. He had driven over to the camp on a number of occasions during the winter, each time counting all the new barracks he could see. Others were being put up over the hill, hard by those two thousand acres owned by Peter Ashcombe.

Intelligent man that he was, Garth realized more men meant more supplies needed. He could supply in volume hemp, corn, oats, straw and hay, and tobacco. The question was not establishing price, it was getting one's money from the Continental Congress, and it was moving the supplies themselves. Fortunately, he wasn't cash poor, because his holdings down in New Bern, North Carolina, and those on Chincoteague Island provided that. Commerce on waterways, or the ocean, gave a man quite an advantage, that is, until a British ship decided to capture your ship and claim all the supplies as booty. So far, Ewing Garth had been lucky on that count. He spotted Captain John Schuyler on the rise above the bridge.

"Ah, Captain. I see progress is being made. The road is much improved."

Tipping his hat to Garth, Captain Schuyler smiled. "With spring, Sir, we should speed along with raising and widening the bridge itself. My only fear is that melting snows will raise the creek too high, too soon."

Nodding gravely, Ewing said, "This was a trying winter. As I age, they are all trying."

Charles West, knee deep in the cold swift-running creek, set thick support logs for what would hold the wider bridge span. Corporal Ix worked beside him. The water coming down from the mountains was so cold that Charles's teeth chattered. Piglet kept running along the bankside, fretting over his master.

"Captain, let us give these men some time by the fire," said Garth. "I can see their distress."

"Of course. Our concern is to set these before the waters rise. You are very kind to think of the prisoners."

"Highly skilled, some of these fellows. I wonder what awaits them when they return to England? This canceling of the Saratoga Convention creates a new complexion, does it not? The Crown refuses to treat with us. Traitors, they say. But, sir, they abandoned their own! If anyone demonstrated tyranny, there it is."

"Ah, Mr. Garth, unlike you, I do not understand politics. I should think the Crown would seek to utilize good men. As for good men with understanding, I wonder that you do not run for congress."

Ewing appreciated this. "You flatter me, Captain. But as I like to get things done quickly, efficiently, I would be woefully out of place in a deliberative body."

The captain motioned for the men to take a break by the fire, then turned once again to the older man. "I believe we can complete your bridge by next month if the weather cooperates."

A large smile covered Ewing's face. "Excellent. Excellent." He placed his hand on his horse's neck. The kind cob took care of Ewing, who was not much of a rider. "Tell me, Captain, what do you think of this war?"

"We will win, Sir. How much time that will take, I don't know, but I do know we have a long, long coastline, and powerful as the British Navy is, they cannot control all of it. And they do not have enough men to land on our shores, nor to take and hold all our coastal and inland cities and towns."

"Yes. Yes. My thought is, and perhaps it is because of my tobacco holdings, that they will shift their thoughts to our South. I would not be surprised to learn they are stealing our tobacco. They know that is how we pay for our supplies. Oh, how they hate the French. Clearly Saratoga dealt the British a grievous blow. But, of course, you were there."

"A great honor. I will be happy when I can again take the field."

Garth shifted in the saddle. "Now that winter is over, can we expect more fighting?"

"No doubt."

Garth turned to see Catherine and Jeddie riding together, coming toward them. Catherine was on the difficult horse, Renaldo, that had terrified her father and had once given John Schuyler the chance to hold her in his arms, however briefly.

"I do wish she would not ride that beast," Garth complained.

John looked at her with admiration.

"She has him under control."

"Well, I ordered her to never ride him alone. Jeddie or her sister must go with her."

"Jeddie has a natural seat," the young captain said and nodded. "Slight fellow."

"He is devoted to Catherine, which gives me some comfort."

The beast Renaldo charged their way, then came to an abrupt stop with an arrogant snort.

On his back, Catherine said, "Hello, Father. Ah, Captain Schuyler. Is this not a beautiful day?" Her deep, liquid voice rang out as she regarded the awestruck captain.

Remembering Charles's lessons, John swept his hat off, dropping his right arm alongside his horse and then raising it and placing his hat under his left arm, the hand of which held his reins. "Miss Garth."

"Father, will you lend me Captain Schuyler for a brief time? I want to show him the back of our lands, where they adjoin the far reaches of the Harvey land and where you can see the Ashcombe land. I'd like to do this before the foliage thickens, obscuring the view."

"Captain Schuyler is in charge of the bridge, my dear. I don't see how he can leave these men."

She looked directly at John Schuyler with vivacious eyes. "Will they do as you say?"

"I think so." He felt a shiver down his spine. "But your father and I must get this done before the snows melt upstream."

She laughed lightly. "Dear Captain, Jeddie and I will have you back before the snows melt." Then she turned her irresistible charm on her father. "Father, I have been thinking how difficult transport can be and how much you must move goods both east and west. At the back of our land are a series of deep gullies. If these men can build a wider bridge over Ivy Creek, why can they not do the same over the gullies and the one ravine? A shallow ravine, thankfully," she said to John, before looking back at her doting father. "Then you could have the wagons go directly into Colonel Harvey's land, where the barracks stand, and the prisoners can unload the provisions. It would save so much time, Father."

The apple had not fallen far from the tree.

Ewing Garth considered her proposal, a slow smile crossing his lips. "Well, my dear, I can rarely refuse you anything, and this is an unusual idea. Perhaps it will bear fruit." He looked at his orchard when he said that, provoking smiles in all.

"Might I take Corporal Ix and Lieutenant West, Sir?" asked John. "The corporal will give us the best advice. He certainly has been right about this bridge and creating the landings on the road. As for the lieutenant, he can make some sketches for you to approve."

"Wonderful idea," Garth agreed.

"Jeddie, go back to the stables and get two more horses for Corporal Ix and Lieutenant West," said Catherine. "Bring them to the pin oak, the westernmost pin oak. We will meet you there." She beamed, turning to her father. "I so want to help you, Father. I know you wanted a son to work with you, but I'm just as good, don't you think?"

Flustered, red-faced, Ewing Garth sputtered, "You're quite better than that, Catherine. Your worth is far beyond the price of rubies."

She smiled at him. "I will pull my weight." With that she turned and trotted off, Captain Schuyler replacing his hat, nodding to Ewing, hurrying to catch up.

Ewing Garth watched them and realized he would never understand his eldest. Her beauty was incomparable, her personality electric. Benjamin Franklin need never have put a key on a kite string. He had only to look at Catherine, Ewing was sure of that. With such prestigious gifts, why did she wish to be useful to him like a son? Well, he had never really understood her mother either.

Nodding to West and Ix as they left the fire to follow Jeddie, he thought better not to trouble himself over understanding his daughter. Better to just love her, which he did.

Back in front of his house, dismounting, his butler's son running out to take his cob, Ewing then walked into his house. He could hear Rachel practicing her French lesson.

"*Mademoiselle*," her tutor addressed her, frustration apparent in her strained voice.

"Oh, piffle! Why can't the French speak English?"

Shaking his head, he walked into his office. A widower with two daughters, he felt outnumbered.

Catherine galloped ahead until John Schuyler came alongside, then she urged her horse to run faster. Side by side they thundered along, the cool April air in their faces. Laughing, she couldn't help herself, she finally pulled up at the huge pin oak. John stopped too, a little out of breath.

"I want to live forever," she declared. "I want to ride, dance, read, and just feel the wind."

Speechless, he smiled, feeling entirely stupid.

She beamed back. "And I really do want to help my father in his successes. Does that surprise you?" she asked.

"Miss Garth, nothing about you would surprise me." He noticed the first blush of spring on foliage, pale green buds on trees.

"I simply cannot swoon over moiré silk, serve tea from good silver, and listen to endless boring, dull chat. I cannot do it. I wish I had been born my father's son."

"I am exceedingly glad you were born his daughter." John grinned, his teeth even.

Looking at this handsome man made Catherine giddy, perhaps even indiscreet. Not that she would compromise herself, or her family name. Still, ideas and feelings erupted, and she made no attempt to bottle them up.

"You flatter me." She inclined her head. "Do you want a shadow, Captain?"

"A what?"

"Do you want a woman who shadows you, does your bidding, keeps to hearth and home?"

"I never thought about it," he truthfully replied.

"Well?"

He thought about it now. "I think a woman's sphere can be taxing, and perhaps for you, as you indicate, boring. I would hate to think of you being bored! I— I am rather afraid I would bore you. I am not a wealthy or an educated man."

"But you are a brave one. You fought, and I suppose you will again." Catherine stared intently into his eyes. "Captain Schuyler, if you would let me be me, you would never bore me. I truly do want to ride, dance, laugh, and I admire my father. He sees opportunities everywhere, and he works for them." She rushed on. "My father is a builder. He is not a man to waste time. He cares a great deal about his place in society, and I don't give a fig, but then I wouldn't have my place in society were it not for him." She abruptly shifted topics. "What is your mother like? Would I shock her?"

He sighed. "My mother is kindness itself. Four of us survived. She and my father taught us, taught us many things. Would she be shocked by you? I do think she would be as dazzled as anyone who sets eyes upon you, but then she would look more closely."

"And would she like someone who serves a perfect tea?"

"Miss Garth, my father is a carpenter. We have a small farm. Farming is much harder in Massachusetts than here. Mother tends the farm. She has rough hands, she walks with a limp, as she broke her leg years ago and it was not set properly. The hard life tells on her, but what she would really want to know is: Do you have a good heart?"

Tears filled Catherine's eyes. "How I envy you. She sounds wonderful."

"She is. And so is my father, although he speaks but little. I fear you would find us, what is the expression, 'beneath the salt.'"

Her face flushed, her eyes flashed. "Captain, I am not that superficial. And I hope someday I will have the honor to meet your mother and your father."

The two sat on their horses. Neither one knew what to say. John felt as though this woman could turn him inside out. He didn't even know what was inside him to turn out.

Jeddie and the two prisoners reached them at last and called out, "Miss Garth, you must have galloped the whole way."

Smiling at John, she turned, now in possession of herself. "I outran him."

The group of five spent an hour looking at the two narrow gullies and the wider ravine.

"It evens out a bit to the east," Corporal Ix noted. "That's a better place."

"It is, but that land belongs to Peter Ashcombe," Catherine said. "We have heard that he was with Howe in Philadelphia. Others have said he went to Nova Scotia. The estate, which is sizable, two thousand acres, is in the care of a farm manager who is for our freedom, but he is loyal to Peter. He betrays nothing."

"I see," the Hessian corporal murmured.

While his legs were still cold and not dry yet, Charles West nevertheless sketched quickly, incorporating the Hessian's suggestions. From her mount, Catherine peeked over Charles's shoulder. "I'll make this tidier for your father," he said.

John Schuyler dismounted, lifted Catherine down. They tied their horses next to the other three, as Jeddie had brought halters and ropes.

"It is possible," Corporal Ix called out at the bottom of the ravine. "Can you tell me, Miss Garth, have you ever seen water flow through here?"

"In very bad storms. Both there in the wider depression, and then also in the gullies, and the waters run faster in the gullies."

"M-m-m," was all the engineer replied.

Once mounted again, they rode back to the Garths' house.

"If you fell the thickest trees, hardwoods, we can sink them into the earth," Ix said. "That will take a great deal of digging, but we can do it, then fill and brace around the logs. The force of the water in the narrow gullies demands a strong underpinning, stronger than the bridge we are finishing. That really is the most difficult part, but the timber is here." The engineer thought it through.

Catherine added, "We can cut our own planks. That will save hauling lumber to a mill and hauling it back . . ."

"The trick is not to be the man in the bottom of the pit," John Schuyler remarked, and the others laughed.

"How long might this take?" Catherine asked Corporal Ix.

"That depends on the number of men available. If I had fifty men, I could sink the supports in three weeks. It's more difficult here than rebuilding the bridge, as I said, and I wouldn't want to build the bridge itself until we reinforced the supports." He added, "All in all, figuring in the weather, three months for the supports and the bed. Remember we have to improve this old road to it. This is just ruts, a farm road."

Catherine smiled. "I think my father will be pleased."

He was. So much so that he didn't notice when Catherine slipped upstairs to her bedroom, selected another book, and gave it to John Schuyler before he departed that afternoon.

# 30

May 5, 2015

"The dogwoods are finally open. It's really spring." Susan glowed as she and Harry, along with Mrs. Murphy and Pewter, bounced on a golf cart to the eleventh hole at Farmington. Ahead of them by one hole played David Wheeler, Paul Huber, and Rudolph Putnam. David, not ready to be buffeted by the winds of Susan's emotion, had quickly organized the afternoon's teams, giving himself Paul and Rudy for mates.

Accustomed to Susan's ups and downs, Harry paid them little attention. Marshall Reese and Nelson Yarbrough, the other two in their group, driving their own cart, carried on a heated discussion about what Virginia football really needed to improve. As they lurched to a halt at the eleventh hole, the subject was whether we need to lure the best high school prospects for defense or offense.

"Defense, Nelson. I'm telling you." Marshall, club in hand, bounded off the vehicle.

Genial in most all circumstances, Nelson just shook his head, saying in his light, gravelly voice, "You guys don't win games."

"Oh? Oh, so how can you say that? How many times did I help take down the opposing quarterback? How many times did I disrupt his timing?"

"Marshall, you were outstanding, but that's not putting points on the scoreboard."

"Will you two shut up and play?" Susan good-naturedly commanded, as she was now near the tee.

Nelson grinned, shoved his tee down into the thick sod, and took a practice swing, saying, "Offense."

Susan pretended to be put out. "You two are overgrown boys."

"All men are overgrown boys," Harry rejoined.

They fell silent as Nelson hit a booming first shot.

Marshall quietly groaned. "If I don't match that shot, I'll hear about it."

Susan goaded the still well-built fellow, "Well, blow right by him, then."

Nelson quietly observed this with a big smile on his face. He respectfully moved out of Marshall's eyesight.

Marshall really did rise to the occasion. While not as powerful as Nelson, he hit straight down the middle, giving himself a good second shot. He landed close enough to Nelson's shot that he needed not be embarrassed. That is until Susan teed up and hit the ball so perfectly it sounded like a deep click. Her ball dropped near Nelson's. Marshall had not played with Susan, as he usually played with his team buddies. He stared, his mouth open.

Nelson hopped in the cart. "Let's go."

Marshall dropped next to him. "Damn, that woman is strong."

"Perfect form," said Nelson. "She's fluid, economical, nothing is wasted. If we had her form, we'd be driving three hundred yards. Ever notice how the best at anything always make it look easy?"

"They do," Marshall agreed.

Back in the "girls' cart," Susan allowed herself a small gloat. "I do so love to drive."

In the back, Mrs. Murphy asked Pewter, *Did you notice that redheaded woodpecker?*

"In the old black gum tree?"

"Right. That could mean the tree will come down sooner or later. Full of bugs." Mrs. Murphy kept a sharp eye on avian behavior. " 'Course the groundskeepers will find it. Must be a lot of work to keep up a golf course."

"It would be better if these were fields of catnip." Pewter's eyes half closed with pleasure.

"Certainly would," Mrs. Murphy readily agreed. "And they could even play their silly game through catnip."

The humans did play through the eleventh hole, pretty happy with their scores to date. Then they teed off on the twelfth hole, the lake hole, which was the fairway on which Ginger McConnell was killed. Not wishing to jinx themselves, no one spoke of it except the cats.

As luck would have it, Marshall hit into the woods. He blamed the bad shot on his sore hands, which Harry noticed were bandaged. Both Nelson and Susan stayed on the fairway, but Susan had a difficult shot up to the green, thanks to the angle at which she found her ball. Such challenges revved Susan's motor.

Marshall, on the other hand, cussed a blue streak in the woods. Harry, taking pity on him, went in to look too. The cats, the best scavengers of all, trotted after her, their tails straight up.

"I knew it," he fumed. "I knew the minute I hit it that it was mishit."

Harry prudently said nothing but continued to search. She saw the sawed-off trunk where she'd found the spike marks right after Ginger's murder. She walked up to it. The cats continued the ball search.

"Harry, I don't think I hit it that far," Marshall called out.

"Right, I was just looking at something." She walked back to continue the search.

"Found it," he said, relieved.

"I found it first," Mrs. Murphy corrected Marshall, as she was sitting right next to the ball.

"*Murphy, don't waste your time. Humans are notoriously ungrateful.*"

Hands on his hips, Marshall mournfully squinted, looking through the trees. "I haven't got a prayer."

"It's a Houdini shot," Harry concurred.

"I'll take the penalty stroke. Otherwise, I'll waste ten minutes of everyone's time."

The rest of the afternoon passed pleasantly enough. Marshall shot in the low nineties. As just lately he played little, he was happy enough—rusty, but he could work on that.

Nelson came in fifteen over par, right on his handicap so he, too, felt he would improve. It was the beginning of May. Lots of time.

Susan shot an 83. Immediately after the game, she was already replaying every hole in her head, figuring where she made a mistake, where she could shave a stroke.

They all sat outside at the Nineteenth Hole. A bit cool, they wore their jackets but enjoyed the beautiful patio views of the golf course. The two cats nestled under Harry's chair, alert to anything dropped.

"Feels good to be back out again," Marshall said as his hamburger was delivered. "So much has been going on, I haven't played for two weeks."

"Has been intense," Harry agreed.

"Thank you for helping me search for my ball back there on the twelfth. What a rotten shot." Marshall pulled a face.

"I wasn't but so much help, I got distracted by a stump in there."

"Harry, not that again." Susan rolled her eyes.

"Are we missing a good story?" Paul Huber smiled. "You know, a remembrance from your wild youth on the twelfth hole?"

"No, after Ginger was killed, I couldn't help myself and I dragged

Susan out to crawl over the twelfth hole and the holes close to it. I found spike marks on this clean-cut stump, the toes of which pointed in the direction where Ginger stood."

"And I told her how lots of people get up on that stump to look for a lost ball," Susan replied.

"If I'd known that, I would have gotten up there," said Marshall. "Might have found my ball sooner."

"Harry, you really can't help yourself, can you?" David teased her. "You've watched too many mystery and crime shows."

"I know. I know." Then, to defend herself, Harry said, "But I think this all has something to do with The Barracks, the prisoner-of-war barracks."

They fell silent, staring at her.

Finally, in a polite voice, Rudy responded, "Going from 1779 to today is quite a leap."

"I know." She grinned mischievously. "But if it's true, what a story."

In the spirit of the teasing, David said, voice commanding, "As an accountant, I can tell you without a doubt, it has to be about money."

This got them all chattering.

Susan said, "Whatever happens, Harry will blame it on the cats or Tucker. You know, the cat found a bracelet or whatever. She can't admit she is nosy beyond belief."

"Hey, my dog and the cats did find Frank," said Harry.

Again the conversation stopped.

"I had heard that," Rudy replied. "Maybe it's best we don't think about it with our food."

"Hear, hear," David seconded the thought.

———

Later, walking back to their carts, out of earshot of Harry, Marshall whispered to Paul, "Where does she come up with this stuff?"

Paul shook his head. "I don't know. But it would make a hell of a story."

The cats, on their way to the truck, took a different view.

"*She should keep her mouth shut,*" Mrs. Murphy grumbled.

"True. *She just opens that mouth and out spills whatever.*" Pewter leapt onto the truck seat as Harry opened the door. "*But here's the thing, what if a murderer, THE murderer, sitting at another table, overheard her?*"

"*She's asking for trouble,*" the tiger sagely meowed as Harry cut on the motor.

"*If she gets in trouble, that's one thing. But she'll drag us through it, and that's another,*" prophesied Pewter.

# 31

"It's so bloody hot even the mosquitoes aren't biting," Edward Thimble cursed.

The men had their shirts off. Sweat rolled down their chests and backs as they carefully fit thick planks onto the last bridge over the ravine.

The bridges toward the barracks, traversing the gullies and the ravine, had been constructed with a mild arch to bear more weight. The task took longer than Corporal Ix anticipated. Delays, while not uncommon in any form of building, rarely bring out the best in people. The men cursed the heat, cursed the long grinding war, and finally cursed one another.

While laying the planks took care—no large gaps should occur—it was still easier than sinking the support beams and positioning the cross beams between them. Three men had broken bones. No one had died, but the incidence of heatstroke, abrasions, and exhausted muscles took its toll.

Charles worked alongside the men. Piglet slept under a large walnut tree, where he had been told to stay. Charles wistfully looked at his dog, wishing he were sleeping there, too.

The men, American and British, knew the French had arrived at Newport, Rhode Island, good news for the rebels. Charleston,

South Carolina, had been captured by the British and the Continentals were crushed at Waxhaw Creek, South Carolina.

Despite Mad Anthony Wayne's being beaten back at Green Springs Farm, east of Charlottesville, the rebels grew more confident. The sheer landmass of the colonies, as well as the territories inland, meant the British would need to commit thousands and thousands of men for victory. And after they won, they would need thousands and thousands of men to keep the peace.

Charles, receiving scant letters from home, more from his elder brother than his father, knew that Lord North's sufferings continued, intensifying unpopularity. His brother, much shrewder about politics than their father, wrote that sooner or later North's government would fall. The British people were weary of a war that was to have been swift. They didn't much like the increased tax burdens. If the colonists wanted to go, let them. The British still held New York, Savannah, and Charleston, but they no longer controlled Philadelphia, the largest city in the New World. The victories they won had little effect upon the rebels, who kept on fighting, wearing down the invaders. Reputations were ruined; a few were made, but very few. Those men who hoped to rise from this war, receiving larger commands and financial reward from a grateful king, had long since realized little gratitude was forthcoming.

Captain Graves called to him. "Lieutenant."

"Yes, Captain."

"Tell your men to take a rest. Wash in the creek. The waters are somewhat cool."

"Yes, Sir." Charles obeyed the senior officer from the Royal Irish Artillery.

He called to his men, and the call went down the line of workers.

Men happily left their tasks, stripped naked, and waded into the swift creek.

"Shall we join them, Sir?" Charles smiled at the older officer, a scar alongside his neck from an old saber wound.

"An excellent idea."

The two peeled off their clothes, which stuck to them thanks to the sweat, and waded in. Piglet ran from the tree, launching himself into the water, where he paddled furiously.

"Come here, fellow." Charles put his arms under the low-built dog, holding him in the water while he sank up to his chin.

How good it felt.

They cooled off for fifteen minutes, then emerged, shaking water off like Piglet himself. Another ten minutes and the men were dry enough to wiggle back into their breeches and torn pants, some shredded tatters at the bottom.

Weymouth, the butler's son, walked along with a bucket and ladle.

Captain Graves ordered them back to work, but held back Charles by his forearm. "A moment, please," he said.

Charles and Piglet followed the short, lean man to the tree where Piglet had been sleeping.

Reaching into his pants pocket, torn at the side, the sandy-haired man pulled out a folded piece of paper. Carefully, Captain Graves unfolded it, handing it to Charles.

"Have you ever seen discharge papers?"

"I have not."

"I took them off one of my men who fell at Saratoga. Cruel. He'd been discharged but could find no way back to Ireland, so he thought one more battle and he'd make his way home. He was killed in the first volley. I thought to save his papers, things."

Charles nodded. "Yes, I did the same if I had time. Thought I'd send them back."

Graves nodded, too. "Bits of paper, a few coins, all to show for a life."

"This war has to end sometime," Charles sensibly replied.

Graves folded his arms across his chest, sighing. "You are well born, Lieutenant. I am less so. To what do we return, regardless of station?" He leaned toward the younger man. "If we go home as part of a losing army, there will be no fetes for us, no rewards. We'll be lucky to collect what pay is due to us. The Valley Road on the other side of these mountains reaches north into Pennsylvania, south down into North Carolina. It's safer across the mountain."

"Perhaps best not to head south, given events."

Captain Graves smiled, revealing a crooked incisor, but he had all his teeth, a blessing. "Wise. I intend to escape, which should be obvious. I need discharge papers and I have heard from the men you have beautiful penmanship as well as your drawing capabili-ties."

"I am flattered."

"You can copy this and insert my name. I have equivalent paper."

Hesitating, Charles replied, "What of the seal?"

"I have wax in my quarters and I paid the blacksmith to make me a seal. Just copy this word for word with my name, Captain Bartholomew Graves, Royal Irish Artillery."

"Captain, what if you are apprehended and taken for a spy?"

He leveled his gray eyes at Charles. "I'll face that if I must."

"You've no provisions, no weapons."

"I can fend for myself. You're a young man and an intelligent one. These rebels will win. Listen to me, Lieutenant, this isn't India, where the people are accustomed to submission, to a potentate. Oh, the people here are alive to wealth and power. They aren't fools, but have you not noticed each man believes he can stand up to any other man? I tell you, Sir, they won't give in."

Thinking hard about this, Charles heard himself utter, "I don't think they will either."

"Then look out for yourself, Sir. I am a man of middle years, but

I think I can thrive here. You are young. This is a place for young men." A flash of passion crossed the older man's face, and that caught Charles off guard.

"I will give your thoughts consideration."

"King and country, is it?" Captain Graves half smiled.

"Yes," Charles simply said.

"If you leave, if you slide into the forests, become a new man, or if you remain Lieutenant West but you do not take up arms against the king, I don't feel you or I have violated our oath." He unfolded his arms. "And why should I stay strapped by my birth, my position, pleasant though it can be? I will never rise above a captain, and should I return I would be a man of some property in Ireland, but there you have it. I was raised in Ireland. It is different for me."

"Yes." Charles struggled. It sounded almost like treason but not quite. What was it?

"Again, Lieutenant, will you draw me these papers? I will pay you fifteen pounds."

"I—"

"Twenty!"

"I will. May I have a few days? I'd like to practice my hand on rough paper."

Captain Graves clapped him on the back. "Yes. And I hope you see reason over time. For yourself."

As they walked back to oversee the men, Catherine and Rachel, with food baskets and cold tea, rode down to them in a wagon, accompanied by Captain John Schuyler. As though overnight, Rachel had matured.

Captain Graves stopped for a moment, then smiled at the sight of pretty girls. "Oh, to be young again."

# 32

*T*wilight's silver-blue gave the early evening a magical feeling. Venus shone brightly over the mountains, but most of the stars would be more visible later as the last reflections from the sun died.

Harry loved this time of day. The foxes, owls, and other night hunters ventured out as the day birds and animals tucked up for the night. She saw a herd of deer way in the back pastures. Deer kept a hunting schedule somewhere, disappearing in mid-October, reappearing in January. Watching them graze, Harry knew they could wipe out an apple grove, grapes, young corn, and yet she never had the heart to shoot them. What she did have was Tucker, happy to be of service and chase them away.

The horses were in for the night. Their schedule would shift as soon as she felt the day's warmth would be steady and the night would be refreshingly cool.

Sliding the barn doors half closed, she walked into the tack room, where Snoop was cleaning bridles and saddles, doing a good job.

Tucker, at her heels, ran out again through the front barn doors. "Intruder."

The cats in the hayloft hurried to the open doors, saw a rooster tail of dust, and noted Cooper's squad car.

"*Let's go down to the tack room.*" The tiger cat headed for the ladder.

By the time Cooper reached the tack room, both cats reposed on saddles. Tucker followed close on her heels.

"Hey," Coop greeted Harry and Snoop.

"Come on in and sit down." Harry motioned for her to step inside. "Snoop's been working with me today."

Cooper nodded to Snoop, now smelling of saddle soap. "Glad you're here," the deputy said. "Let me ask you a few questions."

"Sit down, Snoop. That old chair will hold you." Harry pointed to a frayed director's chair as she took the chair behind the desk.

Flipping open her notebook, Cooper asked, "What made you call Harry, Mrs. Haristeen, yesterday?"

"The guys looking for work crews came down on the mall. They parked up in the lot across from the library."

"Did you recognize anyone?"

"Yes, Ma'am. I don't know who the paving crew boss was, somebody new, and I don't work too much for them, but the landscaping man was Harley Simpson. He's been picking up day crews for as long as I've been down on the mall, eight years."

"Did he speak to you personally?"

"He did. He said the storm caused damage and they could use extra hands, get stuff on the market faster. The storm slowed them down. We'd be paid the day rate, minimum wage at the end of the day. In cash."

"Is that the usual arrangement?"

"Yes, Ma'am. No one would work iff'n it weren't cash. They can screw you with a check."

Cooper smiled. "I understand." She did, too.

Harry butted in. "What about withholding?"

Snoop shook his head. "Don't know about that. At the end of the day I have eight or ten hours, minimum wage. I don't file income tax." He laughed lightly.

Cooper smiled a bit, then kept on. "What did you say to Harley Simpson?"

"I said I had other things to do. I'm not getting back in that truck. Maybe like Frank, I won't come back."

"Were you on the mall the day Frank took a job with Huber Landscaping?"

"No. I never saw him take that job. Frank would work hard for a couple of weeks, then stop working. He needed more money, I think. He was ready to work, but I didn't see him take the job."

"Do you know where he went when he wasn't working?"

He bent over to pick up a rag he'd been using, folded it neatly on his leg. "Sometimes. He'd go to the library. He'd take long walks to see what was happening downtown. Once or twice he even walked out to Pantops Mountain. Or he said he did."

"Ever mention anyone he saw or spoke with?"

Shaking his head, Snoop answered, "No. People don't come up and talk to us."

"But Frank was famous or had been a star," Cooper reminded him.

"A long time ago. When he'd let his hair and beard grow, few recognized him."

"Did you know Professor McConnell?"

"No."

"Did you ever think that Frank had gone to see him?"

"No."

"Did he ever go to charities, places where he might be fed?"

"We'd all go down to the Salvation Army sometimes for a shower."

"Why not more often?"

"They rub the Bible on you."

Cooper had grown up with that old Southern phrase, so she nodded in understanding. "Anyone on the mall that visited him sometimes?"

"No."

"Do you know where he slept?"

"Depended on the weather. If it's clear and warm, we'd curl up anywhere where we couldn't be seen. If it's raining, we'd hang out in the parking garages until they threw us out. Sometimes the stairwells."

"What about when it was cold?"

"The underpass was good. Late at night we could start a fire in a metal barrel and sleep close to it. Until you all would find us, but you didn't sweep us too often."

Cooper smiled a bit. "Most times, Snoop, we have nowhere to put you, especially if the jail is full. You'd be surprised at how often the city jail and the county jail fill up." She looked down at her notes.

"We used to be able to sleep in the post office at night, but not anymore," he said. "There's always a cop who comes in the middle of the night."

"Because the post office is supposed to be open to the public at all hours, the P.O. Boxes anyway," Cooper replied.

"I know. People don't want to step over us. In the old days, some were nice. They'd bring food and leave it if we were asleep."

"Any other places when it was cold or bad weather?"

"We mostly knew where the construction sites were. The ones in town are close, but they're patrolled. If we could thumb rides out of the city or walk, the new subdivisions were pretty good, although we couldn't start fires. That's why the underpass is so good. Nothing to burn except the wood in the barrel."

"Who would want to kill Frank?"

"I don't know. The crew bosses, especially Huber's people, or the big construction dude, they all knew Frank pretty good. Doesn't mean they wanted to kill him. Doesn't mean I wanted to talk to them either."

"Did you ever see Paul Huber or—" She looked to Harry.

"Marshall Reese," Harry replied.

"In passing. I never spoke to them until I found the letter opener in the truck. I told the crew boss; he called the sheriff's office. We waited for you all. Mr. Huber drove in. That's the closest I've ever been to him."

"Did Frank ever mention them?"

He smoothed over the rag again, thought. "He said once that it was easier to work for Huber than Reese. They were at college before he was, but according to Frank, good players."

"Did he say why?"

"Kinda funny, I mean, I don't get it. He said Paul Huber was a halfback like he was. He used the term *same wavelength.* Said Reese was different, defense. Frank said defense people are spoilers. Me, I ran track and field in high school. So I don't know but he believed there was a big difference."

"H-m-m." Cooper considered this. "I never thought about that either." She looked at Harry. "Your husband played football at Auburn."

"Did. Wide receiver. When you're that tall and have good hands, that's where you go."

"Did he ever mention this?" Cooper asked Harry.

"You know, he doesn't talk about it very much except to say he'd rather play offense than defense, no matter the sport."

"H-m-m." She turned her attention back to Snoop. "I will try to find you a safe place. Even if it turns out to be jail, trust me. I don't know if you're in danger, but you found valuable evidence, you knew one of the victims, and the two victims knew one another."

"I think I'm safe here if they'll keep me."

Harry opened her mouth, but Cooper immediately said, "For now, Snoop. But Harry has such a wide circle of friends, sooner or later someone will see you or know you're here. I think we'd better be safe than sorry. Give me and the sheriff a little time to find you another place."

Sensing the interview was almost over, Harry thought she could ask some questions without irritating Cooper. "Snoop, did Frank have any other hangouts?"

"No." He paused. "Sometimes he'd walk down to the courthouse or old Lane High School."

"To get out of the weather? Stay warm?"

"That helped, but he said he was looking for chains."

"Chains," both women said at once.

"That's what he said, but he never brought any back."

# 33

May 9, 2015

*M*arveling at the size of the homes under construction, Harry drove through Continental Estates. As it was Saturday, no workmen labored on rooftops or installed windows in the almost completed section. The subdivision followed a grid pattern, except the roads were curvy to accentuate the country feel.

She wanted to find the border between Continental Estates and The Barracks. Across Ivy Creek, large homes were built about fifteen years ago on twenty-acre lots. East of that rested Ingleside, which was the old Jones land broken up into expensive houses.

The old Jones land once covered both sides of Garth Road. What she wanted to do was look at this new development, paying particular attention to those homes that were ready to go on the market with landscaping finished. She figured it was from one of these sites that Frank was carried off. Where he was killed was unknown. How he was killed was finally known, as Cooper told her he was stabbed and the murder weapon was Snoop's letter opener.

Saratoga Road was the center road, and other roads fanned off of that. Parallel to Saratoga Road was Yorktown Road. Given that only part of Saratoga was nearly finished, she could easily see the layout of the land, as most of the trees had been bulldozed down. Marshall, under the guidance of Paul, did keep all the trees along the creek bed as well as a few magnificent trees that were two centuries old. Once all this was finished, sod on the huge lawns, plantings in place, the old trees would be anchors. Marshall even designed a square such as old colonial towns had. Many were still in use throughout the original thirteen colonies. Around this area, he planned to build houses made to look as though they were from the early eighteenth century. These clapboard buildings, a few stone, would house a pharmacy, a pub, a restaurant, and doctors' offices, and some would be residences.

She'd seen the large plan on a huge sign at the entrance to the estates, the giant wrought-iron gates already in place just like an English country house or the House of Burgesses in Williamsburg.

"He will make a fortune. Beyond a fortune," Harry said and whistled.

"Bet they'll have to walk their dogs on leashes," Tucker crabbed.

"They can fence in smaller portions of their yards," Pewter said.

"What fun is that?" Tucker leaned onto the heavy cat.

"If you're brought up like that as a puppy, you don't know any different," Pewter reasoned.

"We're lucky." Mrs. Murphy braced herself as Harry stopped at the cul-de-sac at the end of Saratoga Road.

The day, pleasant, allowed Harry to keep the truck windows down. She lifted Tucker down once she stepped out, the cats eagerly jumping down.

Harry walked to the very end of the cul-de-sac. The old road, in use until the 1890s, could be seen under the spring grasses, near blackberry bushes pushing out new leaves. In a few places the ruts, deep, were very easy to see.

She walked along the depression in the ground, the animals following along. Stickers and hitchhikers were problems in the fall. Spring's only botanical enemy was the creepers with thorns, and those things would tear at you any time of year.

A mile marker, in place for centuries, stood by the side of the once well-traveled road as Harry neared the steep incline to Ivy Creek.

"Will be there for a few more centuries," Harry commented on the mile marker, a rectangle set in the ground vertically. Numbers were chiseled in the side. Along the old road, the mile markers still stood. She didn't know if it was a crime to remove one, but why bother? They still proved useful if you knew what they were. Fortunately, Harry had been well taught by her parents and by the public schools.

Looking to the southwest, she knew the border with The Barracks was there. If she climbed to the low rise, she'd see the barns. Having grown up in western Albemarle County, the topography, structures, and roads formed part of her memory. Still, she pulled out the oldest map she could find among her father's books in the library. She'd never moved them, nor her mother's. Looking at the map, she then turned toward the east. At one time, three families controlled six thousand acres out here. She stood near the point where all three came together, or so the old stories declared, because she didn't have any map that old.

Standing there, seeing the remains of the old road, this was prime land even then. Goods came in from the Shenandoah Valley. This was an east-west road. Until the railroads were built, hauling by wagon was the only way, or by river, but the rivers didn't always cooperate with direction. Sooner or later goods would have to be off-loaded onto wagons. Ships needed goods hauled inland. Western territories needed produce hauled east.

How precious was a satinwood sideboard or a bolt of fine silk? History books wrote in terms of lumber, corn, iron, but she thought about those women wanting to be fashionable, the men wanting a beaver hat, the top hat before silk became the thing much later. Brass buttons, lace, vanilla beans, a jar of paprika—such things made life sweet and all were hauled along this road and others like it. No wonder so many people had the last name of Carter.

She started to call out to Mrs. Murphy, intent upon something, when she heard a boom, another, and then the ground shook.

"*I told you!*" Pewter had complained about an odd sensation an hour ago.

A small earthquake rumbled through central Virginia, not uncommon by mountain ranges, but not that common either.

Widening her stance to stay upright, Harry listened to the sound of the earth groaning. In a fanciful moment she wondered if it was the Shades crying in the Underworld.

"*Come on,*" she called to the frazzled cats.

Tucker, calmer, had also sensed something.

"*Why didn't you say anything?*" Pewter swept past the dog.

The dog defended herself. "*I didn't know it was going to be an earthquake.*"

Driving slowly, Harry noticed a few cracks in the new asphalt road. When she reached the houses that were near completion she could see one or two broken windows. It wasn't too bad, but if any of the foundations cracked, Marshall would have a lot of work to do.

Before she reached the wrought-iron gates, Marshall, in a company truck, pulled in and stopped.

"Harry, what are you doing here?"

"I wanted to see the place. It's a terrific layout and I wanted to look into the back of The Barracks. The earthquake added to the excitement."

"Hey, will you do me a favor?" He took off his work gloves and she again took note of his bandages.

"Of course."

"Come with me."

She turned around to follow him, stopping at the first house nearest the gate, a completed house. As she stepped out of the car, Paul Huber arrived in his personal car.

Talking as he opened the door, he said, "I was just down at Beau Pre"—he named a nearby estate—"when that damned thing shook. How bad is it?"

"I don't know. Just got here. I was at the club."

"Hello, Harry," Paul greeted Harry, surprised to see her.

"Each one of us take a house, go through quickly, and if you see any damage, write it down. That will save me some time."

Harry ducked back in the truck, grabbed her notebook, a pen. Paul did the same.

"All right. We have twenty finished, or just about. Harry, the keys are under the front-door welcome mats. Look for anything major. I expect there will be small cracks in the walls. Make a note of it. Harry, you take the south side. Paul, let's you and I stay on this side, but you start at the other end and work toward me. We should get through pretty quickly and then we can go over and finish up with Harry."

They broke up as ordered, the cats and dog with Harry. Walking into the first house, she thought the color scheme perfect, the rooms so spacious and the kitchen just huge but inviting, with a fireplace there as well as in the living room. She bounded up the stairs and then down into the basement. By the time she had gone through the two other houses, the men walked toward her.

They gathered in the middle of the street, compared notes.

Marshall, brows wrinkled, said, "No foundation damage, thank heaven. Broken windows, some dust in the fireplace of one twenty-two. Better check that chimney. Given the rumble, it looks pretty good. Still, I better get crews out here tomorrow. Have to pay overtime." He frowned.

"Better than bad press," Paul wisely noted.

Folding his arms across his chest, Marshall nodded. "You're right about that. I'll make an appointment with the county inspector to come out. He'll be backed up, so we can fix these small things. We want a clean report card."

"The trees and shrubs came through." Paul smiled. "They weren't big enough to come down."

"All right, let's hit the off roads. The buildings not under roof, got to see if the trusses are twisted." Marshall thought clearly just as he had on the football field.

"What will you do?" Harry inquired, admiring his nonemotional approach.

"Anything twisted, take it down. You don't need to come with us for that, Harry. I wanted to first go through those houses ready to be put on the market. I'm hoping to open this to the public mid-May. In time for spring fever." Marshall smiled.

Harry mentioned the cul-de-sac. "There's a crack in the road near the cul-de-sac and another one at the back intersection there."

"What were you doing out here?" Paul realized he had no idea what Harry was doing in the middle of all this.

"I'd come out to look over The Barracks and found the old mile-post marker. Curiosity."

"Curiosity killed the cat. In your case, you got an earthquake," Marshall replied. "And thank you for your help."

Driving home, Harry noticed a chimney had tumbled down on an old farmhouse.

"*Wonder if we're okay?*" Tucker looked out the window to see people standing outside their homes or walking around them.

Talking to her animal friends, a habit, Harry said, "Big risk equals big money. If you're smart, read the signs as well as have some luck. I can't imagine how much debt Marshall incurs when he builds these subdivisions. A lot of that is bank money and the clock is ticking on the loan." She exhaled. "And I wonder how many houses he has to sell to draw even? After that, pure profit. But he knows what he's doing. He's been at this since before I was born. Paul has to replace anything that dies within a year, keep up the big nursery, pay the help, pay for fertilizer, keep those greenhouses going. Tell you what, wimps don't go into businesses like that. I know how I fret over my sunflower crop. I don't think I could take the pressure they do."

"You don't have to," Mrs. Murphy reassuringly told her. "You have us."

"Since when do we make her money?" Pewter wondered.

"We don't. We keep her from wasting it." Tucker felt her patrolling alone saved security costs.

"She's lucky," Pewter bragged.

"For now," Mrs. Murphy replied.

"What do you mean?" Tucker's ears shot straight up.

"You know before a big storm or this earthquake we feel things she doesn't?" Mrs. Murphy explained. "When they do feel it, it's too late. I feel something about those deaths. Something's coming."

# 34

*A* boom, a crackle sent Harry running back into the barn from the pasture. No sooner did her feet touch the center aisle than a flash of pink lightning struck the field she'd just vacated.

Mrs. Murphy, Pewter, and Tucker, thanks to speed, preceded her into the barn.

Another tremendous clap of thunder was followed by rolling thunder. Another bolt of lightning struck in the back pastures, white this time.

Within seconds the rains began, large drops, each of which seemed to thud when it hit the earth.

The horses in the barn eating their early morning grain lifted their heads.

Tomahawk, the aging gray Thoroughbred, watched. "*Blast.*"

Shortro, the athletic Saddlebred in the next stall, swallowed his grain, replied, "*No turnout for a while. This is going to last.*"

As the words left his mouth, the rain intensified, slamming the roof, battering windowpanes. The noise sounded like a steady roar. You couldn't hear yourself think.

Walking into the tack room, closing the door behind her once the cats and dog came inside, she could hear better. The *rat-tat-tat-tat* on the roof, loud, let her know the rain poured. The hayloft ran on the opposite side of the aisle, across from the tack room. Over the tack room she stored winter blankets zipped into huge plastic bags. That afforded a bit more muffling, but she sank at the desk, wondering how long this would last.

Her cellphone had a weather map. She punched in the icon, pulled up the map.

"You all, it's a huge green blob with yellow and red parts. Ugly." She commented on the radar map, colorized, to help people gauge timing, danger, et cetera. "Yesterday an earthquake. Today, this."

A warning scroll appeared at the top of the picture. She tapped it, a flood warning.

"Ugh and ugly" was all she said.

The wall clock read 8:30 A.M. Even when the rain passed, which would not be anytime soon, the ground would be too soaked to plow or seed. She didn't want to turn the horses out until the worst of the storm passed. The temperature hovered in the high fifties.

At loose ends, Harry, never happy without a plan, picked up the desk phone and called Susan. "What's it doing over there?"

"Unreal."

"Here, too. I can't get anything done."

"You can always clean out your closet," Susan suggested.

"What an awful thought."

"Well, if you'd throw out all those sweatshirts, including the ones from high school, you'd have more room."

"It's not that bad. I haven't had time to cut them up for rags."

"You've had twenty-five years." Susan wasn't buying it.

"I have not. When we graduated, the sweatshirts were good and so were the tees."

"Will you just go do it and shut up about it? And after you knock that out, throw out half of your shoes."

"My shoes! What, do you want me to go barefoot and get hookworm?"

"You won't go barefoot and you are way beyond Mary Janes."

"Susan, that's unfair. I haven't worn Mary Janes since my mother made me when I was little."

"Some of those shoes are horrible. Don't even donate them to Goodwill. Burn them."

"Aren't you hateful today?"

"Maybe so, but I have organized closets with plenty of room."

"That's because you never come out of your closet."

"Very funny. You're certainly peevish today."

"Am I? Maybe I am. I had the whole day planned to overseed my pastures. Spring is so late this year, I kept putting it off, and I'm glad I did."

"It's a good thing you didn't do it yesterday. It would all be washed away today."

"I might as well surrender and do paperwork, my idea of hell."

"Isn't it everybody's? Call me when you're finished and we can celebrate."

Harry hung up, checked the clock again, pulled out the long middle drawer of the desk and the farm checkbook with it. Maybe she could get a jump-start on the bills.

The phone rang.

Thinking it was Susan, she picked it up. "Now what?"

A long silence followed this. "Mrs. Haristeen?"

She recognized Snoop's voice, became instantly alert. "It is. Sorry, I thought it was my best friend calling back."

"It's hard to hear." He raised his voice. "Can you pick me up?"

"Where are you?"

"Parking lot at the Omni. I'm inside the downstairs door."

"Hang on. I'll get there as soon as I can," she shouted into the phone, hoping she'd be heard over the din.

Throwing on her old Barbour coat, she hurried to the back barn doors, closing them with a slight opening for air. Then she trotted to the door closest to the house, cats and dogs with her, stepped outside, and repeated the procedure.

The four creatures were soaked by the time they reached the truck. Lifting the dog in—the cats were already there—she hopped in, cranked the motor, and drove slowly. She could barely see, even with the windshield wipers on full force.

Driving down the road, Harry saw few cars. Some drivers had parked under underpasses, others pulled off to the side of the road. What kept her going was worry for Snoop plus the sure knowledge that if she waited the creeks would jump their banks. She wanted to get there and back before that happened. With rain sliding across the roads she figured, at best, she had an hour.

Finally reaching the Omni, she turned off into the parking lane, stopped at the meter, unrolled the window, pushed the button, and took the ticket. Brief though that motion was, the ticket and her left arm from the elbow down were soaked. She drove down under the large overhang. Anyone in this part of the parking lot would be dry.

Reaching the door, she rolled down one window, cut the motor, hopped out, and pushed open the glass door.

"Snoop."

Crouched against the wall, he stood up. "Mrs. Haristeen."

"Come on, let's get out of here. You'll have a dog and two cats to contend with, but it will work."

Once Snoop climbed in, she drove out, Mrs. Murphy on her lap, Pewter between Harry and Snoop, and Tucker, heavy though she was, on Snoop's lap.

Reaching the ticket taker in the booth, Harry unrolled the window, leaned way out to give the lady the ticket. As she'd been there less than ten minutes, the lady waved her on, none too happy about her arm now being wet.

The rain pounded on the Ford's roof.

"You okay?" she asked.

He nodded. "Before the storm, I don't know the time but before shops open, early enough, maybe seven-thirty or eight, the Huber truck parked in the lot, the guy came down looking for workmen. I said I didn't want to work. He pressured me a little, said they had repairs to do because of the earthquake. Didn't want to go. Picked up three men and left. Not ten minutes later the paving truck came down. Same story. I said I didn't want to go. Dunno. Don't trust any of those guys. You know?"

"I can see why." She stopped at the stoplight at the top of the hill, the statue at the intersection barely visible.

"How'd you call me?"

He pulled a thin cellphone from his pants pocket. "Made enough to get one. A cheap one, but it works. After our talk, I thought I'd better have one. What if something went wrong when shops are closed? I think a few of the people down on the mall would let me use their phone. But I need my own."

"I'm taking you home. You'll be safe there. I'll call Deputy Cooper and inform her." She thought to herself she'd better inform her husband, too.

"I can work."

"Good," Harry replied.

It took her an hour to reach the farm, the waters in creeks and streams at the top of the beds but not over them yet.

Everyone was soaked running from the truck to the house.

"I need a dryer," Pewter complained in the kitchen.

"Go roll on a rug," Tucker told her.

As that wasn't a bad idea, both cats did.

Harry took Snoop into the basement, where a small room contained a shower, a bed, a dresser. She never used it, but sometimes if Fair had a late night and was particularly dirty, he'd shower down there.

"Snoop, clean up. There's a disposable razor in there and I'll put fresh clothes at the top of the stairs."

"Thank you, Ma'am."

By the time he came up, shaved, in clean clothes that hung on him, as Fair was so tall, he smiled, for Harry had made lunch.

Pewter, fur spiky, sat next to Harry, for she could smell the chicken.

Feeling like a human being again, he finished his sandwich.

"Did the work-crew bosses say what the jobs were?"

"No. Only that there was damage. I don't want to be out there. I don't know if they were looking for me exactly, but they knew where I was."

"*How long before they know he's here?*" Tucker sagely commented.

# 35

*May 11, 2015*

Lilac scent filled the air. A soft breeze gently touched the spring-green leaves of trees, causing a slight flutter. A high spring day almost guaranteed to lift spirits.

Harry, Cooper, Snoop, Mrs. Murphy, Pewter, and Tucker piled into Harry's Volvo station wagon. Although retained for driving people in comfort, it had racked up a lot of miles over the years. The animals had special car beds in the back but preferred to leap over the seatbacks to sit in available laps.

They drove in silence until reaching Crozet. Passing through, they stayed on Route 810, which was getting built up like the rest of the county.

"Turn right," Cooper directed.

Harry bumped along a gravel road.

"*Whoo.*" Mrs. Murphy felt a big bump.

Pewter sat up to look out the window. "*Potholes. Guess they don't want people coming down the road.*"

Pewter was right, they didn't. Up ahead a white clapboard farmhouse with gable windows and maroon shutters awaited them. Parked in the simple driveway rested a van with a big painted blue water drop on it but no writing.

"Here we are." Cooper got out quickly as a burly man opened the farmhouse's screen door. "Hey, Riley."

The porch stairs shook as he stepped down. "Deputy. Who've we got?"

"Snoop, like I said when I called."

Snoop stepped out of the station wagon, as did Harry. The dog and cats looked and listened, for Harry partially rolled down the windows.

Riley grew up here and knew Harry, and vice versa. "Hello, Harry."

Riley worked for the sheriff's department. "Snoop, you'll be safe here," Harry reassured him.

Snoop smiled but said nothing. He wanted a drink. He wanted to stay with Harry, but he understood the wisdom of a safe house. He'd try to stay on the wagon.

"We go around in that van, which looks like an old plumbing van. We don't draw attention to ourselves and most of the time you'll be here. But if there's a baseball game you want to see or something, we try to do it. Put you to work. It's not bad and the food's not bad either." He laughed. "I'm proof."

Harry, sensing Snoop's worry, reassured him again. "You've got my card. You've got your cell and I'll come by. Snoop, we hope this gets resolved quickly, but until then, you have to be kept in a safe place with someone who knows how to protect you and others."

"Who else've you got?" Cooper inquired.

"Only one other guest." He smiled when he said guest.

"All right, then. Snoop, you're in good hands." Cooper spoke to Snoop and then to Riley. "Good to see you."

Harry reached for Snoop's hand, squeezed it, and whispered, "It will be okay."

Bumping back down the road, Harry said, "I feel bad leaving him here."

"You can't protect him."

"Yeah, I know, but he's a lost soul."

"All drunks are lost souls." Cooper, having arrested, handcuffed, and hauled in plenty of aggressive drunks during her years of service, figured they did it to themselves.

"Ever pick up one who froze to death?"

"Not yet. Ever notice how many miserable people there are in the world?"

"Can't say that I have, but then you're in a profession that deals with them."

"Yes, I am. I never thought of that when I went into law enforcement. I thought I would be helping people."

"You do," Harry insisted.

"Sometimes." She avoided one pothole but hit the other, strategically placed. If you avoided the one on the right side, you were bound to thump into the one on the left.

Pewter raised her voice. *"Let's get out of here."*

Harry smiled. "We're getting an editorial comment."

*"You have no idea what I'm talking about,"* Pewter complained.

*"If I were you, I'd be grateful,"* Tucker said.

"Coop, let's drive down to The Barracks. We'll be coming in from the opposite direction. Maybe we'll see something or think of something we've missed."

"'We'? You're on the case now?" Cooper held on to the armrest on the door. "Damn, this road seems longer on the way out than the way in."

"It does. Ever notice how distances seem longer at night?"

Cooper nodded in agreement. "Sure. Let's go on down to The Barracks."

Farms along the way, houses closer to the road, caught the eye as lilacs, dogwoods, tulips bloomed. Especially lovely were lavender lilacs interspersed with the white.

Harry turned left and within a few minutes reached the fork in the road to the stables. Driving up, she saw a fellow she went to high school with on the roof of the office at the stables.

Getting out of the station wagon, Harry called up, "Winnie, what are you doing?"

"Mrs. Bishop wanted the roof repaired. Got to do this in the light, too."

"Still working down at the county offices?"

"Yep," the burly fellow answered.

Cooper, now beside her, looked up. "That's a lot of roof to keep up at the offices."

"I'm a jack of all trades." He stood up, as he'd been bending over.

"Hey, Winnie, you ever see Frank Cresey down there?" asked Harry.

"The old drunk? The halfback?" He started laughing. "Yeah, he'd walk along and he'd break into an open-field run, then zigzag. He'd crouch low. He was a trip."

"Did he ever ask you for chains?"

"No." Winnie was puzzled. "Like car chains, tow chains?"

"We don't know. Did he ever come into the maintenance area?"

"Ah, poor guy, a couple of times he tried when the weather was evil, but the boss would throw him out. Guess he went into the building, curled up in a hall if he could get away with it."

"Do you keep chains there, at the offices?" Cooper asked.

"We do. We have different weights, sizes, depending on the job. A good chain can get you out of a world of trouble."

Claiborne emerged from the office, looked up. "Winnie, don't waste your time on these two."

"Claiborne," Harry asked, "do you mind if we walk to the back of the property?"

"No, not at all." She nodded to Cooper. "Do you need anything?" Claiborne was ready to offer help.

"No. We're going back to see what we can see of Continental Estates. Back near the old milepost."

"You can pretty much see the development once you get over the rise."

"Claiborne, does your land go up to the milepost?" Cooper wondered.

"Almost. That was part of the old Garth estate. It's where the old Garth and the Ashcombe lands joined. I think, anyway."

"I suspect history students must come out here from time to time," Cooper thought out loud.

"They do. When Ginger McConnell was teaching, he always brought his students out. He said he'd been doing that since he was hired at UVA. Before my time."

After a bit more chat, the two women and the animals trekked all the way to the rear of The Barracks on the eastern side.

"There's still dew." Pewter picked up each paw. "Eeew."

"Buy tiny Wellies," Mrs. Murphy said, mentioning the famous rubber boots beloved of horsemen.

"Oh, shut up," the gray cat shot back. "You don't like it either."

Tucker ran ahead of the humans and the cats, ignoring Pewter.

Cooper stopped. "Ah, you really can see the development. This part anyway."

"It's huge," said Harry, observing Continental Estates from this different angle.

"They're working on a weekend."

Harry said, "The earthquake and then the storm did some damage."

"That was some storm, too." Cooper appreciated that. "So where's the milestone?"

"Not far. Let me show you." Harry dipped down into a narrow gulley, worked her way up at a diagonal, then waited.

"No way a car is going through that." Cooper caught her breath. "I guess an ATV could do it. I'm just wondering about a back way into The Barracks."

"There really isn't one." Harry stopped at the milestone. "Isn't it amazing to think that these are still up and down the original thirteen colonies?"

"It is," Cooper agreed. "But I don't see how anyone could travel this way."

"Three bridges had been built, two of short span for this gulley and the one up ahead, and then a longer one for the ravine."

"That makes sense."

"When I was in high school, Ginger took our history class out here as a special treat for our history teacher and us. He loved doing this and what I remember is his saying the bridges allowed foods and supplies to come into the prisoner-of-war camp and save time."

"Efficient."

Harry heard a *whoosh* in the distance. Suddenly, a hot air balloon—colorfully red, white, and blue—came into view.

"*They are so noisy,*" Pewter grumbled. "*I hate those things.*"

"I don't really know when The Barracks fell into disrepair. Guess there was no use for them," Harry said.

They turned, walking back.

Cooper stopped, looked again at the topographical obstacles. "Harry, maybe they used chains and draft horses to haul logs, beams into place."

"Could be, but what would Frank want them for? Or what did he hope to know?" Harry shrugged, then pulled her cellphone out of her jacket pocket. "Maybe Trudy knows." She called her.

"Trudy. Harry."

"I know. Your number came up on my phone. How are you?"

"Fine, and you?"

"Doing as good as I can," Trudy honestly replied.

"Forgive me for asking questions again, and I have Deputy Cooper here with me. Did Ginger ever talk about ironworks, forges, how people made chains, nails, stuff like that?"

"Actually, he visited those that still stand. There's one down at Oak Ridge." Trudy named an estate in Nelson County. "Every big farm had its own forge. The historic places often restore them. In those cases, some are in use only for show, obviously."

"Did he mention any of this close to the time of his death?"

"No, he was focused on prisoners of war, as you know. You've seen his desk and his editor's bin. I expect there was a forge at The Barracks."

"Yes," Harry agreed. "Sorry to bother you. It was a long shot."

"Do you mind telling me?"

"It's odd. Deputy Cooper has questioned the people who live on the mall who knew Frank Cresey. Frank would go to the library and read, read about the Revolutionary War and afterward. Ginger's influence stuck, I guess. Anyway, Frank also mentioned to someone on the mall that he was going down to the county office to look for chains."

"How very odd." Trudy's well-modulated voice registered surprise.

"Again, Trudy, I'm sorry to bother you, and thank you."

As they headed back to the stable area, clear in the distance of a half mile, Cooper sighed. "It was a long shot. Maybe the two murders aren't connected."

"Yeah, I know," Harry said, "but I'm not ready to give up yet." She thought for a moment. "Today is Mother's Day. Did you send flowers?"

"Called. Sent flowers." Cooper smiled. "Mom loves living in New Mexico, but it's so far away. Most older people go to Florida, places where it's warm. Snows in New Mexico. She's happy, that's what counts."

"Does. I miss my mother. You're lucky to still have yours."

Cooper put her arm around Harry's waist. "Your mother did a good job with you."

# 36

*A* light rain didn't dampen John Schuyler's spirits. Hurrying to his quarters, he carefully packed what little gear he had in a small campaign trunk. Kept under his cot, so small his feet hung over the end, the two treasured books Catherine had given him, the paper in which they were wrapped, and the raffia all rested in the trunk, along with a letter from his mother. She had paid to have it written in a good hand. John sent his parents what he could spare when he was paid. Not often.

The second small book on good paper contained two of Shakespeare's plays, *Macbeth* and *Julius Caesar*. Catherine had selected the dramas for him because of their military themes.

Having few possessions, he packed in twenty minutes. He pushed the trunk back under the cot, walked to Lieutenant West's barracks. Although early evening, the air remained warm, a light breeze making all pleasant.

"Lieutenant," Schuyler called, outside West's barracks.

Inside and barefoot, Charles heard the familiar voice and walked from the housing, Piglet at his heels. "Captain."

A broad grin crossed John Schuyler's face. "I have been assigned to Lafayette. The war most definitely is in Virginia, and I leave at daylight." He laughed. "The commandant won't give me a horse."

"That will be a long walk to the coast, I assume." Charles had gained an understanding of Virginia's geography.

John smiled. "I will hire a wagon. I am allowed to do that. Finally, free from this place. You are not the only one imprisoned here."

"Just different sides of the fence, so to speak."

"I am hoping to pass through large towns, and I would like to buy and send a book to Miss Ewing. Can you suggest something?"

The two discussed the contents of *Aesop's Fables* and the two Shakespeare plays. The Englishman was impressed with how the captain grasped the essence of each play, even as he struggled with the language in spots. In this way, those few times when the dark-haired man could speak with Catherine, he could hold his own during literary discussions, constrained though they were. John and Catherine grew closer in mind through the readings. Charles knew how quick her mind was. Schuyler, adept at anything involving arms, was now proving adept at reading for pleasure. He had never before read for pleasure.

"I don't know books," he complained. "What would she like? I can't give her more plays. She's read them all."

Charles said, without hesitation. "*The Sonnets.* Buy her the best bound volume you can afford of Shakespeare's *Sonnets.*"

"Do you not think she has read everything he has written? She prizes him above all others."

"Captain, the volume will be from you and the work is very beautiful. *The Sonnets* it must be." Charles held out his hand. "May my pistol protect you. May you be well."

"And you also."

A mischievous smile played on Charles's lips. "Our paths will cross again. Not in war, I trust."

Impulsively, John took both of Charles's hands in his. "I pray it be so."

He turned and walked off with Charles's good wishes and his father's expensive flintlock.

Walking back into the barracks, the dust still warm between his toes, Charles noticed Piglet standing still, watching the tall captain disappear in the distance.

# 37

*T*he sun, up for an hour, bathed the corn, the apple orchards, the wheat in gold.

Captain Schuyler jumped out of the wagon. He'd had to pay the driver a bit extra for the stop. Fortunately, he had not far to travel, although he couldn't tell Charles West that. He was to connect with a few troops on the east side of Charlottesville. With them, he would be moving to the coast. In Virginia, intent on rampage, Cornwallis was getting his wish. He would also get battle. His commander-in-chief, Sir Henry Clinton, was unable to restrain Cornwallis. The two British generals barely communicated, their mutual disregard having arrived at an unhealthy distaste.

Knocking on the door, hat under his left arm, as he had learned from Charles, John awaited the Garths' butler.

Opening the door, Roger, beautifully dressed, smiled slightly. "Captain."

"Might I have a word with the master?"

"I shall see if he is available. Please, come in."

Within moments, Ewing, an early riser, told the butler to invite Captain Schuyler into the breakfast room for, of course, breakfast.

The room, flooded with light, seemed to create a halo around

Catherine as the good captain walked in. It lent Rachel a glow as well, but John's focus was on Catherine.

Bowing to the father, with a chair pulled out for him by Weymouth, John sat down.

Wonderful though the food was, he was so tense he had to force himself to eat it, or to make conversation. When the dishes were cleared at last, fine bone china at that, he dabbed his lips with a napkin and began, "Sir, you have been so hospitable to me. I can never repay your kindness."

"Oh, my dear captain, after four bridges and two roads, I fear it is the opposite," Ewing nearly gushed.

"I have come to inform you I have been assigned to General Lafayette," John continued, but all he heard was Catherine's gasp. "As you know, the enemy is here in some force."

"Indeed, I had heard that. Destroying everything, stealing horses, and I even heard they slit the throats of mares so we could not continue to breed."

"I would slit theirs," Catherine burst out, her emotion focusing on the horror but really provoked by John's news.

Ewing registered his distaste. "And they call us barbarians."

"I believe, Sir, events will prove otherwise, but I do hope if word should come to you that they are advancing west, hide your horses, your silver, and possibly yourselves. They have not been uncivil to women, but should they experience a . . . a laxity in command, I cannot say."

"Do you think they are loosely disciplined, Captain?"

"Some troops are. Some not. They do seem to lack cooperation with one another and they seem mindless of the French. We have a powerful ally. You would think, of all people, the English would be sensible of naval guns, as well as troops." He paused. "Forgive me." He looked to Catherine and Rachel. "I do not mean to bore you."

"You couldn't possibly bore me," Catherine baldly said, to her father's shock and her sister's and Weymouth's delight.

John registered this then replied, "We do have Washington. The greatest man of the age."

Ewing smiled back. "Indeed." He stood up, and all stood with him as he offered his hand to the captain. "God protect you, Captain." He walked the tall man to the front door, which Roger opened.

Stepping through it, John faced Ewing. "I will write you when I can, and, Sir, might I have permission to write your eldest daughter?"

Struck into silence for a moment, Ewing felt his daughter's hand on his elbow. He thought Catherine had stayed behind, but she had followed at a slight distance.

"Father, please."

"My dear." He looked into her eyes, beseeching him, then turned to John. "You have my permission." After all, Ewing Garth remembered those feelings.

"Oh, Father, I love you so." She hugged him, then followed Captain Schuyler out the door, and Ewing turned back into the house.

John stood by the wagon, ready to swing himself up.

"Return to me, Captain. Be safe."

"John." He smiled. "And I will return to you."

She stood on her tiptoes, wrapped her right hand around his neck, and kissed him, taking both their breaths away.

Releasing him, Catherine looked intently into John's brown eyes, smiled, then turned heel and walked back up the stairs. Opening the hall door for her was Roger. He had seen it all, but would not betray his beloved Catherine.

"Where is my father?" she asked.

Roger tilted his head toward the back of the house, his voice low. "With your mother, Miss Catherine."

She hurried down the hall and swung open the back door. She ran to her father, as he stood in the lovely graveyard, before her mother's monument, a recumbent lamb holding the cross.

Catherine reached him, tears running down his cheeks.

"Oh, Father." Tears now ran down hers.

"I fear I have not been a good father and—"

"You are the best father in the world."

"Ah, you are young and clearly in love with the handsome and brave captain. But I, as your father, should see that you marry well, that you will want for nothing."

"Father, if I don't have love, I have nothing."

Ewing stood silently, then reached for her hand. "Your mother might have said that. When I courted her, she was pursued by so many men, some with wealth, many far more handsome than I. I am not a strapping fellow, but she loved me. We could talk about anything, my dear. That may not sound romantic, but we grew as one, one heart. I may be a fool to allow this friendship, courtship to continue. I don't think the captain has a sou, but if you love him and it is clear he loves you, then I think your mother would be happy." The tears flowed again. "My child, I miss your mother so."

"I do, too, Father, and—" Catherine paused, kissed him on his wet cheek. "I love you."

# 38

*T*he back road from the Charlottesville Airport meandered through a few subdivisions closer to the airport. The farther west Harry headed with the animals in the station wagon, the more the land opened up: revealing plowed fields, and those where the orchard grass and fescue tips were now breaking through the soil. Overhead, enormous cumulus clouds billowed, in contrast to a startling blue sky.

She'd dropped off her husband at the airport, as Fair would be attending a veterinarians' conference in Denver for the rest of the week. Sometimes wives would go to the conferences; other times, not so much. She liked Denver but knew her job was to stay home; her crops would begin their life cycle. Of course, it was too early to tell how each of these crops would fare, but to date the mixture of sun and rain had been perfect.

She rounded a long, sweeping curve. The very back of The Barracks was visible to her left, and farther to her left she could make out the construction for part of Continental Estates. When she reached Hunt Country Store, she couldn't help it. She turned left. This was a long way around to either The Barracks or Continental Estates. It was also the only way. Neither property could be accessed from the west.

Passing the two square blue Barracks signs, she drove closer to Berta Jones's driveway, turned left, and passed individual houses, all large, arriving at last at the great wrought-iron gates of Continental Estates.

"This isn't the way home," Pewter noted from the backseat.

"She likes to wander," Tucker replied, next to the gray cat.

The cat squinted, looking out the window. "Wander? With her, it's a magical mystery tour."

Mrs. Murphy looked on the bright side. "Hey, at least we get to see a lot."

"I can't imagine what these gates cost to make, with the gilded pineapples right in the center," Harry said to them.

For a moment, they thought she was talking about food, but she wasn't, so they lost interest.

"Where are we going?" Pewter demanded.

"Pipe down, Pewter," Harry called to her as she slowed, passing the finished houses on the main center street.

On a whim, she turned left, heading west to see if she could recognize any of the homes whose backside she had seen from the back airport road.

Each home varied from its neighbor and each was set deep on the one- to two-acre lots. A few even had five-acre lots. Not as far along as those on Saratoga, the center road, the dividing line between east and west in the subdivision, where the outsides of the homes were finished. The work here was being done inside. Some had a red-brick exterior, others painted brick. A few even had a stone exterior, and others clapboard. All were built in a style a colonial person, if he came back, would recognize. The subdivision would be alien to them, but its architecture wouldn't be.

Harry ran down her window. The sounds of hammering, electric saws, and drills filtered into the wagon.

"Nasty noise," Pewter fussed.

Tucker, too, found it jarring. "It's the saws and the drills."

Reaching a cul-de-sac, she slowly circled it and headed back out. At the intersection to the main drag, she turned left, driving back to that cul-de-sac. She cut the motor, sat for a moment, then got out, the two cats and dog with her.

They walked across a field and out to the milestone. Standing at it, Harry carefully turned in each direction. The Barracks presented rolling hills. As she turned west, the Blue Ridge came into view. She knew all those homes with great views of the mountains would wear a higher price tag. And why not? It was stunning.

"Come on." Harry moved slightly southeasterly from the mile-post as she followed old deep wagon ruts.

Reaching the shallow ravine, she looked across it, could begin to make out the deep gulley and a deep gulley beyond that.

Tucker looked down into the shallow ravine. "*Long gone.*"

"You know, guys, once upon a time this was heavily traveled," said Harry. "According to Ginger—if I remember, when he gave us The Barracks tour—this was the back way into the camp. Saved time and miles. I never asked him when it fell into disuse. Maybe he didn't know, but Garth Road, along with old Three Chopt Road, were the main east-west corridors. 'Course Three Chopt became Route 250, so anyone along that road could do pretty good with a business. Like goods, wagon repairs, all that kind of stuff. But Garth Road more or less remained large estates. Funny how things happen."

Pewter's stomach growled. "*I'm hungry.*"

"All right, come on." She turned, walking back to the station wagon.

Once Harry and everyone were inside she cut on the motor and the air-conditioning. It wasn't that warm but with the car closed up, it had gotten stuffy.

They sat awhile while Harry tried to imagine the activity here during the Revolutionary War.

Driving back down the center road, she noticed Marshall Reese's car parked in the midst of much activity at one of the finished houses. He and Paul Huber, with his landscaping trucks everywhere, had blueprints unfolded on the hood of Marshall's Mercedes.

Harry stopped. The men called out to her and she walked over, animals in tow.

"Hey, what are you doing here?" Marshall smiled.

Noticing again the Band-Aids on his fingers and a gauze pad on Marshall's palm, Harry asked, "What happened to you?"

"Stupid. Here I have Paul but I decided to plant a quince for my wife at the corner of the yard. Little did I know what I was getting into." He chuckled. "I've gotten soft."

"Yes, but no less stubborn," Paul teased him, then turned to Harry, repeating Marshall's query. "What are you doing here, Harry? We all know you're a curious person." He squeezed her shoulder good-naturedly.

"Wanted to see it after you repaired all the damage from the earthquake, which fortunately didn't affect the landscaping too much." She glanced down at the blueprints. "They're still easier to read than something on a computer."

Paul pointed to the center road. "You can see the homes that are finished are already landscaped. Crepe myrtles for summer, boxwoods, every kind of oak imaginable. Each home has a different palette, so to speak."

"I noticed you haven't put in Bradford pears or Leland cypress," Harry replied.

"Love the Bradford pears," Paul said. "Just love them, but they aren't as sturdy as I would like, and if we use another type of pear, an older type, more work for the owner."

She pointed to rows of trees lining each street. "Each street is different?"

Marshall answered, "We're just firming up putting in the white dogwoods for this street. The first cross street will be pink dogwoods. Some streets will have conifers, others oaks, hickories, even persimmon. It will be beautiful, Harry. Distinctive."

"No locusts?" Harry asked. "They bloom in the spring and smell divine."

"Thorns," Paul quickly replied. "We've narrowed this down to seasons and trees that can't really hurt a child. Those locust thorns do damage. And we tried to avoid trees that have too many droppings, like black gum. Personally, I like black gum, but it creates more work for the maintenance crews."

Harry looked at Marshall. "Maintenance crews?"

"Continental Estates will have a maintenance fee, a garbage collection fee. The monthly bills will be small, especially when the development is completely sold out, but this is the only way to ensure the elegant look. You can't have one person who doesn't trim the street tree in front of their house next to one who does. Just makes for bad feelings."

"Guess it would." Harry then asked, "How's the endowed chair coming along?"

"Tim Jardine raised another million and a half." Marshall broadly smiled. "The response has been strong."

"Did Ginger ever see any of this?" Harry asked, indicating the development.

Marshall nodded to Harry. "He did. Paul and I drove him around, asked advice. He wasn't thrilled with the idea of another development on old land, some of it a land grant, but he knew it was unstoppable, so he accepted a historical look, if you will."

"He even identified for me what was fashionable in gardening then," said Paul. "There we had a lot of help from the Monticello people and Montpelier, too. A lot of help." He put his hands in his pockets.

"A land grant?" said Harry. "I kind of remember Ginger, years ago when he gave us the tour, mentioning it, but, well, like I said, that was years ago."

Ever eager to display his knowledge and his fidelity to his professor, Marshall said, "Continental Estates is on the Ashcombe land grant. A small piece of this is old Barracks land, Colonel Harvey's land that was cut off from the hundreds of camp acres later by a grandson. But I can tell you I have thoroughly researched this chain of title."

Harry's face went white; she swayed a little.

Paul grabbed her elbow. "Harry, are you all right?"

Pulling herself back together, she hoarsely said, "Yes. Sorry. A little light-headed. Made me think of Frank Cresey," she blurted out.

"Frank?" both men said in unison.

"He was obsessed with Ginger in a strange way. Read all of Ginger's books, even after graduation. Would go to the library and read. Read anything about the Revolutionary War. Odd."

"That is odd, but he had been a good history student. Ginger always paid him that compliment," Paul agreed.

"What he was obsessed with was Olivia," Marshall said. "Well, nothing can be done about it now, but Harry, it seems you, too, are focused on Ginger and his work."

"Yes, I guess I am. I feel I have to find out why he was killed. So I come back again and again here to what fascinated him. It's a little crazy. I'll get over it."

"Hope so." Marshall smiled.

After thanking them for showing her the plans, she bid them goodbye, got herself and the animals in the station wagon, and took a deep breath to clear her head. Then she drove out.

She didn't break the speed limit, although she wanted to. She drove straight to Susan's, hopped out of the car, ran in the back door.

"Where you at?" she called.

"In the sunroom," Susan called back.

"Get your purse. Come on."

Susan walked out to Harry. "What's gotten into you?"

"I figured out what Frank was talking about. You drive and I'll call Cooper. Come on. Whatever you were doing can wait."

Within minutes, Susan was driving. The cats and dog, alert, sat in the back. Harry had Cooper on her cellphone.

"Are you sure?" Cooper asked again.

"Yes. Chain of title. That's what Frank meant. Susan and I are on our way to the county offices."

"I'll meet you there."

In the wagon, under a conifer, windows down two inches, the animals fell asleep while inside the nearby building the three women leaned over the counter where land records are kept.

Given that Cooper was in uniform, cooperation was swift. But it would have been anyway.

The older lady behind the counter, Mildred Gianakos, laid out a large copy of an early map.

Pointing out the old roads, she said, "I think this is what you are asking. This is the Harvey land. It stayed in the family for generations. This is the Garth. All of this. Three thousand five hundred acres. Much of it in orchards."

Harry tried to contain her excitement. "And you have the chain of title?"

"Copies. The original documents were fragile and irreplaceable, so way back, when they were photographed. They are all at Alderman Library, along with other early documents, climate controlled."

Harry pointed to where she thought the original land-grant land was. "I thought this had been given by the king."

Mildred went to her computer, pulled up information on original land grants. "Carter, m-m-m, that's to the east." She kept at it. "Why don't you girls flip up the divider and stand behind me so you can see?"

They crowded around Mildred, quite handy with a computer, defying stereotypes about age.

"I had no idea there were that many land grants," Susan said.

"The earliest ones were all east of here, around what is now Williamsburg, called Middle Plantation then; Jamestown, of course; and then once we reached the Fall Line, I mean, once colonists could live there, because it was a war zone between tribes, grants were given there, too. The Crown, depending on who wore it, gave the land grants as rewards, but also the recipient was expected to make the land productive. What the Old World craved was raw materials and exotic, exotic at the time, products from here."

"Mildred, you sure know a lot," Harry complimented her.

"Thank you, sweetie, but I had to learn. We get asked everything in here and lawyers are in and out like houseflies." She giggled. "I didn't say that."

"Who else?" Cooper had been scribbling in her notebook.

"Historians. The late Professor McConnell could have worked my job, he knew so much. And over the last twenty years I would have to say that large home-building companies have been vigilant."

Cooper's antenna felt vibrations. "Like who?"

"Oh, Rinehart, Wade, Reese, even smaller ones. Some use the history as a calling card, but they do need to know where the boundaries are, you know, have there been disputes in the past, how were they settled? Plant a tree or build a fence two inches on the next man's land and you could have a major problem. Hence, the lawyers in here."

"I see." Cooper hadn't thought of that.

"Did Frank Cresey ever come in here?" Harry inquired.

"He did. Poor thing, but he was always clean. Quite the history buff. He would check whatever interested him at the time. Years ago, there were some questions about land out on Old Lynchburg Road. University of Virginia has a polo field there. He looked at those plats and chains of title."

"Do you remember his last interest?" Pencil poised over her pad, Cooper scarcely breathed.

"Not long before he was killed, he was looking at much the same land you are, all the land that belonged to Ewing Garth as the Revolutionary War ended. Thousands of acres."

"Garth?" Cooper knew the name.

"He bought the land grant that the Ashcombes held. Here, I can show you." Mildred pulled up a facsimile. "The land was originally granted by their majesties, William and Mary, to Obadiah Ashcombe. His grandson Peter Ashcombe, a Loyalist, sold the entire grant to Ewing Garth."

"For twenty thousand pounds," said Harry. "My God, that would be millions today!" she exclaimed.

"It was very valuable land," Mildred concurred.

Susan whistled. "Ewing had to be rich as Croesus."

"He was."

"February first, 1782," Harry read the date out loud.

"Here's the grant on the plat, here's how it added to Garth's lands. You can see he controlled both sides of Ivy Creek, the road east and west and a back road into The Barracks. So along with his crops and whatever, he controlled that road still in use today."

"Did he establish a toll?" Susan asked.

"No, from what I understand from Professor McConnell and the other professors who have been in here—curious about the prisoner-of-war camp, that sort of thing—if you used Garth's road, he occasionally would call in a favor. He must have been terribly clever."

"And Frank knew all this?" Cooper asked.

"Yes, Officer, he did."

Cooper pushed the pencil behind her ear. "I don't see any problem with this."

"Marshall Reese bought it for Continental Estates, after doing his research, of course."

"Mrs. Gianakos, what would happen if there were a problem?" Harry wondered.

She frowned. "Well, that would depend on the type of problem."

# 39

May 13, 2015

As Cooper pored over deeds of title Wednesday morning at the county offices, Harry drove to St. Luke's.

The Very Reverend Herbert Jones's reading glasses slipped down near the tip of his nose as he reviewed a national church publication while sitting at his cluttered desk. On the left side, his cat Elocution held down papers. On the right side, Cazenovia pinned correspondence. On the floor, Lucy Fur, on her back, front and hind legs extended, slept soundly.

A knock on the door woke up Lucy Fur. Elocution and Cazenovia were alert but remained in place.

Mrs. Murphy, Pewter, and Tucker preceded Harry into the Reverend's spacious, light-filled office.

"*Let's get some Communion wafers,*" Pewter encouraged the Lutheran cats.

"Locked," Elocution mournfully informed them. "*The closet with all the Communion things except vestments is locked.*"

"*I know that, but we opened it once before. Come on. The humans will just sit here and blab.*" Pewter incited them.

"*That's a fact.*" Cazenovia leapt off the desk, papers flying.

Harry walked over, picked them up, handing them to the Reverend.

Mrs. Murphy followed the cats out of the room with the observation, "No crunch in the Communion wafers. Let's see if we can open a cabinet door in the kitchen instead."

"No." Pewter gleefully skidded down the hallway. "Communion wafers. Drives the humans crazy."

Tucker stayed with Harry.

"I don't know what gets into them," said the Reverend. "Asleep one minute and zooming out of here the next." He pushed his readers up onto the bridge of his nose. "What's cooking? Don't tell me there's a rebellion on the vestry board?"

Harry laughed. "No. We're all getting on quite well." Looking out the window, she blinked. "How beautiful this view is over the first quad, then out to the big one and the graveyard beyond. I bet you never tire of it."

"I don't. If I get stuck on a sermon, I take a walk outside or I stare at the vista. Always figure out the problem. What can I do for you?" He stood up, leading her to the comfortable sitting area. "Would you like a drink?"

"Oh, no, thank you." She settled into the club chair, its leather thin on the edges. "Reverend, remember that last night of wonderful conversation at the dinner table with Ginger, Trudy, everyone?"

He made a steeple out of his hands, sighed. "I do. How quickly life changes."

"It sure does. I think of Ginger and Trudy every day, and I know you do."

"Harry, as a pastor I can offer what comfort the scriptures give us. As a friend, I can offer my time and love, but you know there's no shortcut for those grieving for Ginger. It takes time."

"I've been rummaging around Ginger's last research project. He'd talked about it with us, the prisoner-of-war camp, the confusion once the war ended. I've thought about everything, and Cooper, bless her, hears me out. Nothing in Ginger's past suggests his murder as an act of revenge. Even Frank Cresey's meltdown didn't go that far, and in a way, Frank continued his studies." Harry then told the pastor all they had discovered about Frank from the library and from Snoop.

"You know, we must do something about those homeless people," said Reverend Jones. "We pastors, priests, rabbis need to put our heads together. The city can only do but so much, and same goes for the Salvation Army."

She filled him in on Snoop's memories, how he found the letter opener that murdered Frank and how he was in, for lack of a better word, protective custody. "I like him," she said.

The Reverend smiled. "That's a start. Just because someone has succumbed to drink or other substances doesn't mean they can't be saved. Christ offers us all redemption." He thought for a moment, then added, "Their condition takes more than prayer. It's medical. Well, I got off the track here. I can understand your interest in Ginger, in solving this terrible murder, but Harry, you do blunder into things."

*"You have no idea,"* Tucker seconded that thought.

"Lie down, sweetie." Harry smiled at the dog. Tucker did lie down, even though she could hear, the humans couldn't, some illicit activity at the end of the hall.

"Was there something said at the dinner party that brought you here? Not that I don't adore your presence. After all, I've ministered to you since you wore colored Band-Aids on your knee."

She blushed. "Ginger said he visited graveyards at old churches, he checked out birth rolls and death rolls, as the churches often had better records than the courthouses."

The Reverend flared out his fingers from the steeple, then reconnected them. "True. For the seventeenth and much of the eighteenth centuries, churches sometimes kept the only records."

"Do you have St. Luke's records?"

"I do. Some are even on parchment. Others on heavy paper, but not as permanent as parchment. All this is stored in the big safe downstairs."

"I'd like to look at them." She hastily added, "Not this minute. But sometime."

He glanced out the window. "Tell you what. I've been stuck in this office all morning. I need to stretch my legs. Let's walk down to the graveyard. Maybe that will help you in your quest."

"Really?"

He pushed up with both hands on the armrest. "You'll see."

They walked down the hall. Tucker knew the cats were hiding in the landing on the stairs, one flight up. The Reverend Jones opened the closet, pulled out a light jacket, closing it, but he didn't tightly shut the door. He kept sweaters and jackets all over the office part of the church, the front vestibule of the church itself, closets upstairs. He often felt a chill. He also slept with two blankets and a down comforter. He hated the cold.

They walked out into the interior quad.

"Aren't you needing a jacket? It's a bit brisk."

"No, thanks," said Harry. "Feels great to me."

The mercury hovered at sixty-two degrees Fahrenheit and she wore a sweater over her Under Armour, jeans, kneesocks, and cowboy boots.

The new grass felt soft and giving underfoot as they traversed the large outer quad. Reaching the cemetery, beautiful stone walls encasing it, a wrought-iron gate at both ends, the Reverend reached down, flipped up the latch. They walked in.

Obelisks, large square monuments, and regular-sized tombstones greeted them. The wealthy paid for lustrous white marble statues behind their heads. Angels, lambs, crosses, the entwined Alpha and Omega bid one consider one's spiritual journey. Much of the statuary boasted fine work.

"Let's walk along these first rows." He paused and read out names "Jacob Yost, 1721 to 1778; Macabee Reed, 1759 to 1822; Lavina Reed, 1765 to 1840; Karl Ix, 1761 to 1850. Now, there's a long life, and look here, two wives. The first predeceased him and the second outlived him by nearly thirty years. And here are two little tiny stone markers for two of their children." He swept out his arm as they entered the second row. "You can see most of these early names are German or English. Ginger, having some of the prisoners' names from The Barracks, matched them up to these names. Some of these sleeping souls were either escaped prisoners of war or men who decided not to go home. Over here, a few Italian names. You would think they would be in a Catholic graveyard, but Catholic churches were few and far between back then. Somehow they wound up here. Ginger said Italians did fight for King George, so these people resting here were also, shall we say, impressed citizens."

"If they escaped, why weren't they brought back?" She paused. "Ginger, when he gave us our high school tour, did say The Barracks was overcrowded."

"Here are Irish names, more English ones, too. Yes, The Barracks was jam-packed, even after a thousand men were sent up to York, Pennsylvania, to ease the crowding. Ginger spent time up there himself. When Cornwallis surrendered at Yorktown, more prisoners were sent here."

"It must have been awful."

"Better than losing a limb. Still better than that. Sometimes I'd go with Ginger to visit another old church. I could pass time with the priest or pastor while he would sift through records. I learned a great deal about our country's early days."

She smiled. "I envy you those trips. I bet Ginger never stopped talking."

The Reverend smiled, too. "Well, I could talk pretty good myself." He leaned down for a moment to rub Tucker's ears. "Tucker, best we don't know what you say."

*"You got that right."*

The Reverend and Harry laughed at the dog's light bark.

"Anything stand out in your mind, about what you learned, I mean?" asked Harry.

They continued to walk through the peaceful graveyard, statues shining in the spring light.

"People need God, just as they did back then. Especially then! The distances between people, the difficulties of travel, the church was a welcome place to come together, pray, sing, share joys and troubles. So many worshipped at a church that was close, one where friends gathered. Others, fired up by intellectual considerations, would start a tiny church with maybe three families. The people lying here might have started life as Catholics, Anglicans, I guess I should say, Church of England, but many were true Lutherans. Born Lutheran. Most all the Germans were, except for those few from Bavaria. Bavarians are Catholic, usually."

"Did any of the early parishioners admit to having been prisoners of war?"

"Yes, they did. As generations grew and prospered, it became a matter of pride in the early nineteenth century and really up to mid-century. According to Ginger, who read more diaries than anyone, I swear he did, this was cited as proof that their forebears from the old country, as it was and still is called, saw a New World and much preferred it to the old. Given that most everyone buried here was not on charity, they prospered."

Harry stopped, eyes reading name after name. "Makes you proud, doesn't it? These brave souls."

"It does. They endured so much. They had so much hope and energy. Here they rest some two hundred years later and we remember them. The surnames on these tombstones are still part of central Virginia."

They walked out of the cemetery, back across the lawns.

"It's true we are all standing on someone else's shoulders." Harry drew closer to the beloved pastor. He was a man whose very presence calmed and consoled.

"You think, somehow, this is connected to Ginger's murder?" he asked.

"I do. I've thought of everything, academic revenge, but everyone loved him and he never wrote monographs attacking someone else's work. Even the uproar over Sally Hemings was resolved and he was even tempered about it all."

"He was that. But you think his murder was connected to these prisoners of war?"

"I do. The path keeps bringing me back to The Barracks, Colonel Harvey's lands, Ewing Garth's, and the Loyalist, Peter Ashcombe. And then, poof, dead end."

"Well, you know St. Luke's was designed by a prisoner of war after the war's end, in 1781, really. The treaty, I think, was 1783."

"I sort of knew that, but didn't pay much attention in school."

"Well, let me show you." They walked into the church vestibule, high-ceilinged, a floor of black and white marble squares, lovely touches of woodwork where the ceiling met the walls, with a recessed alcove holding a statue of Christ as the Redeemer. Their footfalls echoed softly on the marble.

"How many times have you walked past this?" The Reverend pointed to a black, high-gloss marble rectangle set into the wall. "Charles West, Architect and Benefactor. This was set in when the church was completed."

"I read the name, but I didn't know he was a prisoner of war."

"Ginger often remarked on fate. Anyway, West was young, nine-

teen, I think, captured at Saratoga and marched here with hordes of others, all the way from Boston. Here he discovered his talent for architecture, and at war's end he learned this trade. He did a beautiful job."

"He certainly did."

"He married the younger daughter of Ewing Garth, and that was a leg up. Ewing introduced him to everyone. Commissions dribbled in and then flooded in."

"Garth. Yes, his lands backed up on the camp."

"Rachel and her older sister were great beauties, so I expect at some point the young fellow lost his heart to her. Well, I'm always a sucker for a love story, but they're buried out in the graveyard. The large mausoleum with the winged angel, hands outstretched to heaven. They had eight children. Eight, and five survived into old age. We all are standing on someone else's shoulders, as you said."

As they left the church and walked through the arcade and back to the office part of the complex, a soft breeze lifted Tucker's fur.

"When you get the time, maybe Ginger has papers on West," said Reverend Jones. "I know he researched anyone involved with the camp and it's a good story. I doubt it has any bearing on his demise, but still, it is a good story. And West was so artistic, many of his pen-and-ink drawings are scattered throughout the county. He made drawings of estates for a little money."

"I'm sure I've seen them and never known."

Once inside, walking down the hall to his closet, the Reverend noted, "I didn't leave the door open."

Tucker noticed light paw prints all over the place but not a cat in sight.

"Those devils!" He knelt down to pick up a box of consecrated wafers.

Harry, now on her hands and knees, handed box after box up to him. "Some are torn open. Others just have teeth marks."

"I will swat them. I will smite them. Damn those cats!" He swore, then caught himself. "Sorry."

She laughed. "I'd have said worse."

"Elo, Cazzie, Lucy, where are you?" he shouted.

"Mrs. Murphy, Pewter," Harry called out.

*"They aren't that stupid,"* Tucker opined.

"Kitty, kitty, kitty," the Reverend Jones's deep voice sang out.

Silence.

Harry, standing now, looked at the Reverend. "They had their first Communion."

"Won't do them a bit of good. They weren't confirmed, so they're still going to Hell," he shot back, and then they both laughed until they ached.

"So let's hope they really do have nine lives," added Harry.

## 40

December 21, 1781

Cornwallis surrendered at Yorktown on October 19, 1781. The victory brought with it many decisions, one of those being what to do with the large number of prisoners of war.

Word of Washington's victory reached The Barracks three days after the British laid down their arms, some of the infantry so furious they broke their muskets, then threw them on the pile. The Continentals, wisely, let it pass as they stood in rows, watching their defeated enemy, a fine army defeated by people called barbarians, rabble, and traitors, and even worse, cowards. The soldiers and sailors of the New World had proved their worth.

A cheer went up at The Barracks from the Americans. The British, the Hessians, and the Italians, all of whom had fought for the king, remained silent. Many were dumbfounded. Others, such as Captain Graves, expected something, perhaps not the surrender of an entire army, but something to finally bring this conflict to an end. The night of the announcement, Graves slipped away.

Over the summer, many prisoners remained at the farms where they had been loaned out. Others left, using papers forged for them by Charles. No one guarding them appeared upset. A few broadsheets were printed describing the missing. That was the extent of the search. Fewer mouths to feed, plus many of the guards had grown fond of their captives. They didn't want to hunt them down. If nothing else, they could rely on the Irish for a rollicking good laugh.

When word arrived that a portion of Burgoyne's army was to march to York, Pennsylvania, to a new camp, again not many were surprised. The Barracks was filled to overflowing and there was little choice but to send some soldiers away.

The march through beautiful country in high fall proved too taxing for those already weakened by captivity and not enough food. The constant fevers that would often rage through the camp also claimed victims.

Along the march, other prisoners silently slipped away, their first thought being to find decent clothing, to get rid of what was left— often very little—of their uniforms.

Lieutenant West, young and strong, kept moving, keeping Corporal Ix and Samuel MacLeish together with the remnants of Captain Graves's Royal Irish Artillery, but many of those men left shortly after the captain escaped from the camp. If their captain was going, so were they. The more phony discharge papers Charles created, the better he became at it. He could now mimic any signature.

Watching men literally fall by the wayside deeply affected him. He was told to keep moving, that wagons would come to pick up the weak and sick. Piglet marched along, too, no longer resembling a piglet but still healthy, ready for whatever life threw at him.

Once Charles reached Camp Security in Springettsbury Township just west of York, the frosts and cold had taken their toll. Trees denuded made the trek even more mournful.

Camp Security differed from The Barracks. A stockade of chestnut logs encircled the perimeter and the camp itself was divided into different sections. The captured officers had been billeted all throughout Virginia, Maryland, and Pennsylvania. Charles and a few others marched with the men, refusing the officer-class courtesies.

A giant rectangle, Camp Security looked foreboding. Its well-constructed cabins helped house the men, but Charles and the others knew life would be different from life in Charlottesville. Given the overcrowding, they expected some of them would be sent out to farms.

For the first time since he was actually captured, Charles felt downcast, worried. Eight hundred prisoners from Cowpens, South Carolina, had arrived shortly before the prisoners from The Barracks.

"It will be dark soon," Corporal Ix noted. "So little light now."

Walking along the symmetrical pathways, Charles agreed. "The winter solstice. As a child I looked forward to it. Christmas, you know, and I would be home from school."

"I'll be going tonight, Sir." Corporal Ix nodded toward the guards. "They'll all be bunked up."

Although Joseph Reed, president of Pennsylvania, had objected to the Continental Congress about the large number of prisoners housed in his colony, congress adamantly refused to offer other locations.

The job of building a new, large camp fell on Lieutenant William Scott of the York County Militia. Colonel Wood, in charge of the camp, did all he could to see to further construction, proper food and water. As it was, even though the pay for guards was decent, three and a half shillings a day, there weren't enough guards. The war siphoned off men. Often those left behind were injured, formerly wounded, or aged. Then, too, the overburdened colonel had to face the fact that Continental money was worthless. Congress blithely ignored this unpleasant reality, shifting the financial burden onto the people of Pennsylvania, much of it borne by those in York County.

Sharp in gathering information, Charles surmised this. He'd also heard that Cornwallis had burned all the tobacco warehouses in Petersburg during his campaign. He wondered if Ewing Garth's tobacco had been stored in those enormous warehouses.

"Corporal, I don't see how the war can continue, do you?" Charles asked Ix.

Piglet barked, for a rat shot in front of him, which he dutifully chased.

"No," said Ix. "The Crown has to reach some agreement, and I fear that will take as long as the war."

Ruefully smiling, Charles nodded. "You and I are all that remain of the marksmen."

"Perhaps we should have escaped when Samuel and Thomas did, or Captain Graves." Ix rubbed together his hands, wrapped in rags. "Tonight is a good night. I have my papers. Better than the real ones, Sir. Your hand is better." He smiled.

"All right."

At midnight, it was below freezing. The sentry at the front gate was dozing in his box. The camp was quiet, tendrils of smoke curling from the chimneys.

Charles and Corporal Ix left their cabin. Not unduly worried about awakening other prisoners, they still moved cautiously, fearing a stray guard. Piglet kept extra-alert.

Moving to the back of the camp, Charles said, "Up and over, Corporal."

"What about you, Sir? How can you scale the wall? It's too high to jump up and grab the top."

"I can't leave Piglet, Corporal. He's been by my side since I came to this land. I'll get on all fours. Step up on my back and over you go."

The corporal looked intently at Charles. "I hate to leave you, Sir."

"Go, make your way. I will escape in good time with Piglet and we will meet again." He held out his hand, which Corporal Ix took in both of his.

"God bless you, Sir. We will meet in Virginia."

"We shall." Charles dropped down as the Hessian, thin, as they all were now, nimbly leapt off the lieutenant's back, grasped the top of the palisades, hoisting himself over. Charles heard him drop on the other side, then he turned back toward the cabin.

The cold air filled his lungs; he felt as though they were expanding with the cold. Piglet's breath emitted in tiny puffs.

"We're together, Piglet. Forever, you know."

The sturdy fellow looked up. *"Forever."*

Being the second son of a baron meant something back in England, poor or not. Charles considered his life, something that being a prisoner gave him much time to do. Was it to be a life of service in the army, promotions painfully won, if at all? Anyone with more money could move ahead of him, despite lack of training or ever having been tested in battle. With luck, Charles might be promoted to major at the end of a long career. His only hope for some financial gain would be through the spoils of war. None of that here. Or he could hope for another posting, wherein conflict promised goods that could be exchanged for cash. If he lived through this adventure, that is.

He imagined attaining some success. Who could he marry? The great heiresses would be sold off to first sons of titled men. Every now and then a love match would spice up the marriage market, but he could hope for little in that department. Perhaps a suitable wife, herself of good name, would have a bit of a dowry, but the prospects before him dimmed. Could he ever return to the formality and suffocating social demands? Suffocating to him anyway.

Ideas battled one another after the first year of his capture. The eight-hundred-mile march from Boston awakened him to the richness of this raw land. The Barracks taught him how any man with a trade, a bit of boldness, might flourish. A man with gentle manners, good breeding, and a fine education had a great advantage. Charles never thought of himself as handsome, but he was, and that confers advantage as well.

He had made up his mind to stay, to study draftsmanship and architecture. Such an idea would horrify his father, but in it Charles found excitement, a kind of fulfillment he did not find in the army, although he liked the army. Anything was better than sitting idle.

He would leave before the fevers returned.

On Christmas Day, Camp Security's guards and prisoners relaxed as best they could. Charles and Piglet presented themselves at the sentry box. Charles carried his portable drawing box, nothing else.

"Where do you think you're going?" the sentry asked, his vowels quite broad.

"To deliver a present to the Wolf family, Sir. Here." He reached inside his worn, torn coat and pulled out a forged pass signed by Colonel Wood, the signature more clear than Wood's own signature, giving Charles freedom to deliver a gift from the colonel to the Wolfs.

Charles knew the Wolfs to be a prominent York family. He also knew the sentry, any sentry, would know that. And a sentry wouldn't wish to run afoul of their commanding officer's desire to please the wealthy Wolfs on Christmas.

The sentry read the paper, handing it back. "You may pass."

"Happy Christmas to you, Private."

The private touched his forefinger to his cap.

And Charles West, formerly of Captain Alexander Fraser's Company of British marksmen, began the long walk back to Virginia, various forged papers in his pocket, his faithful dog by his side. He had not a penny to his name, all he had was youth, strength, intelligence, hope, and, of course, Piglet.

# 41

$\mathcal{S}$tanding once more at the milestone near the eastern end of Continental Estates, Harry spread facsimiles of two old maps on the back end of her F-150. She'd copied the maps from Ginger's editor's bin, along with the old highways maps, like that for the Valley Road. Trudy happily allowed her to do so.

Harry had studied the documents at her kitchen table and now on the site of those old properties. The first hand-drawn map showed the Harvey lands, the Garth lands, and the Ashcombe lands. An east-west road, now called Garth Road, was a rude scribble. This map was dated 1774. The second map, dated 1794, showed a widened road. The black line was thicker and had more offshoots: one being the road that this milestone marked, the road into the back of The Barracks passing over lands marked GARTH. Garth had absorbed the Ashcombe lands. The back of Continental Estates rested on the old Ashcombe/Garth land.

She also noticed two smaller holdings on the other side of Garth Road. Cited as being owned by Garth in 1774 was one now owned by West and the other by Schuyler. This had to be the Charles West who designed and built St. Luke's.

The 1794 map showed more estates than the 1774 map, but Garth remained the largest landholder.

Hammering and sawing could be heard in the background. Driving through Continental Estates, Harry saw how quickly the men worked. Of course, framing goes up fast. The interior work takes forever, but still, three new homes were being framed. She also noticed that the neighborhood square now had a cross through it of trees with a smaller cleared square, no shrubs or anything in the middle. How beautiful it would be someday.

Walking to the shallow ravine, Tucker skidded down. He was followed by Mrs. Murphy and Pewter. There were enough bushes and saplings here to entice them to hunt.

Harry figured the ravine had last been cleared maybe ten years ago. The gullies, with less growth, had been cleared by faster rushing waters sweeping everything before. They were proof of the term *gulley washer.*

Her cellphone rang.

"Harry, it's Snoop."

"How you doin'?"

"I'm doin', but I need a break. Can you pick me up just for a ride, just so I can get out of here?" He paused. "Too much goodness."

"Sure. I'll be right over and you can help me."

"Right."

Harry then called Cooper. "Hey, Snoop needs a break. I'm going to pick him up, give him a ride and a late lunch. Will you clear it with the house mother or house father?"

"Sure."

The house, which Harry thought of as Snoop's holding pen, wasn't far. Within fifteen minutes, Snoop, scrubbed, wearing a new T-shirt and jeans, sat in the truck. Pewter was on his lap, Mrs. Murphy and Tucker were between him and Harry.

"It's good to see you looking so well," said Harry.

"It's good to see you. Don't get me wrong, I've been treated well, but . . ." His voice trailed off.

"This won't take long. But I can use your eyes."

"Yeah, sure."

They drove through the open, huge wrought-iron gates, down the main strip of Continental Estates, as Snoop intently observed the activity. "Man, they sure done a lot of work."

"Wait until you see the square."

Just as she drove toward the square, Marshall drove past and waved. Paul and six other men were working in the square. Harry also waved at him. He smiled, returned the greeting.

Another five minutes, and she was back at the milestone. Hopping out, she unfolded the two maps as the animals again rushed into the ravine.

The sound of an approaching car turned their heads. Marshall pulled up in one of his company work trucks painted Continental blue. He stepped out onto a gleaming chrome step, then onto the dirt.

"What are you doing out here, Snoop? If you want work, I've got it. And Harry, I can hire you, too." He grinned.

She spread out the two maps. "Look at this. Well, you may have seen this in your research."

"Sure. The old Garth estate. Huge." With his bandaged hand, Marshall pointed to the second map.

"If you compare this to the first one from 1774, you can see how Garth expanded his holdings. Continental Estates is on a large portion of Garth's land." She swept her arm outward.

"A very good businessman, Ewing Garth. Ginger and I talked about him a lot. He was so shrewd. He picked up properties owned by Loyalists when the tide turned in the war. They were glad of the money."

"What if they hadn't sold?" Harry queried.

"The colony, soon to be the state, would have taken possession. Garth beat them to it, and so did other men who could tolerate risk. After Yorktown, it wasn't as big a risk, obviously, but still the terms of disengagement, if you will, drug on for two years."

Knowing little history, Snoop said nothing but observed. He could read a map well enough.

"I bet Ginger loved going over all this." Harry smiled. "Researching new things."

"He'd light up like a Christmas tree. Now, I enjoy it, but I also enjoy the historic tax credits, so my research, which often was his research, borrowed, has to be impeccable."

Harry put her finger on the WEST name, then moved it to SCHUY-LER. "A West was the architect for St. Luke's. Herb said he married one of Garth's daughters."

"Ginger loved that story. Charles West escaped from the prison camp in York, Pennsylvania. He'd been confined to The Barracks first. Anyway, he made his way back here, offered his services to Garth, who somehow or other was able to keep him from being sent back to The Barracks."

"Wasn't the war over? Really?"

"That was part of it. At least that's what Ginger thought. They had enough mouths to feed, and Garth, a very important man, vouched for West. West created new barns for him, outbuildings, an addition to his house, and he also fell in love with Garth's younger daughter. Curiously enough, the captain who captured him had fallen in love with the older daughter. He fought so bravely at Yorktown that he was upped to a major, brevet major. He and West got along famously. One of history's oddities."

"I hope you put this on a plaque somewhere in Continental Estates."

"I promised Ginger I would. It's such a good story. The older Garth daughter, Catherine, took over all her father's businesses when he died. Both she and Major Schuyler ran them, but she was the brains behind it."

"Love is always a good story."

"She also bred good horses. Her favorite slave, Jeddie Rice, worked with her on this. Seems he, too, had a real gift. Well, I've nattered on, but you can see that Continental Estates has a rich history and hopefully a wonderful future. I'm going to re-create the stables, riding trails. I'll try to duplicate those structures for which I have drawings or photographs, as many remained standing once photography was invented."

"That will be fabulous." Harry thought it sounded like a fitting tribute to the early owners.

"That it will, but historical fidelity distinguishes my developments from all the others. Now, don't get me wrong, there are some very good builders out there, but they don't have a theme."

"I guess you could say that Ginger made your career," Harry replied.

"He did. Otherwise, I would have been just another high-end construction firm, development firm, after college." He looked at Snoop. "Sure you don't want a job?"

"Not right now." Snoop tightly smiled. "When I'm free, maybe. I remember that I liked working out here." What Snoop didn't say was that whatever is out here may have killed Frank Cresey.

Harry folded up the maps. "I like coming to look at the milestone."

"You come on in here anytime you want. I'd be happy to sell you a house, but I know you'll never leave the farm. Tell you what, if I had inherited that farm I wouldn't leave it either."

Marshall bid them goodbye. Harry, Snoop, the two cats and dog crowded back into the truck. She drove to Blue Mountain Brewery on Route 151 to take Snoop to lunch, first dropping off Mrs. Murphy, Pewter, and Tucker, not at all pleased that they wouldn't be having lunch.

"*After all we do for her,*" Pewter groused.

Sitting outside, the Blue Ridge Mountains were a stunning back-drop behind a greenhouse called AM Fog. The rolling hills were greening up to the mountains. Harry devoured a hamburger. Snoop did also, and although this was a brewery, he didn't seem tempted by beer. He drank an iced tea, as did Harry. She found she much enjoyed his company.

"Being a cabinetmaker, you must have a feel for the properties of each different kind of wood."

He nodded, swallowing. "And the beauty. Some wood sings in your hands."

"What a wonderful thought. Okay, maple."

"Hard, lasts."

"Heart pine."

"Not buggy like some wood. It sort of glows. Soft, but people have loved it since way back when. I do, too."

Harry, as always, was curious about everything. "What about the imported woods like mahogany, zebrawood, stuff like that?"

Snoop shrugged. "I'll work with anything, but we have so much good wood here, why spend the money on that stuff?"

"You have a point there." She wiped her fingers on the nap-kin. "My farmhouse and barns, outbuildings, everything, are built from trees, stones taken from the land. I think when the house was built they struggled to pay for glass, but they were frugal and obviously good builders. The house is still standing and it was built in 1834."

"They knew what they were doing, the old people."

"What do you think about the houses at Continental Estates?"

He thought about this. "Big. He's not cutting corners. I don't think the landscaper is either, but I know less about that even though I've done what they asked when I would get day jobs out there."

"Marshall asked you back."

He folded his arms over his chest. "Harry, I'm not going back there until Frank's killer is found."

"I can understand that. This does seem to be about that development. Deputy Cooper, my friend Susan Tucker, and myself went down to the county offices and traced back chain of title. Legal."

His eyes opened wider. "That's what Frank meant by *chains!*"

"We think so, but we can't find anything."

"Ma'am, I trust Frank. I don't know squat about this sort of thing, but I do know this: When there's a lot of money on the line, life is cheap."

"You mean like the tax credits, the historic tax credits."

"I don't know about that either. Today was the first time I ever heard of that. Sounds like a good idea, and I bet Frank knew something about it. What does it mean, these credits?"

"Well, in North Carolina, for example, they used to have a program, maybe they still do, where if you bought a dilapidated historic house and revitalized it according to historical records, you received tax credits, so ultimately you saved a bundle of money. Many states have variations of that, Virginia being one. But if you can prove the background of a place, you keep much of it intact or preserve some of it, the federal and state government will again give credit and also money, real money. Marshall gets millions in tax credits."

He whistled. "Millions. So these murdered men, the history professor and Frank, might have known something to ruin that?"

"We've checked everything and everything is aboveboard and legal, the property transfers, all the historical research done on Continental Estates, all properly done. And there's also the fact that Marshall and Paul studied with Ginger and loved him. It seems unlikely that either one, and I expect Paul has benefited as well as the paving contractor, would kill Ginger."

"Millions of dollars seem like a powerful motive to me."

Driving back from dropping off Snoop, Harry checked in with her husband. Fair was enjoying the conference, happy to see colleagues and even a few people who were at Auburn when he was. He rattled on about how high-tech veterinary medicine is now and he had to run to catch up. She told him everyone felt that way. He also said Denver was as great as he remembered and he even had a little time to tour the state house.

Pressing the phone's off button, she considered how good it was to be married to a man who wanted to learn and who loved what he did. They were both lucky that way.

It was three o'clock as she turned on the two-lane highway to the farm, then abruptly turned around. She called ahead to Trudy and then she looked out for anyone from the sheriff's department because she was speeding.

Parking in the driveway, Harry sprinted to the door.

Opening it, Trudy couldn't help but notice Harry's flushed face. "Are you all right?"

"Trudy, forgive me. Remember our dinner at Reverend Jones's?"

"Yes, of course."

"Do you remember Ginger speaking about a professor, a don, I don't know, a research person at Cambridge who was going to call him before his golf round the next day?"

"Yes."

"Did that person call?"

"Oh, yes. Ginger took the call in his office and later he came out smiling like the Cheshire cat."

"Did he tell you what it was about?"

"No, Ginger was on the phone so long he was afraid he'd be late for his tee time. He hurried out of here."

"Again, forgive me, do you have that person's number?"

"Let's look. I know where he would keep it."

They hurried into the office, late-afternoon light flooding the room. Trudy pulled an old Rolodex from the deep drawer.

"He liked this best. Never put numbers on his computer or his phone. Ginger always said, 'What do you do when the power goes out or the battery dies?'" She smiled.

"Do you know the person's name?"

"No, we can figure it out. I know how his mind worked. He would have this under three categories: the person's name, Cambridge, and the research itself, which I would assume would be either under The Barracks or something close by." She flipped first to CAMBRIDGE, where a list of names, neatly written, were listed in alphabetical order, fortunately with the project behind it. "This has to be the one."

"A woman?" Harry exclaimed, as her vision of Cambridge was crusty dons in flowing robes teaching hard-partying male toffs.

"Harry, Ginger would want you to know some of the best academic work in England is being done by women, many of them young. The world has changed, well, North America and Europe. I don't know about the rest of it."

"Brazil, Argentina, for starters. Women presidents."

Trudy smiled. "Sooner or later I expect we'll catch up, but here she is, Sarah Lincoln."

Harry scribbled down the number. "Let me hurry home and call her. I just might make it because it's nine-thirty there. Hopefully this second number is the home number."

"Don't wait until tomorrow." Trudy grasped the significance of this as well as the danger, which Harry ignored. "Call her from here."

Harry dialed 011, then the number. Waited. To her joy, a lovely voice answered the call. "Hello, Sarah here."

"Miss Lincoln, forgive me for calling you in the evening. I am Harry Haristeen, a friend of the late Professor Greg McConnell."

A sharp intake of breath told Harry that Sarah didn't know Ginger was dead. "Oh, no. Oh, I am so very sorry. He was so helpful to me in my work on Lord Cornwallis, and I even had the good fortune to meet him when he was visiting Cambridge. I am so sorry."

"We all are, Miss Lincoln. It was a profound shock. And recent, so his obituary will most likely be in next month's various academic publications. It's probably on the Internet, too, but let me tell you why I am calling. This will further upset you. He was murdered."

"What! I can't believe it."

"We can't either, but I'm wondering if you can help me. I'm looking into some of the professor's research when he died."

"Of course, anything." The young woman was terribly upset.

"You called him on Saturday morning, April eleventh. Do you recall the conversation?"

"Vividly. In my work over the last few years I have discovered many Loyalists who returned to England, some of whom flourished, some not."

"Were any of these families from Albemarle County?"

"Yes, there were a few fearing increased hostility and even violence, as Albemarle was considered one of the hotbeds of sedition. One of these men had connections to Lord Cornwallis through his wife. She died early in 1779. Cornwallis had rushed back to England to be with her. It was a true love match. Peter Ashcombe, the Loyalist related to Lady Cornwallis, gave the general some trinkets from his wife's childhood. He appears to have been a decent man, Ashcombe, and he left behind thousands of acres under care of a farm manager."

"And it was this that Professor McConnell was interested in?"

"Yes, and it is a great curiosity. You see the bill of sale, I assume it's called that there, but the purchase of those thousands of acres was made, according to Professor McConnell, on February first, 1782. A Mr. Garth purchased Peter Ashcombe's land for twenty thousand pounds."

"Yes, he did. I've seen the sale papers and the subsequent deed in the records at the county offices here."

"But Peter Ashcombe had died January twenty-second, 1782," said Sarah. "Sailing the North Atlantic in winter takes longer than in summer, and even then you must figure two or three weeks."

This time it was Harry's turn to sharply breathe in. "Miss Lincoln, this is almost as much of a shock as Professor McConnell's death."

"I doubt a man can sell property from the grave, and Ashcombe had no heirs."

"Thank you. Thank you so much. When we get to the bottom of this, either myself or Mrs. McConnell will call you."

"I'm glad to be helpful. He was one of the most delightful men I have ever met." Then she added with a light laugh, "It was hard to believe he was a professor."

After bidding goodbye, Harry turned to Trudy. She had heard most of it, but to be certain, Harry repeated the dates.

Trudy's face flushed for a moment. "My God. But why kill Ginger?"

"If Ginger told Marshall, Paul, or Rudy, I would narrow it down to those three. A lot of money could be lost, and as Continental Estates is owned by Marshall's company, well—"

Trudy protested in disbelief. "But it's been centuries."

"Has, but think, Trudy. Who really owns the Ashcombe land? Probably the state of Virginia, once this all comes out."

———

Harry hopped in the truck, heading back to the farm, calling Cooper on the way. She didn't like talking and driving, but she felt she had abused Trudy's hospitality enough. Best to call Coop from her cell.

After telling her everything, Harry added, "You're almost off duty. Stop by. Maybe we can figure this out."

"Be there."

As Harry pulled up to the barn, out rushed Tucker.

"There's an intruder in the hayloft!"

Bending over, Harry smiled. "You're excited."

Poor Tucker did all she could. She'd run a few paces ahead, stop, turn, bark, but her warnings were useless.

When Harry walked into the barn, the cats in the hayloft leaned over. "Run!"

"Aren't you two the busybodies?"

"She is abysmally stupid," Pewter wailed.

Harry walked to a hanging tack hook by the corner of the tack room, slipped halters over her shoulder, when she heard a creak. Looking up, she saw the barrel of a gun pointing right at her.

"Harry, I'm sorry to do this," Marshall Reese apologized. "I like you. I've always liked you."

Keeping calm, Harry replaced the halters with which she would have led the horses back in. She was glad they were out in their paddocks just in case he started shooting wild. She put her hands on the ladder, began climbing up. Harry was nothing if not brave. She also bet on Marshall's desire for her information. More important, even, who did she tell?

"Let's talk about this," said Harry. "You don't know what I know."

Keeping the gun level on her, his curiosity aroused, Marshall warned, "You know enough."

"I know you killed Ginger and Frank. Is that the gun that killed Ginger? Is three the charm?"

In a way, Marshall admired her. "You're cheeky, you know that? Why tell you about the gun? It's unregistered, I'll tell you that."

Mrs. Murphy edged closer to his left leg. *"Pewter, take the right. Don't do anything yet."*

While poor Tucker howled in the center aisle, Pewter did as she was told without argument.

Harry took a small step toward Marshall. He stepped back. "Ginger told you about his phone call from Sarah Lincoln of Cambridge, didn't he?" she asked.

"He did. I had to act quickly before he released his research. I told him this could cost me untold millions. I would have to stop the project, spend years in court with the state while the homes disintegrated without proper care. Millions. And that's not counting the historic tax credits."

"Did you tell Ginger this?"

"I did." As Harry had stepped toward him again, he stepped back. "Don't push, Harry. I will shoot."

"I know you will, but you want to know what I know, don't you? Or who I've told? I mean, how many people can you kill?"

"As many as I have to kill. But I told Ginger, and he said all would be well. The state would drop it. They might after I shelled out millions, if they didn't drag me through court. It's not like I'm a criminal. I didn't know. No one knew, but when Ginger found out when Peter Ashcombe died, he would have to write about it. He was a historian. It makes a great story about those days, but the man had no business sense at all. None. He would have ruined me."

"Do Paul and Rudy know?"

"Nothing. The fewer people who know, the better."

"Which means you need to know who I have spoken to because one of them will tell." Taking another step forward, she was guiding him bit by bit back to Matilda, who watched the entire drama with great interest.

Matilda tolerated the opossum, ignored the cats, tolerated Harry because she put out food to help her in early spring. But one human was the limit. Matilda curled up, ready to strike.

"Well, who did you tell?" asked Marshall.

"Put down the gun and we can discuss it."

"Harry, I'm not a fool. I'm not putting down the gun."

She shrugged as though this was of no account. "All right, then. You killed Ginger. You killed Frank. Killing Ginger, thanks to the woods at the country club, all the people playing golf that day, was pretty easy especially since you're a cool customer."

"Thank you for that." He kept the gun leveled at her.

"And I figure you probably lured Frank with some kind of promise."

"Jim Beam." He smirked as he mentioned the brand of bourbon. "Too easy, really."

"But exactly how did you bury him under the tree?"

"Killing Frank was the easy part. Burying him was hard. Remember all the Band-Aids and the gauze on my palm? From burying Frank. First I had to dig up the tree which, although newly planted, took a lot of effort. Then I had to fold him up and tie him up. Otherwise, a rectangle would have been noticeable. So I pulled the tree out, dug deep as I could so I could put the tree back. Fortunately, he was pliable. No rigor mortis. Tied him up, dropped him down, put the tree back, covered it all up. Even though I wore gloves"—he sighed—"it tore my hands to hell. And you know that would have been the healthiest tree in the line. Nothing like good compost." He laughed. "Your damn dog and cats figured it out. Never underestimate the olfactory powers of dogs or I guess cats. So you see you've been a thorn in my side one way or another."

"Still am. You need to know if I've told Coop or my husband or anyone. If you put the gun down, we can discuss it."

"Harry," he replied with some disbelief, "I can blow a hole through you. You do what I say."

"It's kind of like offense versus defense, isn't it?"

"What?"

"Nelson Yarbrough says that defense men are spoilers. They have to get whipped up, especially in the locker room. The offense can stay quiet and calm."

"What does that have to do with this?"

She took another step. He moved within Matilda's striking range. Matilda eyed the two cats, then returned her concentration on the man's leg moving closer.

"But I'm offense," she said. "I have the ball, so to speak. I have the information. You want it. Offense versus defense." Harry spoke as though they were chatting in her kitchen, anywhere but here with a gun pointed at her. She figured if she was going to die she wasn't going to be a ninny about it. She took one more step toward him.

"Stop right there." He was right in front of Matilda's hay bale with his left foot.

"Now!" Mrs. Murphy commanded.

Each cat clawed a leg, which made Marshall step back again. Matilda struck, sinking those long curved fangs into his right calf.

Screaming, Marshall lurched forward, gun firing into the air. Matilda wasn't finished yet. She sank those fangs as deeply as she could while the cats shredded his pants and then his legs.

Finally released by Matilda, Marshall stumbled forward. The snake slithered back into her home.

Emboldened by Marshall's scream, Mrs. Murphy and Pewter chomped their fangs deeper into each leg. He ran a few steps, cats hanging on, then tottered, falling over the edge of the hayloft onto the aisle below. Below, his gun clattered across the concrete surface.

Harry looked over, then slid down the ladder, hands and feet on the outside. She didn't waste time on the rungs. The cats climbed down on the rungs. Tucker growled in Marshall's face, ready to tear him apart.

Harry picked up the gun first thing, then turned to Marshall. From the angle of his head, she knew he was dead. He'd broken his neck.

Cooper pulled up in the driveway. Harry ran outside, gun in hand. Cooper jumped out of the car, saw the gun, looked at Harry, and sped inside the barn.

Kneeling down over Marshall, she felt for a pulse. "Dead."

"Good," Harry succinctly replied.

"*I did it.*" Pewter puffed up.

"*We both did,*" Mrs. Murphy corrected her.

"*He's lucky I couldn't get to him.*" Tucker regretted not being able to inflict damage.

Harry suddenly felt the gun in her hand; she hadn't been paying attention to it. She turned it around, handing the butt end to Cooper.

"You could have been killed." Cooper was a bit shaken herself.

"But I wasn't. I have two cats and a snake to thank for that. Coop, while you call the department, let me tell you what happened. By the time the other officers get here, you'll have the whole story."

"First, did he act alone?"

"He did, and it was all about greed."

"One of the good old seven deadly sins." Cooper stared at the sprawled figure who seemed to have had everything except morals.

"In this case very deadly," Harry agreed.

# 42

*W*alking in wagon ruts and a foot and a half of snow, Charles was in front. Piglet trailed behind. Finally, he reached what Charles hoped would be some sort of refuge.

Pushing through the snow, he arrived at the shoveled-out meandering walk to Ewing Garth's imposing house. Shivering in the pale morning light, he climbed the front stairs, lifted the shiny brass pineapple knocker, and rapped loudly three times.

The butler, Roger, answered. Looking at Charles, Roger paused, his mouth dropping open.

"Pardon my appearance. May I speak to Mr. Garth?"

"I . . . I, come in, Sir. You'll freeze to death out there." The elegant older man saw Piglet. "The dog, too, Sir."

Charles stood in the hallway, the warmth heaven-sent. Roger stared at his wrapped boots, the paper and cloth worn, too, and the rags wrapped around his hands.

Footsteps boomed down the stairway.

John Schuyler hurried to the still-shivering man. "Lieutenant!"

"Captain. I mean Major. I heard of your exploits."

"Sit down, man, for God's sake." John turned to Roger. "Surely there's biscuits left. Something. This man is starved. Hot tea."

"We do meet again, God be praised," Charles said to John, tears in his eyes. "Please don't send me back to The Barracks." Painfully he reached into his coat, handing John forged discharge papers.

John flipped them open. "Yes, fine. Lieutenant, the war is over and the camp doesn't need one more man. Plus, you have your papers. Here, let me help you into the kitchen. Best we go there."

With his hand under the elbow of Charles, who did not protest his assistance, John got him back to the kitchen. The cook, a slave with a gorgeous face, Bettina screamed when she saw him.

"Oh, Lord, let me help you." The middle-aged woman grabbed some biscuits, cold bacon, put the water up, looking for anything to nourish this man who was in sorry shape.

Bettina was one of those women who knew only how to care for people. Fortunately, the centuries consistently produce such souls, regardless of station or gender.

Hearing the commotion, Catherine came down the back stairs, Rachel behind her. They too stared in shock at Charles West.

Rachel went over to Bettina. "Another pot of water for when he's finished."

"Yes, Missus." Bettina nodded.

Catherine took one look and hurried back upstairs, returning with a shirt, underclothes, and a pair of breeches that might fit. "This will help after food and a bath. Where have you been?"

"Camp Security," Charles said with a bit of renewed vigor, thanks to the hot tea and the food being brought to him.

Bettina winked at him, putting down food for Piglet. The little beast lived up to his name.

Charles slowly felt his bones warming. The shivering stopped, the ice melted on his mustache and beard, for he hadn't been able to shave in weeks. Bettina kept handing him towels to wipe the water off.

Sitting opposite him, John smiled broadly. He looked at Catherine, who returned his smile. "I have stopped here before returning to see my mother and father," he explained. "I have sought Miss Ewing's hand in marriage, and she has accepted me."

"Congratulations." Charles grinned at them both. "Fate. You are fated to be together."

"When you are thawed, bathed, and shaved, I will tell you about the campaign here and at Yorktown. Unless you would rather not hear of it." John leaned forward, accepting a cup of tea, as Bettina poured another for Charles. "And your pistol did indeed save my life."

"Where is Mr. Garth?" Charles, although interested in his pistol, tried not to sound nervous, but he knew his future depended on Ewing Garth.

"In his greenhouse. A new interest. It's small, but affords free rein to his curiosities." Catherine smiled.

Weymouth, a slender fellow, appeared. "Roger says I am to bathe and shave the lieutenant."

Charles laughed. "I think Piglet needs to get into the bath with me."

An hour and a half later, Charles, limping slightly, appeared downstairs in the library. The breeches bagged a bit, but the socks and shirt fit well enough. Surprisingly, Ewing Garth's shoes fit him perfectly.

Ewing awaited him in the library, greeting him with open arms. "Lieutenant, I trust you have decided to become a Virginian."

"I have, Sir."

"Good, good. We need skilled young men." He smiled. "The major has explained to me your situation. He said you had proper papers. No need to report your return to The Barracks. All is well."

"I take it the camp is still full."

"Indeed it is. Until a proper treaty is agreed upon, those men remain here, although I do hear many stay on the farms where they are working."

"May I ask, Sir, if anyone has seen Corporal Ix? I know he was trying to make his way to you."

"And so he did. Like you, half frozen, starved, but he did arrive, and with his discharge papers as well. He will be back tomorrow. I sent him down to Scottsville to purchase tools. He lives in one of our dependencies. He has already improved his quarter and those of my other dependents, especially the draws in their fireplaces." Ewing, a Virginian, did not like to use the term *slave quarters*.

"I hope I may be able to see him. I have come seeking employment with you, Sir."

Ewing smiled reflexively, looked at Weymouth and down at Piglet. "Might I have Weymouth fetch your papers?"

"Yes. What remains of my pitiful belongings are next to the tub."

"I see that your dog has been properly beautified." Ewing chuckled.

"Piglet appreciates looking his best. I barely recognized myself when I looked in the mirror. Thank you for having Weymouth shave me. He's an excellent barber."

Ewing inclined his head. "He will be glad to hear that." Then he took the papers that Weymouth, just entering the library, handed him.

Unfolding them, tears along the cracks, Ewing read with care. "I see both you and Corporal Ix were discharged by Captain Alexander Fraser, your commanding officer at Saratoga."

Charles swallowed, glancing at John, who betrayed no emotion. "Yes."

Both Ewing and John knew perfectly well that Captain Fraser was nowhere near Camp Security. But the papers looked convincing. Even the sealed stamp looked right.

"Major, would you excuse us for a moment?" Ewing asked his daughter's fiancé.

"Mr. Garth, of course." John slightly nodded and withdrew.

Charles noted that the tall major had absorbed much of his gentleman's training.

Indicating that Charles sit closer to him in one of the large chairs, Ewing folded his hands together over his stomach. "You have endured much."

"I have learned much. I see clearly why you and others were willing to risk everything to break with the Crown."

This pleased Ewing tremendously. "What would you want of me?"

"The opportunity to be your architect. To work with Corporal Ix and to work with your people here. I believe we can build anything, anywhere."

"Yes, yes, I quite agree. And what would you ask for compensation?"

"I—" Charles stumbled, for his enthusiasm almost overtook him. "Sir, I am so grateful to be here, to be a new citizen of a new country. I never thought about compensation. Perhaps learning from you, such a successful man, will be compensation enough."

"Come, come," Ewing indulgently replied. "I can and will do better than that, but you must make a bargain with me."

"Yes."

"Your hand is remarkable. You can create anything." He tilted his head. "Indeed, your hand is better than the clerks who write all these papers, writs, and so forth." He waved his hand, as though dismissing hordes of clerks. "If you can create such papers for me, I will be happy to have you in my employ."

Charles couldn't help smiling. "I trust, Sir, you need no discharge papers."

Ewing laughed uproariously at this. "My, my, no, but I need a bill of sale. Peter Ashcombe, a Loyalist, owns two thousand acres. He will never return to claim them and he has no heirs. He left in haste and in anger and unfortunate feelings still persist. Indeed, he would be foolish to return. I have taken the precaution of retaining his farm manager at a higher salary than that which he formerly enjoyed. I've told him I am in contact with Peter to effect this sale, but alas, that's not true. I haven't been able to reach Ashcombe. I would like to buy those acres, and with you, I shall."

"Have you a model?"

"I do. I have had copies made of every land transaction I have ever concluded to my satisfaction." Ewing emphasized the word *satisfaction*.

"Have you parchment or vellum?"

"I do, and I have good ink, sharp quills, and wax."

"Ribbons, Sir. We need ribbons."

"Ah." Ewing sprang from his chair, opened the door.

"Roger."

Immediately, the butler appeared.

"Will you find one of my daughters and ask for fine ribbon?" He looked to Charles.

"Silk," Charles added. "Or satin, but good ribbons. In red."

Roger bowed and left.

Ewing returned to his chair. "I can see you are a businessman."

"I have not your gift, but I do hope over time some of it rubs off." Charles smiled, as did Piglet, at his feet.

Once Roger returned with the ribbon, Charles, sitting at the large, lovely desk, began work on a good sheet of vellum, using Ewing's most recent land purchase as a model. He added flourishes of his own, quite happy that, although they were cracked a bit, his hands hadn't been ruined by the cold. Cutting two ribbons set at an angle, he took a candle and dripped red wax where they joined, turning the stamp to smear it a bit, as they had no good stamp with the correct symbols on it. Gently shaking some sand on the document, he waited a bit, then carefully tilted the vellum so the sand would go into the wastebasket.

"Mr. Garth, according to your instructions."

"Yes, yes. Now, what is this?"

Charles read, "'In the year of our Lord one thousand seven hundred and eighty-two, February first, in the twenty-second year of the reign of His Majesty George the Third.'" Charles looked up. "Ashcombe is a Loyalist—this is his version from England. Now I must make one that records it for this country. You see, the record-keeper will be either amused or angry at the mention of the year of George the Third's reign. He probably will not look closely at these documents."

"Ah, Lieutenant, you are exceedingly clever."

Within short order, Charles completed the transfer for the county clerk. Both papers would be taken down to his office tomorrow.

Ewing was barely able to contain his excitement, reveling in Charles's fine work. "Those years when I thought I might be hung. And now this." He looked at Charles. "Shall we start at ten pounds a month, living quarters and food, of course?"

"Ten pounds." Charles couldn't believe it, for this was a very generous sum that he would be able to augment with drawings of people's homes, carriages, plantings.

"For your first year. I believe over time you will see thankful increase."

"Sir, I thank you."

"And I thank you. These are remarkable." Ewing took a deep breath, then laughed with joy. "No one will ever know."

Dear Reader,

In 2005, the National Trust for Historic Preservation named Camp Security in York County, Pennsylvania, on a list of America's eleven most endangered historic places. For two hundred twenty-five years, the prisoner-of-war camp had suffered nothing other than normal farming disturbances. A local developer wanted to build a 105-house subdivision on this land, thereby rendering it useless to archaeological examination.

In 1979, a team of professional archaeologists examined just two acres of the camp, recovering more than fifteen thousand artifacts. Given the severe time limitations under which they worked, there was no way to discover what remained hidden on the thirty acres remaining.

Carol Tanzola, a luminous soul with a passion for history, for finding out just who we were and who we are, couldn't abide this. Like many people who think about civilizations, the past, wars, et cetera, Carol knew that one can judge a time, a people by how they treat military prisoners, to say nothing of how they treat women, animals, or those unable to compete due to physical or mental infirmity. A woman with a deep sense of fairness as well as curiosity, she started Friends of Camp Security.

As with all such nonprofit organizations, they discovered that fund-raising is the second oldest profession.

Undaunted, they pressed on. The developer was not charmed. The Friends never gave up and over time the local newspaper began to keep track of goings-on. The York Historical Society also took note. (This organization is housed in a wonderful home off York Square.)

More than twelve years later, Carol and the Friends have finally saved Camp Security for all Americans. Over the years much will be unearthed about how people lived, their pastimes, their old pipes, et cetera. There's hope that the grave sites of those who died in the unfortunate sweeps of fever will be found. Perhaps the archaeologists will find medical information, as well. It's quite exciting.

On a personal note, Carol is a fellow foxhunter, and we met through this rapturous love at the Pennsylvania Horse Show held at the end of October. It's the last of the great indoor shows. Madison Square Garden is gone. Washington hangs on but changes venue. But the Penn National remains what it has always been: fierce competition, elegance, and fabulous horses.

Over the years we stayed in touch. I should add here that Carol, Jim, and their two daughters are all crazy fun so I looked forward to any communication and always to the big show.

I could never write big checks. I live with the typical writers' curse: chicken one day, feathers the next. But I promised Carol that I'd find a way to put Camp Security into a mystery. And so I did. I will continue to revisit the camp and York in the future. In fact, I'm surprised that York County, in particular, and southeastern Pennsylvania, in general, haven't been the backdrop for more novels. Apart from the area's physical beauty and history, the people present an array of delicious contradictions. What writer could ask for more?

Well, I've nattered on but the long struggle to save Camp Security reaffirmed my faith in Americans. One person can make a difference.

In this case, it was Carol Tanzola.

Well done, Madam.

Always and Ever,

## Acknowledgments

Nelson Yarbrough, D.D.S., and his wife, Sandra, also D.D.S., have put up with me for just about four decades. Last year, I inflicted myself on Nelson, the quarterback of the 1959 University of Virginia football team, for an overview of UVA, as well as college football, during that era.

Not only did he teach me, delight me, and make me think on topics I had not examined, but I stayed so long that he fed me. Because of his insights and his gentle way of getting his point across, I will come back to this generation again. It seems to me there has been a significant break in behavior since Nelson's college days and today. I could have sat there and listened until the cows came home, and when I left, my cows were coming home.

As always, I thank him for his time and patience. So many of us in central Virginia thank both Drs. Yarbrough for their countless acts of unobtrusive kindness.

## About the Authors

RITA MAE BROWN has written many bestsellers and received two Emmy nominations. In addition to the Mrs. Murphy series, she has authored *A Nose for Justice* and *Murder Unleashed*, the first two mysteries in a dog series, and the Sister Jane foxhunting series, among many other acclaimed books. She and Sneaky Pie live with many other rescued animals.

SNEAKY PIE BROWN, a tiger cat rescue, has written twenty-five mysteries including this one—witness the list at the front of this novel. Having to share credit with the above-named human is a small irritant, but she manages it. Anything is better than typing, which is what "Big Brown" does for the series. Sneaky calls her human that name behind her back after the wonderful Thoroughbred racehorse. As her human is rather small, it brings giggles among the other animals. Sneaky's main character—Mrs. Murphy, a tiger cat—is a bit sweeter than Miss Pie, who can be caustic.

## About the Type

This book was set in Joanna, a typeface designed in 1930 by Eric Gill (1882–1940). Named for his daughter, this face is based on designs originally cut by the sixteenth-century typefounder Robert Granjon (1513–89). With small, straight serifs and its simple elegance, this face is notably distinguished and versatile.

DON'T MISS THE NEXT BOOK FROM

# RITA MAE BROWN

## & SNEAKY PIE BROWN

# TALL TAIL

A MRS. MURPHY MYSTERY

SPRING
2016

A Bantam Books
Hardcover and eBook